# The Pond

## By Michelle Dubois

*So spellbinding and adventurous,*
*you won't want to put it down!*

authorHOUSE®

*AuthorHouse™*
*1663 Liberty Drive*
*Bloomington, IN 47403*
*www.authorhouse.com*
*Phone: 1-800-839-8640*

*Published by AuthorHouse    05/25/2012*

*ISBN: 978-1-4685-3862-5 (sc)*
*ISBN: 978-1-4685-3861-8 (e)*

*Library of Congress Control Number: 2011963748*

"Miguel, please don't leave!" she whispered again.

Just as she pulled some ferns apart to look deeper, she gasped and jumped back! It was her brother Miguel standing right in front of her.

Staring into her face he said to her in a soft deep voice, "Hello my sister, you should not be here. The Amazon is no place for you."

# Chapter 1

Michael, Allen and Quinn ran down the steps of their Alma Mater in New York jumping and shouting with their diplomas in hand.

"We did it!" shouted Allen.

"We're going to be doctors!" Quinn yelled out.

Michael ran in front of them while slapping fellow students and professors on the back as he ran by them.

Everyone laughed as the three of them descended down the stairs catching up to Allen and Quinn's parents with Michael's brother, John.

"Congratulations Men!" John said while patting all three on the back. "I wish mom and dad were here to see you graduate Michael."

"I know, I wish they were here too," as Michael sadly smiled at John.

We're so proud of you!" Allen's mother, Rita cried out.

Allen's father, Abraham, nicknamed Avi, nodded his head to confirm what Rita said.

"You all deserve it!" smiled Quinn's father, Tom.

Mary walked up to Quinn, "Mark wanted to be here but someone had to run the store for your dad. And Katie wanted to be here too but Courtney has her first piano recital of the year tonight. They both told me to tell you they send their love and they are so proud of you! They're going to call you later."

"Thanks mom, I talked to them both this morning and got their cards," smiled Quinn.

Tom fiddled with his video camera and said, "I got it all on tape."

"So guys, where do you want to go for dinner? It's on me!" said Avi.

Michael, Allen and Quinn all looked at each other smiling while removing their caps and gowns.

Quinn excitedly said back, "How about sushi?"

"Sushi it is!" said Avi.

Everyone piled into the limo that Allen's parents arrived in. Once they were all inside, Michael turned to Allen and Quinn and gave them a quick stare.

Quinn and Allen looked at each other, and then Quinn asked, "Why did you look at us like that?"

Michael shook his head at them, "How in the hell did the two of you ever graduate?" as everyone laughed!

Michael Sinclair, Allen Greenberg and Quinn Adams were best friends. They met playing rugby on the university rugby team and decided to share an apartment together. They all had steady jobs to support the three bedroom apartment they had over a kosher deli owned and operated by an old Jewish man and woman.

Catching the subway back and forth from university to their jobs, they would sometimes pass each other laughing while trying to hike the next subway train.

Allen worked in a men's department store, while Michael took a job flipping hamburgers at a diner, and Quinn worked in the university library. They also tutored other students in their spare time for extra money.

None of them had to work since all three had quite successful parents. But they didn't want to completely depend on their parents so they took jobs to prove their independence.

Between their studies, work and tutoring, it didn't leave much time for socializing, so they hung around the apartment with their three desks set up in the living room and talked about women, travelling and becoming doctors. All three were very intelligent and by the time they graduated, they graduated with honors.

Michael and Quinn did their internships at the same hospital in New York while Allen did his internship at a children's hospital in New Jersey.

All three went on to be very successful doctors, and even though they had busy lives, not a day went by they didn't talk on the phone or send out an e-mail to each other.

They met up at the country club they belonged to on Park Avenue at least twice a week for dinner or lunch. All three still played rugby in a men's league and played golf as much as they could with fellow friends and doctors. Life was good for all three of them. Quinn got married to Catherine, but for Michael and Allen, they were at the stage in their lives that it was time to focus on settling down and having families.

Michael Sinclair specialized in Nephrology as a kidney specialist. He opened his own private practice and he worked long hours between his practice, surgeries and seeing his patients at the hospital in Manhattan.

Michael wanted to settle down with a family someday. Although he wanted a family life, he hadn't found the woman he wanted to spend the rest of his life with.

He moved to Amherst, New York, a suburb of Buffalo at the age of eleven where his parents and brother, John, settled after leaving Australia when his father became a Professor of Science at a local university.

When Michael first moved to Amherst, kids at school teased him because of his accent, but eventually he made many friends through playing soccer and being on the honor role year after year at the private school he attended. Michael learned being a great rugby and soccer player from when he was living "Down Under."

Michael tragically lost both parents to cancer. He was only fourteen years old when his father, Zerek died of pancreatic cancer, and then lost his mother, Althea to ovarian cancer at the age of seventeen. He and his brother John remained very close. John became like a brother and a father to Michael before he entered university.

John met his wife in college and they got married six months after graduation. He became a high school football coach and his wife, Laura, was a history teacher at the same school. They had two children, Megan who was six, and Christopher who was eight. They loved Uncle Michael and he sent them gifts everywhere he went.

At the age of thirty-one, Michael stood 6'1" with olive color skin and black hair. And even though his parents claimed Australian citizenship, his parents were originally of Greek heritage. He was strikingly good looking and his body was in perfect form. People envied him because he was ideally fit from years and years of playing rugby and soccer.

Michael began to wonder if he would ever fall in love. He wanted to get married and have children, but wanted the right woman to be able to live with the commitment involved in being married to a doctor. He saw too many doctors lose their marriages due to the stress in their relationships and he knew being married to a doctor took a lot of dedication and a special kind of woman to make it work.

Being a doctor and as handsome as he was, he had lots of opportunities. He had sexual partners but never made any kind of commitment. He was very cautious.

He knew what he wanted and he wasn't going to settle.

Quinn Adams became a Radiation Oncologist. He grew up in Martha's Vineyard where his parents owned a hardware store. His father had a sailboat and he and his parents, his brother and sister went out sailing practically every weekend during the summer when they lived at home.

His older brother Mark became the general manager for the family hardware store and married Angel. They had two sons Mark Junior and Thomas. His younger sister Katie was a housewife, who married Jason. Jason was a general manager for a packaging firm. They had a daughter Courtney who was very musically inclined and played piano and the violin.

Quinn was 5'10" tall. He was thirty-two years old and came from an English background. He had a thin build and wavy dark reddish brown hair and hazel eyes.

Quinn didn't have the same poise as Michael and Allen had, and he had no fashion sense at all! Once when he got dressed and went to walk out of the apartment with Michael and Allen, they turned and shook their heads and laughed. He stared at them with a perplexed look on his face and asked, "What, what's wrong with this?" pointing to his clothes.

Quinn started dating an Oncologist nurse. Her name was Catherine Huard. They met in the hospital cafeteria and they sat and talked for three weeks before he asked her out. Quinn nicknamed her Cath.

Catherine was petite and stood about 5'4" tall with big blue eyes and blonde shoulder length hair. She fell in love with Quinn but she wasn't sure how he felt about her.

One evening she put some candles on the table with some romantic music. She tossed rose pedals all over the white table cloth and got out her fine china and crystal. When Quinn walked in and saw the table he wasn't sure what was going on. And then a big smile came over his face, "Don't tell me, it's my birthday, right!"

Catherine loved his humor and she always laughed at his wit. He leaned over and gave her a very soft kiss on her lips. She looked up into his eyes and nervously announced, "I'm in love you Quinn, but I understand if you don't feel the same way."

He smiled and then he reached into his shirt pocket and pulled out a little black velvet bag and handed it to Catherine. When she slowly opened it, she pulled out a one carat diamond ring.

Quinn looked at Catherine while she was totally fixed on the ring, "I've loved you since we met in the cafeteria. I just didn't think you felt the same way. So I've been carrying this ring for over two weeks now and I was just waiting for the right time to give it to you. I love you too Cath. Will you marry me?"

Catherine and Quinn were married three weeks later at a small Lutheran church in Albany, New York where Catherine grew up. Allen and Michael were both his best man.

Allen Greenburg was also thirty-two years old. He stood 5' 11 and ½" tall. He was very athletic like Michael and he worked out four times a week at a local gym.

He was considered be very good looking with dark green eyes and he always kept his dirty blonde hair neatly brushed back.

Allen had no siblings; his mother Rita was Italian Roman Catholic originally from the Tuscany region of Italy where her parents were grape growers on a small quaint countryside farm.

Avi Greenberg was Jewish and was the youngest of three sons. He was the only one to be born in Canada and was ten years younger than his two brothers. His family immigrated to Canada from Israel where they became jewelers in downtown Toronto. Avi took over the business with Rita when his brothers retired.

Rita and Avi met in Italy while Avi was in the Canadian Reserves. And when he left to return to Canada, they wrote back and forth for almost a year. On a surprise trip back to Italy to see her, he proposed in front of her parents kneeling on one knee. Two weeks later they were married in Italy and they left to live in Toronto.

Allen and his mother visited his grandparents in Italy every summer and when they passed away, his grandparents left the family farm to Rita and her brother Amadeo, where she and Avi vacationed for two months every year.

Allen grew up respecting both religions, but raised Catholic since he and his mother attended the Roman Catholic Church every Sunday. He entered prep school in Connecticut and loved the United States so much he decided to finish his studies in New York. Once he completed his degrees and internship he opened a private practice as a pediatrician.

Allen was the only one who fell in love while attending university. Allen's girlfriend's name was Stephanie Williams. They were together for a year and a half before she was killed in a car accident while heading home on Thanksgiving weekend. Allen never got over her. He still loved her and not a day went by he didn't think of her.

Allen became a pediatrician since he and Stephanie always talked about opening a practice together to help under privileged children. So in her memory, every Saturday morning Allen headed to the Angel Care Shelter in New York to administer medicine and examine the children. This was his way of still being part of her and letting her live on through him.

Every year Michael, Allen and Quinn took a week's vacation together. It was going to mark the 10th year and they decided it would be in Brazil right off the coast of Manaus to sightsee the Amazon Rainforest.

They enjoyed making plans and they would meet every week at the country club and go over the details.

Their vacations were always just one big party which included water sports, volleyball, food, beaches, bathing suits and beautiful women! They jammed as much fun into one week as they possibly could and always boarded the plane home totally exhausted from their excursions.

They knew someday as they all got married and had families these vacations would not be possible anymore. It was hard for Quinn to get Catherine to let him go since she knew how they partied and womanized. But Allen and Michael promised her on their lives that they would take good care of him and not let him out of their sight. So Catherine agreed to let him go this one time. They all talked about the possibility of this being their last trip together and agreed they would all make it their best!

# Chapter 2

They flew into Manaus and then shuttled to the resort with eight other people. They introduced themselves on the bus and planned on meeting up for drinks and dinner once they settled into their rooms.

When everyone got off the bus at the Tishi Amazon Resort they were amazed at the beauty that surrounded them. It was one of the most beautiful destinations Michael, Allen and Quinn had ever seen. They twirled around as they took in the beauty of the rainforest jungle. Their eyes widened as they looked at each other knowing it was going to be a great vacation!

The Tishi Amazon Resort was ten kilometers from Manaus right off the banks of the Rio Negro River. The complex was surrounded by its own grounds of more than two square kilometers. The resort was built around a beautiful natural lake that surrounded the resort. At the edge of the lake, there were twenty double huts with thatched roofs built on poles which would be their accommodations.

Each accommodation had a bed-sit with a spacious deck above the lake. There was a lovely wide sandy beach with small motor boats anchored walking distance out. There was one shower a day of heavy saturation and it could get very humid, but other than that, the weather was beautiful!

The resort had a large swirling swimming pool with a bridge over the pool that led to the Tishi Cabana Bar surrounded by beautiful palm trees. There was also a restaurant, a water sport center and an amphitheater. And everywhere around them they could see, hear and smell the Amazon jungle.

Their quarters were spacious double rooms, made entirely from wood and perfectly finished with local Teak and Mahogany woods. It was without a doubt one of the nicest accommodations they ever stayed in. The rooms had twelve feet high ceilings which vaulted to the center and gave the rooms a fantastic feeling of spaciousness.

The French doors gave them access to the large deck overlooking the beach. The bathroom was five star with a beautiful separate hot tub and their room also had a bar with sink and compact fridge.

Each day their breakfast, lunch and dinner were included and in addition all of the guests were offered various recreational and activity programs which was a large part of the vacation and included in the trip.

Once the three of them settled and unpacked in their rooms, they headed separately down to the resort to meet the other people from the bus for a drink.

Michael was dressed in a white linen loose button down shirt that opened from the neck to his breast line with a pair of tan linen designer slacks with a pair of canvas tan shoes for a more casual look. He always wore a thin gold chain around his neck that carried a symbol of the Australian flag.

Allen wore a pair of red and blue plaid shorts with a tight dark blue tee shirt, dark leather sandals and a Panama hat he bought on their last vacation in Ecuador.

Quinn never knew what to wear so he resorted to putting on a Hawaiian shirt and white canvas shorts that Catherine packed for him. His outfit looked surprisingly good for him. As he walked up to Allen and Michael at the bar, they started to clap and whistle surprised to see him dressed so nice. Quinn did a quick turn and a short bow and moved towards them while giving them the finger and rolling his eyes in the air.

Once they were seated in the restaurant, they were matched up in tables of eight people. Cindy and Alex, who they met on the bus from the airport, were seated with them. They were all having a great time getting to know one another.

At the end of the dinner, Cindy leaned over to Michael as she sat next to him on his right side. She whispered in Michael's ear, "Michael, do you get high?

Would you like to join me down at the beach and we can just sit and relax and then."

Her words stopped there and Michael knew where she was going with the conversation as he was approached countless times from women wanting the same thing. She wanted to get high on some local dope she purchased from one of the native people and make love through the Euphoria of it.

Michael was very attracted to Cindy's friend Alexandria. When he got on the shuttle bus to the resort he couldn't take his eyes off of her. But Cindy wasn't his type.

"Look Cindy, I don't want to insult you and I hope we can still be friends and have a good time together. But I don't get high, I'm a doctor, but I'm sure there's someone else who would love to take you up on that!"

Cindy stared into his dark eyes as she paused a moment at his breathtaking face. She wanted him and he wasn't interested. That just didn't happen to Cindy!

Cindy was a very smart career woman and a financial advisor for a national bank in Amsterdam. She was 5'6" tall and twenty-eight years old. She had breast implants and rhinoplasty with injected collagen in her lips. She was tanned with mid length light brown hair with blonde streaks around her face. Her eyes were light hazel and lined with dark brown eyeliner. She wore light pink lip gloss with a darker liner around her lips. She worked out every day and she was in very good shape. Men looked back over their shoulders to watch her go by.

Alexandria was a beautiful natural blonde with a very natural build. She had a very carefree attitude and a pleasure to be around.

Unlike Cindy, Alexandria could throw her hair into a ponytail and she was ready to go anywhere. But when she dressed in high heels, all eyes were on her long and thin shapely legs.

Alexandria was 5'8" tall. She was naturally fit and toned since she was always on her feet being a flight attendant for a European airline.

Cindy told Michael if he changed his mind she would be down on the south side of the beach. Michael shook his head to acknowledge what she said. She got up from the table and excused herself and left.

Michael had a small grin on his face as he looked over at Alexandria.

"Hello, are you in there?" Quinn asked as he shook Michael back to reality.

"Yes, I was just daydreaming."

Quinn looked curiously at Michael, "It looked like you were a million miles away."

Michael smiled at Quinn then he got up from the table to head back out to the pool. Allen and Quinn followed him out as they finished the night partying at The Tishi Cabana Bar with Alex and some of the other people from the bus.

# Chapter 3

The week was half over and they all took part in special day programs such as rainforest treks and survival programs. They participated in special theme programs on most afternoons such as dancing lessons, playing in a steel band, and rainforest nature lessons.

In addition they took part in lively evening beach parties, especially the one on Praia Da Luna, which was a beautiful moon lit romantic beach. There were lots of music venues, dance and cultural shows. They did so many interesting activities and were having the time of their lives with the new friends they made.

Every night they met everyone at the Tishi Cabana Bar and they danced, ate and drank into the night.

They had four days left in their vacation and the next day they were to head out for a three day excursion into the Amazon Rainforest.

They got up early to leave for their three day trek. This excursion would take them to the source of the Amazon down the Rio Negro River and into Lake Januari, which was a very cultural swamp lake and village of Irandavu where they could get to experience its rich traditional lifestyle of an Amazon tribe.

They would also visit the caves and waterfalls of Presidente Fiquereido, and a night cruise on the Amazon River. They would also take a trip searching for crocodile and fishing for Piranha. The natives working in the resort told them that they had to taste the Piranha soup and Tucanare fish that can grow up to a meter and a half long.

They talked about the three day excursion into the Amazon for most of the year. It was going to be their most adventurous and exciting vacation that they ever had. But at the same time they were a bit leery of some of the dangers that lurked in the Amazon.

They were told by Yurah, their guide about some of the dangerous animals they may encounter while on the tour. There were also many poisonous insects and reptiles they were warned about and what to do in case they were bit or encountered by them.

They all had their malaria and tetanus shots so they were protected from many of the diseases carried by the jungle swamps and insects.

They saw many salamanders, iguanas and beautiful birds including many Toucans, butterflies and other creepy crawlers while they were in a protected environment inside the compounds of the resort. But once outside they were warned of the many dangers they could encounter.

By 7:00 a.m. they met with the other parties and the tour guides, including three other couples and Alexandria. Cindy was also going to go but she got sick the night before and was fighting Montezuma's revenge mixed with a bad migraine headache. She told Alexandria to go on without her so not to spoil her vacation. Alexandra, being a very independent, spontaneous and adventurous person had no problem going on the tour on her own. So she met the others with excitement and ready to take on the challenge of the Amazon!

All together, there were ten tourists, two tour guides, whose names were Yurah and Davi (Dah • vee), and two fourteen year old native boys, Tutu and Nino (Nee • no), who would carry the food and supplies. They put Alexandria, Michael, Allen and Quinn with Yurah and Tutu in one green 23' motor boat, and then the other three couples with Davi and Nino in another white 23' motor boat. If they split up for a bit one team had to stay together. It would be safer and that way everyone was accounted for.

By 7:30 a.m. they left the resort and loaded onto the boats at the bank of the Rio Negro, better known as the Amazon River. As they floated down they could see the resort getting further and further away. Once they had no sight of the resort they all turned to look at each other as if to say, "What are we doing and will we ever come back alive?"

The first trip down the river was to Lake Januari. It was a very muddy swamp lake. Some of the inhabitants' they encountered travelling into the lake were Manatees, large catfish and a school of Piranha.

The trip got very dark and somber as they entered the lake. They could hear the paddles of the oars in the water as Yurah, Davi, Tutu and Nino stood rowing the boats through the narrowing of the lake. They turned the motors off not to disturb the animals once inside.

There were also sounds of insects buzzing around their heads, and birds and monkeys in the background. Then a sound came from the edge of the river and when they turned they could see the large body of an Anaconda slither into the water. Everyone gasped at its size as one of the woman clung to her husband in terror at the sight of it!

Everyone looked down into the water trying to see the bottom but couldn't. Yurah said that many Cayman crocodiles lived in the lake of the black muddy water. It gave them the protection they needed against predators and the natives.

Just as Yurah was narrating, a big bang hit the bottom of the boat! The force plunged everyone forward! Yurah and Tutu hurriedly sat down not knowing what it was.

Yurah and Davi started the boats engines and sped away as fast as they could! Everyone was terrified and looked back to see if they could see anything but nothing was there. Then Yurah yelled out laughing, "Everyone, welcome to the Amazon!" while he and Davi sped the boats forward.

A while later Yurah and Davi turned the engines off again, and Yurah said they needed to be very quiet and sit very still until they got to the large opening in the lake. They all looked at one another as their nerves mounted. One of the women in Davi's boat started to tear up she was so afraid. Davi told her she was okay and they were safe. He said that the crocodiles have much food in the waters and they have no need to attack humans unless provoked.

Further into the river it darkened and they saw a few crocodiles on land. They were basking in the sun on rocks where there was a very small clearance of the sun coming through the trees. They were a bit nervous, but since it looked as though the crocodiles were all asleep and too comfortable to leave their rocks they were sunning on, no one panicked. But once passed them everyone was relieved!

Hours later they came to a large opening where the water had a faster current. As they crossed Lake Januari they could see in the distance small huts built on high piers near the water's edge. They could see little children of the Cavairi natives and the village of

Irandavu. Other natives came out of their huts to see who was coming.

The huts were built on stilts to avoid the heavy rain period between December and July. They could expect up to twenty-five feet or more per season so the huts were built high off the river to survive the rainy floods. Sometimes up to twelve inches per day!

By the time they reached land the natives were standing on the shore excited to see them. Two of the native men helped to pull the boat up to the docks as everyone got off. The last two to get off were Michael and Alexandria.

Michael was being a gentleman letting her get off first, but while he stood there she reached down for her backpack and opened it. Then she unbuttoned her sweaty shirt and slipped it off and bent over to put her shirt in her backpack. She was wearing a bikini bathing suit top underneath with low rise denim shorts.

Michael could feel the excitement in his body as he watched her. But shaking his thoughts from his head he put his hand out, "You go first Alexandria."

As she passed by him she said softly while looking into his eyes and holding on to his hand, "My friends call me Alex."

He loved her casual yet beautiful demeanor. She was a true lady with simple elegance. He stayed close to her as much as he could for the rest of the day. As they toured the little village and ate on an old floating restaurant for lunch he sat himself down next to her.

By now Allen and Quinn definitely took notice of Michael's attraction for Alex.

They went on an afternoon excursion and got to see beautiful birds and flowers that embanked the river's edge. They had dinner that a few of the native men and women cooked over an open fire. It was fish again but cooked very differently with local spices and other herbs, nuts and fruits they had never tasted before. They had salads that were topped with herbal oils and dressings. They drank coconut water right out of the coconuts, and tried Tacacá, an Amazon local soup. The soup's broth was made from the root, Tucupi, and garnished with salted jumbo dried prawns, Jambu, a leafy green, dried shrimp, and some tapioca gum added for thickening.

They were all amazed at how this civilization survived hundreds of years in the depth of the Amazon, and how they depended solely on the land to provide food and materials to build their houses. It truly was incredible!

They went for a tour and stopped at a floating pier and walked on a skywalk to a lookout post to see down the swamp lake and marvel at the large lily pads. So large that people could walk on them.

When they got back they went on a little ferry boat down the river and got to marvel at giant Victoria Regia water lilies. They also saw a spectacular sight of three pink dolphins jumping out of the water acting as though they were happy to see everyone. The native man driving the boat opened a burlap bag and pulled out a few fish and threw them up in the air to the dolphins. The dolphins jumped up and caught the fish midstream in the air like they were trained to do it.

When they got back to the small village they were taken away again in their boats. They finally settled on land to some accommodations for the night. The huts were also built on stilts with thatched roofs and the accommodations were simple but quite clean and comfortable. There was one accommodation for the men and one for the women. There was a one rod shower on the ground on each side of the huts, and two out houses with a wooden fence all around them.

After they had breakfast the next morning they went Piranha fishing, and as soon as they put their make shift fishing rods into the water with some fresh cut up dried meat, hundreds of the Piranhas surfaced and flapped hungrily in the water after the bait.

Yurah warned everyone that if a Piranha jumped into the boats to move away from it since they were known to attack people while flopping on the deck floors.

Michael was the first one to catch one and then Quinn and Allen. Alex caught two. Each person in the other boat caught one also.

Yurah, Davi, Nino and Tutu didn't fish to keep an eye on everyone. They told everyone Piranha stories and how they bit toes and fingers off some of the native people. And how some natives went out to fish Piranhas and never came back!

Yurah and Davi wrapped the Piranha in wet burlap and paper to have for dinner that night. They all would have lots to feast on with having caught eleven Piranhas all together!

# Chapter 4

Back in the muddy water of Lake Januari, the trip out seemed much calmer. Everyone was much more relaxed enjoying the jungle tour as they passed back through the swamp that led them in the day before.

They got glimpses of things they never noticed on the way in. They spotted two Golden Lion Tamarins which are beautiful bright orange monkeys with manes like lions, and weighing about two pounds each.

Just as they were watching a river otter making a dam, they were all paralyzed in their seats from loud roars just feet from the river's edge as one of the women in Davi's boat started to scream!

"What the hell is that?" her husband cried out!

Panicking, everyone covered their ears from the frightening sounds.

As everyone was terrified waiting for an attack, they jumped up from their seats nearly tipping the boats over!

Yurah shouted as loud as he could, "Everyone, sit back down right now, or you'll get eaten by the crocodiles!"

In fear of tipping the boats over everyone took a moment to settle and then they sat back down into their seats. The animals were coming closer.

Yurah and Davi stopped the boats and everybody looked at them in terror!

"Have you lost your minds?" another man shouted at Yurah and Davi, "Get us the hell out of here!"

"It's okay!" yelled Yurah, "They're monkeys!"

"What are you talking about?" shouted Quinn. "Those are not monkeys! Those are wild animals that are going to attack us if we don't get the hell out of here!"

Yurah laughed, "Look, look over there about three feet inland just passed that big tree. Look up in the tree behind it and you'll see one of the monkeys. It's called a Howler monkey!"

They all looked up where Yurah was pointing and there was a monkey in the tree with its mouth wide open roaring down at them. And then they spotted others in the trees.

"Are they harmless?" another lady cried out still in fear of the monkeys.

"Yes, they won't hurt or attack. They are just warning us that they are there. I haven't seen them in these parts of the Amazon in many years. The Howler male monkey is one of the loudest animals in the world, and they use their loud harsh voice to ward off danger.

I guess they heard us and wanted to take a look," Yurah laughed.

It took minutes for everyone to compose themselves, but once they realized what it was they all started to settle down.

Alexandria was the first to compose herself. She was highly trained to stay in control being an airline flight attendant. She wrestled for her backpack and pulled out a camera and started taking pictures. After her the others joined in.

Everyone was starting to really enjoy the trip again as they realized they were in good hands with Yurah and Davi. They had been doing these tours for years, and even the animals were probably used to them by now. It was quite an exhilarating experience and they were all glad that the experience was over.

Once they reached the waters of the Rio Negro River again they all took a sigh of relief! The landscapes around them took their breaths away as it was one of the most beautiful places they had ever seen.

The sun beamed down with extreme heat on their bodies and faces. They all had lots of sun screen, hats and mosquito repellent or they wouldn't make it out alive!

Even though the waters were black, the foliage and flowers inland were that of a pure tropical paradise. The colors were so vast that even the beautiful toucans and other tropical bird's complimented the colorful landscapes. And heavy moss grew on the ground of the river's edge making it look like a giant dark green carpet.

The rest of the early day was spent in the boats travelling along the river's edge admiring its beauty while eating cheeses, fruits, and canned sardines, red wine and chocolate treats.

Once on land and all unpacked, Yurah told them they were going to take a walk inside the jungle. Everyone was very nervous accept Alex and Michael. The rest were not sure if they were ready to go on that trek yet.

Quinn asked if it was safe. Yurah said that it was never safe in the jungle, but he had done this many years and never had any problems he couldn't handle.

The other couples were very nervous, but then Alexandria spoke out and said, "Come on everyone, this is what we're here for!"

As they all lined up and started, Michael found himself again walking right behind Alex. As they went deeper, they spotted a pair of sloths and everyone stopped to laugh at them because of their very slow and passive nature. They laughed at one of the sloths scratching its head with its foot. But still respecting their territory they moved on after taking many pictures of the humble funny looking critters.

Spider monkeys hopped over their heads like they were flying through the air. They were all around them and very curious of the humans. They made a racket and pounded down some leaves and twigs over the marching brigade as they walked deeper and deeper into the jungle.

As they walked it got more humid and the plants and trees got larger and greener from the moisture inside the Amazon jungle.

A while later, Yurah motioned for everyone to be silent and stop! When everyone was standing still, Yurah reached to his back and slowly pulled out a rifle, and then Davi did the same. Everyone watched them while not moving a muscle.

With slow and heavy footsteps, Yurah and Davi joined together back to back moving around in a circle while they could hear something coming closer.

Then in the dark green camouflaged hedges, they could hear a massive animal growling as it slowly stalked towards them.

Terrified, everyone else turned towards the noise as they all band together in a closed little circle. Michael grabbed Alex's hand and put her behind him.

Michael, Allen and Quinn all looked at each other not knowing what was going to happen.

Then out of the bush came a two-hundred pound leopard running towards them!

As some of them screamed, Yurah took one shot in the air and the leopard turned and ran back into the hedges as fast as it came out!

Everyone was in a panic!

Davi tried to calm everyone down while Yurah ran into the bush shooting his rifle to scare the cat farther away.

A woman screamed out, "Get us back to the resort!" as she cried uncontrollably."

Everyone took a deep breath while some sat down to settle their nerves.

"We are half way in." Davi said while Tutu and Nino ran to give everyone water.

"There's no reason to turn around now. Now that it knows we're armed and dangerous, it will flee into the jungle and not return again."

Everyone looked at each other hesitating to go any further. They were all shaken and worried the leopard would return. But they trusted Yurah and Davi. They had not steered them wrong yet.

Once everyone settled down and drank some water from the canteens, they began their journey again walking on nervously with very watchful eyes!

# Chapter 5

When they arrived in the city of Presidente Fiquereido, the main attraction was the city's one hundred beautiful waterfalls that have won the town the nickname, "Terra das Cachoeiras," which means "Land of Waterfalls."

They all pulled out their cameras and started to take pictures right away! Alexandria asked Yurah if it they could go into the water as they approached a large waterfall with a big deep pond of water. Yurah said yes, and Alexandra ran into the water jumping and shouting, "Last one in is a rotten egg!"

They all laughed as one after the other piled in. They all jumped and swam around and went from waterfall to waterfall. Others jumped from the boulders to dive in. They were all like school children and none of them wanted to leave!

A while later Michael asked, "Where's Alex?" as he looked around for her. Everyone else stopped and turned to look for her but she was nowhere to be seen.

Then all of a sudden from just above them they heard Alex yell down, "Hey everyone, Come up here! Look what I found!"

Everyone quickly scurried out of the water and ran up a path to the top of the waterfalls. When they got to her she was standing in an opening of a very large cave. Everyone was mesmerized looking at the amazing sight of it! The cave had a large opening and the ceiling was at least thirty feet high.

"This is so cool!" said Allen as he turned around in a circle.

Everyone wandered around looking at the high ceilings of stone and little ports of other caves that ran off of it.

Alex ran up to Michael and grabbed his hand, "Come with me!" leading him to the back of the cave.

Once inside, they went down a narrow opening. When they got to the other side Michael couldn't believe his eyes! It was a beautiful waterfall rushing down across from them. It was like standing in front of a large movie screen while the waterfall plunged down and landed in a pond of water about twenty feet below.

"This is amazing!" said Michael.

Then all of a sudden Quinn ran in and shouted, "There you are!" And just as he shouted, loud screeches and blackness instantly surrounded them.

"Get to the ground!" screamed Michael. Michael grabbed Alex and pushed her back before she fell over the twenty foot cliff. He knocked her back so hard she hit her head on a rock going down.

No one could move off the ground as it seemed like minutes. They could hear the screams coming from everyone still inside the other side of the cave. Then in an instant the light came back and the loud screeching sound was gone.

Michael lifted his head slowly, "Bats!" yelled Michael, "We woke up the bats!" Then he remembered pushing Alex down to the ground! He and Quinn ran to her side.

"Are you okay love?" Michael cried out!

"Yes, I'm fine. I just hit my head a little."

He saw the small gash just inside of her hairline. He grabbed his tee shirt and ripped the pocket off and placed it on the cut.

Alex smiled at him, "Wow, what a rush!"

Michael looked down at her while holding the cloth on her forehead. He shook his head laughing, "You're too much!"

As everyone walked out of the cave, Quinn walked up to Michael and put his hand on his shoulder and said, "Love? You called her love?"

The next day, morning was half past and the sun was starting to burn as they headed back down the river. Tonight was going to be their last night before heading back to the resort.

As they headed back they saw a Kinkajou stretching itself awake. The Kinkajou is a monkey like animal that also resembles a raccoon, and Tutu explained that the native people also keep them as pets.

And then a Harpy Eagle flew over top as if watching them in their travels. They took pictures of the beautiful bird as it hovered over top with its expansive wings that spread open at least six feet wide. The eagle started to spiral downward as it looked fixed on something in a tree. The bird swooped down and grabbed a baby Callithrix Jaccus monkey right off of its perch and flew away with it in the grasp of its large sharp claws.

Everyone gasped at the sight of the bird while the tiny monkey screamed and tried to get away. But the eagle held on fast with a tight grip of its claws. As it flew away the monkey stopped fighting. And the eagle flew into the rainforest to finish its prey.

Everyone got over the sight quite quickly. After all, it was the Amazon and they had many experiences along their travels. Everything they saw just reinforced that it was Mother Nature and it was how it was meant to be.

An hour down the river the boats stopped for their last excursion. This was going to be the last night and they had to survive on their own. It was all up to them to provide for their own food and shelter.

Davi told them that they had to gather their own food and make their own fires and do it as teams. They also had to build a make shift shelter which the natives call a Bivouac. It's made of twigs, mud and topped with leaves for camouflage.

The area was surrounded by the Amazon jungle and they all were very hesitant about the location. It was very open and it seemed like anything could just walk out at any time during the night.

One of the men in Davi's group asked Davi if it was safe being in the open. Davi said yes, and he had been there many times. While everyone ventured out to find the materials to make their Bivouacs, they all tried not to wander too far from the camp.

They also agreed that Alex would stay behind with Yurah so that she could get a fire and start gathering food. Yurah would stay back with her and help.

"Who will go with us?" asked Allen.

Yurah laughed. "Com'n men! You are strong and brave. You don't need our help. Just go and stay close. Don't wander too far and you'll be fine."

Michael, Allen and Quinn looked at each other.

"Yurah's right, we'll be fine!" said Michael smiling at Allen and Quinn.

Quinn and Allen looked at each other, then looked back at Michael shaking their heads okay.

Michael, Allen and Quinn wondered towards the edge of the jungle looking inside. They were too leery to go too far so they tried to stay near where they entered.

They started to pick up broken twigs, leaves and other debris they could use for their shelter. Michael also looked for berries and other edibles to help Alexandria prepare a meal.

He wasn't too happy leaving her behind with Yurah. But he felt that she was in safe hands since he had a rifle just in case.

Turning to look back behind them there wasn't any sight of the camp anymore. They scanned their eyes through the jungle to see if it looked safe to enter.

When all three decided it looked alright they made their way in. As they walked, they picked up leaves, branches and other materials. And then they thought it would be a good idea to make a little skid to pull their findings back to camp. So they gathered some small vines and some branches and tied the branches together, totally unconscious of the fact that they had wondered quite deep into the thick foliage and trees.

"I'm going to cut one of those vines near that big tree to use to drag the skid," said Quinn.

"Okay, but stay close," said Allen while picking up some branches.

Quinn nodded okay walking through the Liana vines and pushing them out of his way towards the big tree.

All of a sudden Michael and Allen heard a large moan, and then a distant thump on the ground! Michael and Allen dropped what they were doing and ran after Quinn.

When they got to Quinn he was lying on the ground white as a ghost with his eyes wide open and frothing from his mouth. His lips were blue and he looked like he was in pain. They reached down and shook him but there was no response. Allen hurried to take his pulse but he couldn't get one. They looked at each other in panic!

"Quinn's dead!" shouted Allen.

Allen and Michael were mortified and in shock! They were stunned for a few seconds, but then their medical instincts kicked in to resuscitate Quinn. Allen started CPR to try to revive him but Quinn wasn't responding. Michael kept calling his name and checking his vitals with no response. Not thinking to call for help they ripped his clothes off of his body.

They looked all over and finally discovered two large holes on the left thigh of his leg. Right away Michael and Allen knew that Quinn was bit by a large snake. Allen began to cry silently as they tried to save the life of their friend.

All of a sudden from a small distance they heard something running towards them! Allen and Michael looked at each other eye to eye with terrible fear on their faces.

Michael cried out, "What the hell is happening now?"

Thinking it was a wild animal plunging towards them, they jumped up to see what was coming. They were frozen in their footsteps it was coming at them so fast! But they couldn't leave Quinn's side to run! In just a few seconds while their hearts were pounding like drums, they hurled around to the sound of something behind them! There stood a man standing in the distance.

He was a man in his late twenties. He just stood there and stared at Michael and Allen with a heavy breath and not moving a muscle. His stance was tall and solid.

He was wearing tight light colored straight leg blue jeans that showed his long legs and a rip across his jeans that exposed his large right thigh muscle. He wore a black leather vest that exposed his massive chest and a tight v-neck white tee shirt underneath. Like his vest he had leather boots that came midway up his calf with his jeans tucked inside of them. He had a strap over one shoulder on his back that had a bag with some hunting apparatus inside of it. He had another leather pouch joined to his hip.

His thick wavy hair was jet black and it was just to his shoulders and pulled back behind his ears. His chin and cheek bones were chiseled as they could see the man was in perfect form. His nose was of a Greek God and his skin was dark tan. He stood at least 6'2" tall and his muscles were as tight as they had ever seen. He was very strong and they could tell he lived in the Amazon.

Michael and Allen knew they would have no chance to survive a struggle with this man in front of them. Michael reached his hand towards the man to make peace with him.

Allen motioned to him to help Quinn since he knew this man was quite a survivor.

The man just stood there and stared at them. Finally after a few seconds, he looked down at Quinn as if he was assessing the situation. He then turned and with large footsteps and headed back where he came from.

Michael and Allen looked at each other and then turned their attention back to Quinn. They tried to get Quinn onto a hollow broken log that was cracked in half so they could carry Quinn back to the camp.

Just when they were ready to pull Quinn up onto the log the young man reappeared. This time he was wearing thick black leather gloves on his hands. He walked up to Allen and Michael and pushed them with both arms to pass by them. Michael and Allen couldn't believe the man's brutal strength. He leaned down in front of Quinn and pulled a jar out of his bag.

The jar was filled with a purplish grey fluid. The man opened it and poured it into Quinn's eyes, ears and mouth. Then he moved his leather vest open to show his massive chest and pulled out a knife from a strap he had around his chest. He took the knife and cut an "x" between the two bite marks. He then opened another jar and took out six large leaches and placed them on the wound.

Then after a few minutes he pulled the leaches from Quinn's skin and threw them to the ground. Then he poured the rest of the sludge over the cut. He massaged Quinn's cut with his hands and then ran his thumbs over Quinn's eyes.

He got back up and moved back standing in between Michael and Allen. All of a sudden there was movement coming from Quinn's chest. Michael and Allen took a deep breath and realized Quinn was breathing. They ran to his side and started trying to revive him again. After a few long seconds Quinn opened his eyes.

He looked up at Michael and Allen then spit the fluid out of his mouth onto the ground. He said with a soft weak voice, "I'm thirsty."

Allen and Michael grabbed Quinn and gave him a hug and pat on his back. They both turned around in excitement to thank the man but he was already gone. They couldn't believe what just happened! But they knew they had to get Quinn back to their camp for more evaluation. They lifted Quinn to his feet and walked him back to camp each holding on to him.

When all three men returned to the camp the others could see something was wrong. Alex ran to them and walked right next to Michael as she worryingly looked into his face.

"What happened?" asked Yurah.

"You won't believe us when we tell you," said Allen.

They helped Quinn down on a blanket. Everyone in the camp ran to his side. He was very weak but still very alive. His vitals and blood pressure had all returned almost normal. When everyone was seated around them, Allen and Michael told them what happened and all about the mysterious rainforest man. They all looked on with disbelief while the three doctors just kept reiterating that it really happened.

About a half hour later Yurah spoke out, "He wasn't dead and he wasn't bit by a snake."

Michael looked at Yurah for a few seconds then stood to his feet. Michael knew that it did happen, and didn't like Yurah challenging the truth about what they were saying.

"Are you calling us liars Yurah?" Michael spoke in a harsh voice. "We know what we saw and what happened! How could you even say that? You weren't even there!"

Allen knew that Michael was very upset. His nerves from what happened got the best of him. He saw Michael like this once before in a bar when a man slapped his girlfriend across the face. Michael jumped over a table and punched the guy so hard the guy was knocked out cold! He could see that look in Michael's eyes so Allen grabbed him by the shoulder to back him away from Yurah.

"Michael my friend," said Yurah, "I understand what you think you saw. But the truth is what you saw was nothing more than an illusion. It was an illusion that was bestowed on you by Natowa (Naht • ow • ah). He's a spirit that lives in the Amazon."

Everyone looked at Yurah with their eyes and mouths wide open except Michael.

"What are you talking about Yurah?" contended Michael, "Look, I'm not into voodoo or spirits or ghosts or any other phenomenon you can think of. It was as real as all of us standing here!"

"Michael, you must understand and you have to believe me or he'll haunt you for the rest of your life! He's a spirit who helps people to survive in the rainforest. If he stops he'll be doomed to hell forever. So he makes people illusion bad things so that he can make them well and roam the rainforest. He blew finely ground opium in your face. So fine you cannot see it. He leaves it on the ferns that you walk through so it falls all over you and you breathe it in without knowing it. It's an opium so strong only one little dusting of it will make you hallucinate. He has done this to many of our people. We consider him to be friendly. But don't cross him or he can become evil!"

Michael, Allen and Quinn looked at each other. They were in total disbelief of what Yurah was saying.

Michael shook his head, "I don't want to talk about this anymore. We'll keep an eye on Quinn for the night. If nothing comes of it, then we'll forget about it."

Michael turned around and his first thought was where did Alex go? As he looked he could see a fire down at the water's edge. He walked towards it and saw Alex standing cooking over the fire.

"I think you all need something to eat, It's been a long day and I hope you're hungry," said Alex as Michael approached her.

He looked over on a blanket and there was a feast fit for a king! She cooked the Piranha they caught, lobster and crab legs, avocados, fruits and berries. A big salad with nuts and herbs in an oil dressing in hollowed bowls of coconuts. There was a big jar filled with the coconut milk. Everyone had joined them by now and they were all amazed at the food she found and prepared. She told them that Yurah was a big help!

After dinner Michael, Allen and Quinn were exhausted from the episode they encountered. No one had time to make the bivouac shelters because of all the commotion. They all slept around the fire in their sleeping bags.

The next morning everyone was up at the crack of dawn to head back to the resort. The trip back was long for Michael, Allen and Quinn. They were looking forward to getting back to the resort and enjoying the comforts they were accustomed to.

The experience with Quinn made them realize how lucky they were to live in a country like America. Even though the Amazon was beautiful and filled with excitement and adventure, it was a hard place to live and survive. And everyone on the boats all agreed that the people of the Amazon didn't know any other lifestyle because of how isolated they were. It made them sad to think they all had to live such a hard and constrained life.

They were just minutes away from the resort now and everyone was anxious to get there. As soon as the resort was in sight when they came around a bend they all cheered and clapped their hands!

All of a sudden Alex stood up in the boat and ripped off her shirt to expose her bathing suit top. She jumped off the boat and into the water. The water was up to her hips as she started wading towards the resort splashing the water about, "Last one in is a rotten egg!"

Michael laughed and jumped in after her. Then Allen and Quinn followed too. They all raced each other to shore while the others in the boats just laughed and watched on.

# Chapter 6

After everyone returned to their rooms, they were all exhausted from the three day excursion. Michael laid in his bed as he stared up at the ceiling of his room contemplating the events that happened with Quinn and the man in the Amazon jungle. And he thought about Alex and how happy he was he got to know her even more without having Cindy's interference all the time.

As his mind drifted into sleep he woke a few hours later with a soft knock on the door. As he tried to shake himself awake, he got to his feet and walked to open the door.

When he opened it there was Alex standing there in a beautiful red sequined dress and matching stiletto heels. She had her hair twisted up in a bun on top of her head and she looked at Michael with a big smile.

"Hi Michael, are you coming down for dinner?"

He shook his head again and asked, "What time is it?" If he was only asleep for a few hours then it wasn't nearly time for dinner yet.

"You must have been very tired. It's time to go for dinner and Allen and Quinn are already waiting for you. I told them I would come to get you."

He turned to look at the clock on the desk and it was 7:00 p.m. He remembered now that he could hear the phone ringing but he was too tired to wake up. He apologized to Alex for over sleeping and he told her that he would be right down.

Alex said, "Then why don't I come in and have a drink while you get ready."

Michael was surprised Alex would invite herself in, but he was glad to see her take an interest in staying to be with him, so he opened the door and let her in. As she passed by him he could see the long slit down her dress exposing her long and shapely left leg, and when she walked her firm muscles popped out from her calves as she stepped in her stiletto heels.

Michael had just woken and his body was very sensitive from the sight of her. He felt himself swell under his robe. He had never had a woman at just the sight of her make him excited and lust for her before she even touched him. He was enjoying his feelings for her as he never thought any woman could make him feel this way.

By the time he took his eyes off of her body she was standing at the bar pouring them both a glass of

Chardonnay. She walked up to him and held out one of the glasses. He took it from her hand as he gently touched across her fingers. She wasn't wearing a bra and he realized she was very excited about his touch.

Michael was again excited by the sight of her, and he leaned down over her and kissed her lips. He gently pulled the elastic from her hair and her hair fell in waves down her back and around her face.

Alex reciprocated by pressing very firmly an open long and hard kiss over his mouth.

While he was lost in his thoughts, Alex pulled him back a bit and said, "I think you should get ready for dinner now."

But Michael's thoughts were not on dinner. He leaned over and kissed her again and again. Finally he knew that he had to pull away or he would take her into his bedroom. He drank down the rest of the wine and then headed towards the shower.

The phone began to ring again. And as he went towards the phone he lost his step and somehow fell! When he got back up he didn't know where he was for a minute. He turned to look at Alex but she was nowhere to be seen. He couldn't understand what was going on as he looked around the room. And then his heart fell as he realized what happened. Alex was never there. Everything that happened was only a dream!

Once Michael was over the disappointment, he got ready and joined everyone for dinner.

As he sat at dinner staring at the empty seat where Alex usually sits, Allen leaned over and declared to Michael, "There's Alex."

Michael's eyes went straight to the door and there was Alex and Cindy entering the room. She was as beautiful as always and even though she wasn't wearing the red dress from his dream he still could see her in it as she walked across the room. Her presence made him smile and all three men stood and pulled the two women's chairs out as they sat down at the table.

This time Alex seated herself next to Michael as she looked into his eyes and asked, "Did you have a good sleep?"

He chuckled and commented, "It could have been better."

She smiled back at him for a few seconds and then Cindy noticed the two of them. Cindy knew the look on Alex's face when she was in love with a man. Cindy met Alex's last boyfriend whom she dated for two years. He was an airline pilot and Cindy and Alex flew a few times on his plane. He would have them come up to the cockpit and fly with him. Alex would give him that same kind of smile and glimmer in her eyes. Cindy was pissed! She wanted Michael, and now Alex was getting in the way.

As the night went on Michael moved himself next to Alex again at the cabana bar. There was something that was building between the two of them and Alex felt it too.

Later, Michael took Alex by the hand to slow dance. He held her firmly in his arms as he swept her across the room. They danced like they were a match made in heaven and people looked on admiring what a stunning couple they were.

Allen and Quinn were really taking notice never seeing Michael act this way.

As they danced Michael whispered in Alex's ear, "How's your night going beautiful?"

A smile came to her face as Cindy watched on with malice in her eyes.

As everyone was having a great time, Michael felt a pat on his shoulder. It was one of the bell boys from the hotel, and he told Michael that he had an important phone call. Michael excused himself and asked if the phone call could be transferred to his room.

When he returned to his room he was waiting for the phone call to be forwarded when there was a knock on the door. When he opened the door Cindy was standing there with a bottle of Merlot and her blouse unbuttoned below her breast, staring at Michael like he was her prey.

"Cindy! What the hell are you doing?" Michael blurted out at her, "I already told you that I'm not interested! For you to trick me to come to my room only reinforces you are not my type!"

Cindy had quite a few drinks and was swaying a little as she stood in her four inch leather sandal high heels. Cindy paid no attention to his words and cried out to Michael.

"Michael, come on! Why don't you want me? "It doesn't have to mean anything. Just you and I have to know!"

He pulled her into the room to not make a scene outside. His brow was beaded with sweat as his anxiety got the best of him.

"Look Cindy, I already told you I wasn't interested and you should have left it at that!"

Just as he was ready to speak again, Cindy wrapped her arms around his shoulders and stole a deep hard kiss. As he tried to push her off of him, he grabbed her by her shoulders and tried to shake her loose. But she was quite strong from working out as he struggled to pull her away!

All of a sudden the door slowly pushed open and there stood Alex. The look on Alex's face suddenly changed to disgust as tears filled both of her eyes.

Cindy hurriedly buttoned her blouse while Michael wiped the sting of Cindy's lips from his. He was still shaken by Cindy's actions and had no idea what was going on in Alex's mind.

Alex gave them both a deep long hard stare and then turned and walked back out. Michael tried to compose himself and then walked next to her going down the stairs trying to explain. Then grabbing her arm he spun her around to look at him.

"Wait Alex, where are you going? You can't leave!"

Alex gave him another deep stare and pulled her arm out of his grip. She left towards the beach as fast as she could.

Cindy stood there staring down at Michael. "Is there something I should know Michael? Is there something going on between Alex and you?"

Michael turned to look up at Cindy with rage in his eyes. "Get out of here Cindy!" as he climbed the stairs towards her. When he got to the top he went inside his room then he slammed the door behind her!

Later that evening Michael tried to call Alex's room but he couldn't get a hold of her. He tried her cell phone but just got her voicemail. He left a message and told her he could explain and he was going to tell her what had happened. He hurried down to the bar where Allen and Quinn were still drinking.

"Hey Michael, get over here!" called Allen. "We miss you!

He walked behind Allen and patted him on the back. "I think you guys have had enough to drink," as he watched Quinn across the pool doing the limbo with a native woman dancer. Then he preceded passed Allen.

He was looking everywhere for Alex, but she was nowhere to be found. He waited up until 6 a.m. camped outside her room. But she never returned.

He was very worried about her and he started down to the beach to look for her. He called up to Allen and Quinn's rooms to see if they had seen her but there was no answer. He went to the front desk and asked the clerk if she left any message and the hard words of the clerk rung through him.

"Oh yes Mr. Sinclair, Ms. Van De Meer checked out at 6:30 this morning. She told us she had an emergency."

He was numb from the disbelief that she left without giving him the time to explain. But then his mind wondered and thought, "What if I would have seen Alex and Allen like that? What would I have thought?" He knew she had every right to feel the way she did, even if it wasn't his fault.

He never spoke another word to Cindy for the rest of the trip. And Cindy knew what she did was horribly wrong. She knew there was no chance with Michael after what she did.

# Chapter 7

When they got back to New York, Michael told Allen and Quinn that he had fallen in love with Alex, and what had happened with Cindy the night Alex had left. Allen and Quinn felt bad for Michael. They knew that he must have really loved her since they had never seen him like this ever before.

Allen especially knew what Michael was feeling with the loss of Stephanie. Over the next few weeks, Michael left countless messages on Alex's cell phone but they were never returned.

A month went by after Michael, Allen and Quinn's vacation. They tried to get together for dinner since they had many things to catch up on. This was the longest they had ever gone without seeing each other. They all stayed in touch by phone and tried to make some plans. But Michael had to cancel time and time again since he wasn't feeling well.

Allen and Quinn thought that he just needed some time after all that happened with Alex. They tried to encourage him to see a doctor and he promised he would.

After Michael cancelled their last dinner engagements four times in a row, Allen and Quinn decided to pick up a pizza and beer to surprise Michael at his house. When they arrived they rang the doorbell three times. They knew Michael was home since his car was parked in the circular driveway, rather than his three bay garage that was located at the back of his house.

Quinn thought it was strange that Michael's car was parked in the front. He drove a brand new black Aston Martin fully loaded. It was Michael's pride and joy. When Quinn walked to the car to check the hood he could tell the car hadn't been driven.

Quinn and Allen went around the back of the house and could see a light on in Michael's room. Quinn picked up a soccer ball that was in the back yard from the neighbor's young son and threw it and hit Michael's bedroom window.

When Michael appeared to look out the window to see what was going on, Quinn and Allen couldn't believe their eyes! Michael looked as white as a ghost and as though he hadn't taken a bath in days.

Quinn yelled up to Michael. "Michael, open the door!"

Michael turned slowly from sight and finally opened the door.

Allen and Quinn were devastated at the sight of their best friend. He looked gaunt and lost at least ten pounds and could hardly stand up on his feet. When they rushed to his side they helped him back into the house and onto the couch.

"What the hell is going on with you Michael?" asked Allen extremely concerned for him.

"I'm not sure. I think I have some kind of flu bug. I went to see my doctor last week and had some blood work and an MRI done. I'm just waiting for him to get back to me with the results."

Quinn and Allen were quite upset and knew what Michael had was more than the flu. They even thought for a moment that he may have Malaria from their trip to the Amazon, but he was vaccinated and thought it would be highly unlikely.

Allen and Quinn insisted on taking Michael to the hospital right away to do their own tests. Quinn went to Michael's home phone and picked up the receiver to call an ambulance. There was a fast blinking light which meant Michael had messages on his answering machine.

When Quinn listened there were four messages from Michael's doctor. All the messages from him were urging Michael to call him. The doctor stated that he was trying to get a hold of him all weekend and he needed to see him as soon as possible!

Quinn knew Michael's doctor and called him on his cell phone, "Hi Dr. Richardson, this is Dr. Quinn Adams calling you. I'm calling in regards to Michael Sinclair. I know you've been trying to get a hold of him. My friend Allen and I are with Michael right now and he's not doing very well. Did you get the tests results back yet?"

As Quinn stayed silently on the phone for a few minutes, Allen could see Quinn's face drop then tears filled his eyes as the doctor gave him the diagnosis.

Allen stared at Quinn knowing something was very wrong. Michael was already back asleep while looking weak and pale on the couch. When Quinn hung up the phone, he put his head down and he tucked his hands into the pockets of his jeans.

"Tell me what's going on," pleaded Allen.

Quinn slowly looked up at Allen and said, "Michael has cancer of the pancreas, and it has gone to his liver as well."

Michael lay in the hospital bed and was feeling much better with the small doses of morphine the hospital was administering.

A week passed and Michael was begging the doctors to let him go home. But they all urged him to stay in the hospital until further tests and MRI came back.

Allen and Quinn came early each morning, during lunch and after work. They knew the chances of Michael recovering from his prognosis were very slim and they wanted to spend as much time with him as they possibly could.

A few days went by and all Michael's tests came back. The doctor wanted to perform surgery to cut out as much of the cancer as possible and then after Michael recuperated he would need chemotherapy. It wasn't going to cure him, but it would buy him some time. Michael had a long rough road ahead of him, and Allen and Quinn were there for him every step of the way.

After Allen and Quinn left the hospital on one of their visits they stopped by a local bar to grab something to eat. They talked about trying to get a hold of Alex, but wondered how Michael would feel if he found out.

Michael was a very proud person and he certainly wouldn't want anyone to feel sorry for him. He would tell Allen and Quinn at each visit to go home and not to worry so much about him. He hated how he was inconveniencing his friends and how much they were doing for him. But they both ignored him and stayed by his side.

As they talked Allen reflected on the last vacation they all had together, and all the wonderful memories of all the years they had as friends. After they ate and had a few drinks they were feeling their spirits.

Quinn joked and half seriously said, "Maybe we should go back to the Amazon and get Natowa who saved me in the rainforest."

They both laughed!

A few seconds went by and then they looked at each other like they were thinking the same thing.

"Should we?" added Allen.

Quinn stared down at his drink, "There's something I have to tell you."

"Okay, what is it?"

"Well, do you remember when Yurah alleged that Natowa was a spirit? Yurah said that he sprinkled us with opium, and that what we saw was only a hallucination?"

"Yes, I remember."

"Well, it wasn't."

"What do you mean?"

"It really happened."

Allen looked at Quinn confused, "How do you know?"

"I know because I had a hair follicle test done when we got back to the hospital, and it came back negative, which means there was no opium in our systems like Yurah said."

Allen looked surprised! "So it really did happen!"

Quinn shook his head yes.

"I had to know," said Quinn. "Was I really dead or was it a hallucination?"

"Why didn't you tell us?"

"I just wanted to forget what happened. People would think we were crazy if we went around saying that I died and then I was brought back to life by some guy by the name of "Natowa!" We're doctors for God sake! So I thought it was best to leave it alone."

Allen plunged back hard in his bar seat. His shoulders hung heavily down as he went deep into thought. Then he lifted himself up and gulped down the rest of his drink. He stood up and put his leather coat on. "Come on, let's go. The only way we're going to save Michael is to go back and get Natowa. We have a plane to catch!"

Sitting by Michael's side in Michael's hospital room, Allen and Quinn told Michael that they had to leave for a week or so. Michael was a bit puzzled and asked them where they were going?

"Well" said Quinn, "We know someone that can help you."

Michael looked confused, "What are you guys talking about?"

Quinn told Michael about the hair follicle test he had taken and the fact that the test came back negative.

"I don't understand what you guys are talking about?"

"Natowa is real. He wasn't an illusion," said Allen.

Michael stared at them with a blank look on his face. Then realizing what they were talking about he started to laugh. He was laughing so hard that he was holding his stomach from the pain.

Allen and Quinn just looked at each other and shrugged their shoulders. Then they got up and leaned over Michael and gave him a pat on his shoulder and then walked out of the room.

As Michael yelled after them to come back they stood for a second at the door and waved good bye to Michael. Michael first thought it was a joke, but then after a few seconds he realized they were serious! Michael was in no position to argue. They were already gone.

# Chapter 8

When Allen and Quinn arrived at the airport in Manaus, Yurah, Nino and Tutu were waiting for them to drive them to the resort.

"Hello my friends," Yurah boasted! "How are you doing? So nice to see you arrive so soon after your last vacation!"

Allen and Quinn looked at Yurah knowing this trip wasn't going to be any vacation.

"Thanks for picking us up Yurah," said Allen, "But we need to tell you something."

"Okay what is it?" asked Yurah.

Quinn said, "It's Michael."

"Yes Michael! Where is my friend Michael? I thought he would be with you."

Allen looked sadly at Yurah, "Michael is very sick Yurah. He's dying in the hospital from cancer."

Yurah, Tutu and Nino looked surprised and very sad to hear the news.

"So why do you leave your friend to come on a vacation?"

Quinn said, "We're not here on a vacation Yurah. We need your help. It's the only chance we have to save Michael. Yurah, we've come back to hire you and Davi to help us go back into the Amazon."

Yurah looked puzzled. "You want to return to the Amazon jungle?"

Allen said, "Yes, we need to find Natowa. He's the only one that can help Michael."

"Natowa," Yurah shouted! "No man, Leave him alone or he'll possess you!"

Allen and Quinn ignored what Yurah contended and then told him that they knew Natowa was human. They have proof that he exists and they have to find him to save Michael. Yurah kept shaking his head no, but Allen and Quinn were relentless!

"Yurah," said Quinn. "If you don't help us we'll do it anyways. We're willing to give you a year's worth of pay to help us. If not, we'll find someone else."

Yurah looked at Allen and Quinn with dismay in his face. But thinking of a year's worth of pay was too hard for him to turn down.

Tutu and Nino were pushing Yurah to say yes, so he agreed reluctantly to help them go back in the Amazon to find Natowa.

Carrying their luggage to the jeep with Nino and Tutu, Yurah walked ahead of Allen and Quinn shaking his head and then said, "You have both lost your minds!"

As they loaded up the boat the following morning to head into the Amazon, Allen and Quinn were much more at ease and knew more about the dangers. The noises that were heard this time were more familiar to them, and returning to the Amazon again was quite spectacular as they admired it even more than the first time. As they travelled down the Amazon River they fell on many sights that they remembered and many new ones discovered.

As the day passed and the sun set they stopped along the water's edge and made camp for the night. Allen and Quinn were exhausted from the flight and didn't have much sleep to prepare for the journey. They knew that they could go out fast asleep but tried to keep one eye open just in case a wild animal wandered nearby. They slept in sleeping bags near the fire to be safe.

Quinn woke before Allen and could smell ham and other foods cooking.

"Good morning," said Quinn.

Allen pried his eyes open and gave Quinn a soft nod to acknowledge him. Then they walked together to the open fire where Yurah, Davi and Tutu and Nino sat.

They sat down in a circle around the fire and feasted on some left over ham, fish and rice that Yurah and Davi prepared for dinner the night before.

Yurah went over the day's agenda and what time they should be arriving at their destination. They planned to head back to the same place where they had camped the day Quinn was bit by the snake and Michael and Allen met Natowa.

They needed to find the exact place hoping that Natowa lived or travelled nearby. Yurah told them that it was quite unlikely that they would see him again, and kept reiterating that Natowa was a spirit and not a person.

Being doctors, Allen and Quinn knew that the science of the hair follicle test proved that Natowa was alive and as human as they were. And they knew they were not doused with opium which caused them to hallucinate as Yurah believed. These were old wives tales, and Yurah was brought up to believe that spirits exist. After they ate, they immediately packed up and headed back down the river.

It seemed there was no time for anything else but making camp, eating and sleeping. They made camp again the next night at the same camp where they found Natowa. They intended to head out the next morning to look for him.

When everyone was sound asleep, Yurah sipped on water to help him stay awake. He had just one more hour to keep watch when Davi would take over. His eyes were beginning to feel very heavy as he had been up for twenty hours so far. But he fought his deprivation by standing much of the time almost feeling his body topple over from being so tired.

Just as his eyes started to drift again, and maybe for the last time before he would have fallen to sleep, a loud screech just a few yards away came barreling towards their camp! Then two large screeches as they neared the men as if they were communicating to each other. Everyone knew they were wild boars!

Everyone jumped up from their sleeping bags knowing there was danger coming right towards them. Tutu and Nino screamed in terror and started to run from the camp.

Yurah yelled to the boys to come back! Nino stopped as he was half in shock and ran back to stand between Allen and Quinn. Allen put his arm around the young man to compose him, but there was no sight of Tutu.

They all feared the worst! Yurah already had a rifle in a halter he wore on his chest and rifle in his hand. Davi ran to get two rifles and threw one of them to Allen.

Allen looked in shock as he had not shot a gun since he was sixteen years old on a fox hunt with his father. But knowing that he had to use the rifle to save their lives, he cocked it and got ready to aim and shoot.

Quinn stood looking around with a large knife in his hand.

The noise stopped! And Yurah motioned to everyone to be very quiet. As they all stood like statutes back to back in a small circle to protect one another from the beasts, the screeches began again. This time it was so close that any second the animals would be breaking into their camp.

As they all aimed the guns towards the noises, a wild boar plunged into the camp screeching and running so fast that Yurah and Davi fired their rifles and missed. The wild boar acted as if he didn't even know they were there as he went running past them straight out and back through the other side of the camp.

Before they could turn around, a jaguar was staring straight at them just fifteen feet away. None of them had their rifles aimed. He slowly snarled as he stalked towards them. It was ready to pounce at the first move.

All of a sudden Tutu ran back into the camp and stopped behind the jaguar not even knowing it was there! The cat turned and slowly stalked towards him. Tutu screamed for help crying uncontrollably. Just when Yurah got a clean aim at the jaguar, it leaped at Tutu and dragged him so fast into the thick marsh that Yurah didn't have time to shoot!

Yurah and Davi repeatedly shot aimlessly hoping to hit the cat as Tutu screamed and fought for his life! Allen not knowing where to aim couldn't do anything. They all looked at each other in shock as they heard the young man get ravaged by the jaguar. They couldn't go after him for other animals by then could smell the blood and they would all become their prey.

Allen and Quinn were numb from what just happened. Yurah and Davi sat Allen, Quinn and Nino down to compose them. For the rest of the night no one said a word. Still watching for predators Davi and Yurah were on the alert. They were armed and prepared for another attack!

The next morning and after what had happened to Tutu, Allen and Quinn decided to end their journey. The Amazon was just too dangerous and they were too heartsick with what happened to Tutu. His screams haunted them and it was best for everyone's safety to head back to the resort.

Back into the river, a terrible feeling came over Allen. He was thinking of Michael.

"How are we ever going to tell Michael?" Allen asked Quinn.

"I don't know how we're going to tell him, I don't really want to think about it right now."

"I know, but we're going to return with the bad news. Michael might be hanging on to his life thinking were going to find a cure to save him. How are we ever going to tell him that we had to quit and return without trying to find Natowa?"

"We'll think of something even if we have to lie."

"Allen looked at Quinn "Lie to him?" And when he dies do you think I'm going to able to live with that?"

"No!" snapped Quinn. "I didn't mean it like that! I just don't know what to say. I'm totally exhausted and someone died because of us, and I just want to stop thinking about it for awhile."

Yurah and Davi listened on to Quinn and Allen's conversation.

Then Yurah said, "Allen and Quinn, Michael is very lucky to have the two of you as friends, and what you're doing is very noble to say the least. Tutu did not die because of you. It was his time to go to the mighty kingdom, and that's the premise that the natives live on in the Amazon.

We cannot question when and how we will die for many of us die of many causes in the Amazon. So we have a way of coping with our grief to say that his spirit will live on and it will protect the Amazon and all of its elements. Even though his mother will grieve, she'll not blame you or anyone else for her son's fait. It was his time!"

Yurah's words brought Allen and Quinn some comfort. And realizing that they had come this far and return without any hope gave them second thoughts as whether to leave or stay.

"What should we do?" asked Quinn to Allen.

"Yurah and Davi, what would you do?" asked Allen.

"I would not give up," said Davi. "You have come this far."

Yurah said, "If Natowa is alive and he is not a spirit, we will find him. And if he can find a cure for Michael, then the young man did not die in vain. His death will become a legend to his people.

Allen and Quinn with the encouragement of Yurah and Davi decided to stay. They would give it one more chance to find Natowa. They were even more driven now to find him, not only for Michael, but in memory of Tutu also.

They decided not to delay or waste any more time. They would enter the jungle as soon as they reached their destination again.

They all settled in for another night into their sleeping bags. Davi and Yurah agreed they would take turns watching the camp and relieve each other every four hours. So as everyone else slept, Yurah stayed up first by the roaring blazing fire they built to ward off the animals.

One fear that the animals of the Amazon had was a fear of fire. It was nature's way of keeping the rainforest healthy from sickness and disease. The strong ones could run for protection while the weak ones couldn't make it out.

The Amazon had an incredible way of taking care of itself. And with every rain and fire, the Amazon grew stronger and stronger and grew more and more herbs, plants and trees while keeping the wild animals and disease under control.

The morning dawned and the wetness of the jungle's dew woke everyone from their sleep. The heavy dew chilled them to get up and go and stand by the fire.

While Davi and Nino prepared breakfast, Allen, Quinn and Yurah talked amongst each other about entering the Amazon jungle again.

Allen looked out into the clearing and then followed his eye exactly where they entered into the jungle the day Quinn was bit by the snake. He knew that once inside he would remember the place where he and Michael witnessed Natowa bring Quinn back to life.

Allen and Quinn missed Michael, and reflecting on the last time they stood in that clearing, they could hear Michael's laugh as he was always ready and willing to take on a challenge.

He was the first one to want to enter the Amazon jungle. Whether they were on vacation in Bora Bora or Hawaii or the Fiji Islands, he was always the first to take on the endeavor which led Allen and Quinn to join in. It felt strange to them that they were on their own without him.

Too far into the Amazon to use their cell phones, they lost connection with the outside world. They prayed Michael was okay, and they knew being doctors that he could take a turn for the worse at any time. They just wanted to be able to return before Michael's fate took him. And even if they could not find a cure through Natowa, they hoped they could return to be there for him as he passed.

They were very confident that they were going to find Natowa. So with that in mind, they embarked back into the jungle with Yurah and Davi leading the way while Nino walked sadly thinking of his friend Tutu behind them.

The sounds of the tropical jungle were calling them again, and as they walked they could hear the familiar sounds that echoed through the ferns, vines, and trees. And jumping from tree to tree the Spider monkeys and their curiosity called the other life from the rainforest to their attention.

As they walked, the sounds got louder and louder. And they could hear a waterfall in the distance that represented they were getting nearer to their destination.

"Stop!" shouted Quinn.

Everyone turned to look at him.

"What's the matter?" Allen looking at Quinn very worried.

Quinn stood in one spot nearly frozen to the ground. "I don't want to do this!"

Allen looked at Quinn in surprise! "What's wrong?"

I don't want to die again!" The terror and panic on his face was evident he didn't want to go any further.

"Quinn," said Allen, "We came this far! Trust me, everything will be alright!"

But Allen's words didn't comfort Quinn. He wasn't moving another foot.

Yurah walked towards Quinn and then stood right in front of him. "Come Quinn," said Yurah. "Just take one step at a time. It's natural that you would be fearful but you can do this. We're not too far away from where we need to stop, and we will see from there if Natowa will show up. If not, we'll return back to our camp."

Quinn looked at Yurah still not wanting to move. Then Davi and Allen walked up alongside of Quinn as if to protect him from outside danger.

Nino walked up behind him and gave him a gentle nudge. Nino added, "You need to do this for Michael."

As Quinn looked down at Nino, he moved forward behind Allen and Davi as they led him closer to their destination.

After a short walk, he regained his confidence. He gave everyone a sigh of relief that he was okay.

They all smiled at him and walked on with their heads high and not worrying anymore of what the Amazon would have in store for them. They knew that they came this far and had to complete the journey whether they ever got to see Natowa or not. They were almost there!

As Allen motioned with his hand for everyone to stop, he recognized they were at the location. He remembered the large tree that Quinn slipped behind, and then the sound of the thump he heard when Quinn hit the ground.

"This is it!" Allen cried out. "This is where it happened!" Allen was full of excitement as he led everyone to the spot where Quinn laid when he and Michael found him.

Quinn looked on from a near distance not wanting to step back into the tracks that took his life. The last thing he remembered was waking up after the pain stopped. That's all he wanted to remember.

Allen stood looking around wondering if Natowa heard them enter and maybe following them. He knew that Natowa had very keen instincts and senses since he found them the first time. He also wondered if Natowa would remember them. Even though Allen was anxious to see Natowa return, he was cautious and somewhat fearful at the same time.

Quinn was even more nervous for he never got to lay eyes on Natowa. He was afraid that Natowa might be angry for them returning. After all, it was where he lived to be apart from humans and the danger they may bring.

After a little while, they decided to have lunch, and then they looked around to see if they could find any tracks that could lead them in the direction of Natowa.

Yurah was a great hunter and tracker. He grew up tracking animals with his father and kin. He could tell by the way the ferns bent and leaned and stones were turned. He could tell what kind of animal it was or whether it was human. As he looked around, he was looking for leads that may take them in the direction of Natowa.

Yurah still wasn't sure if Natowa was human or a spirit? He just knew that he was being paid a lot of money to find the answer. So he did whatever was needed to find the truth. Yurah ran his fingers over ferns and pushed them to the side to look at the ground.

"What are you doing?" asked Quinn.

"I'm looking for damaged ferns and footprints."

Davi was doing the same thing on the other side of the opening while Nino packed away canteens and food from their lunch.

Davi walked towards Allen and Quinn with a fern in his hand. Then Yurah and Nino joined in. He held it up to show Allen a long black hair on the fern. "Does this hair belong to Natowa?"

"Yes!" Allen shouted in elation. "That's his hair!"

"How in the hell did you find It?" Quinn shrieked in surprise!

"Eyes like a hawk!" laughed Davi. Then he handed the hair on the fern to Allen.

Allen was so relieved to know that Natowa could possibly be near. "How long do you think the hair has been here?"

"It could have been there since your first encounter. But most likely it's recent. How recent I cannot determine until we find more tracks."

Quinn was beginning to get excited too. Although still nervous of their fate, he hoped that Natowa would resurface and show himself again.

Hours went by and they were getting a bit tense to stay in the jungle much longer. As they looked most of the day for more evidence, the hair was the only thing they could find.

It was time to return to camp. Allen and Quinn were very disappointed that they didn't have more progress that could lead them to Natowa. They only had two days before they had to return back down the Rio Negro to return to the resort, and then leave back to New York the next day. Timing for them was everything!

# Chapter 9

Back at camp they sat around the blazing fire, and everything was calm and peaceful. Yurah and Davi knew this was a pretty safe place since it was one of their destinations as tour guides from the resort. Other than snakes and insects, this part of the rainforest was a good location to make camp.

Davi believed more than Yurah that Natowa did exist. Although his parents and culture talked about the spirits in the Amazon, his family was more modern in their beliefs than Yurah's.

As Davi thought about finding Natowa's hair, he also knew that Natowa was human now and in a fairly close area nearby. Was he watching? He knew that if Natowa knew they were there, he would be watching and keeping an eye on them. So he settled into his place near the fire always looking around behind him, wondering if at any time Natowa would make his presence.

As soon as the dawn broke, the men were up and packed for another excursion into the jungle. Knowing where they were going, they moved quickly through the thick tropical jungle. They were at the location within less than an hour.

As soon as they were there they could feel the relief and energy since they knew that they had many hours ahead of them to make headway. So they started right away to look for more tracks and evidence of Natowa.

A screech came from a nearby cockatoo. It was a noise they made when danger was nearby. And then the Spider monkeys started to jump from tree to tree and signaling down at the men that something was nearby.

They all stopped and looked at each other, and Nino was frightened again for fear of what happened the last time.

Allen put Nino next to him as he looked around to see what was going on.

"There is something coming," whispered Yurah.

Allen whispered to Yurah, "What is it?"

Yurah listened as it neared them. "It's a human. I can tell by the way the monkeys are acting."

Allen began to get excited thinking it was Natowa.

And then from the ferns from a distance, they could see someone getting closer but still too far away to see who or what it was.

Quinn's heart was pumping so fast he couldn't hear anything else. He felt weak at the knees wondering if they were in danger again. Then all of a sudden they could hear someone calling them.

"Hey! It's me! It's Tutu!"

They could hear his laugh and excitement of spotting them!

They all stood in shock as he ran towards them.

Dropping the cargo that Nino was carrying, he ran into the ferns after Tutu. "Tutu, Tutu!" yelled Nino. And then ran after him so fast he was gone before anyone could stop him.

Yurah yelled to Nino, "No Nino! Don't go! Come back!"

But Nino was so happy to see Tutu he didn't listen. Then all of a sudden there was a loud scream and Nino disappeared!

Yurah screamed out, "It's the spirits! They have Nino!"

Everyone looked on in horror again, not believing this could happen a second time!

Quinn started to panic! "No! Not again!"

Allen ran to Quinn's side and shook him until Quinn composed himself.

Then Allen and Quinn sat down next to each other totally stunned.

"Maybe they aren't dead," said Allen a few minutes later.

Quinn answered back, "Maybe Natowa has them and he's using them for some kind of ransom or as a lure to get something he wants. We thought for sure that Tutu was dead, but he's not!"

"Or is he?" asked Yurah still believing Natowa was a spirit. "No one knows for that's a trick of the evil spirits."

Allen and Quinn didn't know what to believe. Davi didn't say a word but was thinking instead.

"I think it's Natowa," said Davi. "I think he has them until he knows what we want."

Allen thought about what Davi said and thought it made sense. He thought to himself, "But how did they get them back? And what does he want with them? Or will he hurt them?"

With the men believing that their two young friends were still alive, they had to get them back!

Now with Tutu and Nino both missing, the men were now even more desperate to find Natowa. Standing in the middle of the clearing next to the tree where Quinn laid, Allen and Quinn were hoping Natowa would show up.

They knew Natowa had something to do with Tutu and Nino being taken. Were they alive or dead? Either way, they needed to find the answers. Their days were numbered and with each day they had no success, the chances got smaller and smaller of finding him.

They waited for hours but there was no sign of him. Yurah and Davi looked for more tracks but didn't find anything. Sitting on a log, Allen had his arms folded together. He was in deep thought and Quinn knew that Allen was trying to come up with an idea.

Then Allen said to everyone, "What if we set up a trap for Natowa?"

"What kind of trap?" asked Quinn.

"Well, he seems to come when people are in distress or injured. So why don't we pretend that one of us are injured and see if he comes to help."

Quinn thought for a minute. Then he agreed that it was worth a try. So did Yurah and Davi. They decided that Allen would be the decoy. He would cut a small superficial cut on his wrist and pretend he was injured. It would be just enough for Natowa to see Allen was bleeding.

Allen went into the shrubs and cut two small slits into his wrist. Being a doctor and surgeon he knew exactly how deep to cut. Then he covered it with a white cotton cloth. He probed it over and over to get the sight of the blood on the cloth so Natowa could see him bleeding.

Once he made spots of blood all over the cloth he ran shouting out of the shrubs, "Help me, I'm bleeding!"

Quinn, Yurah and Davi ran to Allen's side.

"What happened?" shouted Quinn!

"I don't know. I don't know if I have been bit or if I'm cut!"

Pretending to be frantically worried, they laid Allen down on the ground.

Quinn slowly removed the cloth from Allen's wrist and by this time it was saturated with his blood.

"It looks deep, whatever it is," said Quinn. "I hope you didn't puncture an artery!" Quinn shouted into the rainforest jungle so that Natowa could hear what he was saying.

They all stayed still for a few minutes pretending to administer first aid to Allen.

Allen pretended to be very faint and weak. He lay very still and kept looking at Quinn as if to say, "Do you see anything?"

But Quinn just stared back at him as if to say, "Nothing yet."

"Move away from him!" A voice called out from behind a tree.

They could hear the voice but couldn't see anyone. Allen knowing it was Natowa, motioned for everyone to move away.

Natowa came out and into the clearing. He stood just outside for a few seconds assessing the situation and looking over all the men. Once he felt safe, he walked with a large stride towards Allen.

Allen's heart was pounding out of his chest. He was nervous and elated at the same time. He was afraid what would happen if Natowa knew they tricked him.

As Natowa stood over Allen, he scanned his eyes up and down Allen's body.

"Where are you hurt?" he said in a deep voice.

"My wrist," cried Allen. "I'm bleeding!"

Natowa lifted Allen's wrist and looked over his wound carefully. He then stood up and said, "You will live!"Then he turned away from Allen's side and walked towards some thick Bromeliad bushes.

"Stop!" cried out Allen. "We need you Natowa!"

Natowa turned and looked at Allen as Allen lifted himself quickly off the ground.

Natowa looked confused. "How do you know my name?" Natowa said in a deep harsh voice.

"You're a legend in the rainforest," said Yurah as he stepped closer to Natowa. "Many of my people talk about your healing powers. But it was believed that you were a spirit!"

"You think I'm a spirit?" Natowa laughed as he continued to walk and kept laughing about what Yurah just said.

"Natowa wait!" Allen pleaded with him again. "Do you remember this man?" Allen grabbed Quinn by his shoulders and gently nudged Quinn to stand in front of Natowa.

This was the first time Quinn ever laid eyes on Natowa. And even though Michael and Allen told him over and over about his strength and size, Quinn still couldn't comprehend it until seeing him for himself.

Natowa stared at Quinn for a few moments. Then he slowly walked up to Quinn. He stood right in front of him staring into his face. He looked Quinn up and down. Then he reached down and pulled up the left pant leg of Quinn's pants. He pulled them up until he reached the spot where Quinn was bit by the snake.

"I remember," said Natowa. "It was my snake that bit you. He got away from me."

"Why do you have a poisonous snake?" asked Allen.

Natowa said, "I use his venom for my medicines."

Then Allen realized that Natowa "was a" medicine man. And from what Allen witnessed, he was a great healer that could probably cure cancer, viruses, and many other diseases.

"Natowa, you have a vast knowledge for healing," said Allen. "You have an antidote that could save millions of people all over the world. Will you help us by sharing your cure with us? Would you help us save our friend Michael who is lying in a hospital dying from cancer?"

"I can't help you," said Natowa.

"Please Natowa!" Allen pleaded once more.

"I can't leave the rainforest. I help keep the natives and the rainforest clean of disease and infestation. I cannot leave!"

He turned again and started walking away behind the bromeliad bushes.

"Wait!" shouted Yurah. "Where are the two boys?"

Just after Yurah said the words, Natowa walked back out from the bushes holding the hands of Tutu and Nino.

Everyone looked astounded for they couldn't believe their eyes! They heard the screams of Tutu that night he was killed by the jaguar.

"How could this be? How did you save him? How can he be alive?" questioned Allen stumbling on his words.

"The same way I saved your friend from the venom of my snake," said Natowa. "I have healing remedies way beyond what your doctors could even understand. I was taught the healing powers of the plants, animals, and venoms that inhabit the Amazon. I have thousands of years of remedies and cures."

Nino and Tutu ran to Davi who was motioning the boys to come to him. He threw his arms around the young men.

Natowa looked at the young boys as they smiled back at Natowa.

"You will be safe now."

Tutu's eyes welled up as he looked at Natowa.

Allen told Natowa that he could be a very rich man if he shared his remedies with doctors around the world. But Natowa stated again that he could not leave the rainforest.

"There's a whole world for you to discover Natowa. And even though the rainforest is a beautiful place, there's so much more of the world to see. If you have brothers and sisters . . ."

Natowa broke through Allen's sentence and said, "I have a sister."

"Does she live in the rainforest?" asked Quinn.

Natowa strongly shook his head no. "My sister lives in Rio de Janeiro. I must go now!"

Natowa turned and leaped into the Bromeliad bushes and ferns and he disappeared.

Minutes went by and all the men looked disappointed that even though they had a chance to see Natowa, they couldn't convince him to help them. As they turned their thoughts to the two young boys, Davi asked them if they were okay, and what happened to them and how they wound up with Natowa.

Tutu stated that the night the jaguar dragged him into the rainforest Natowa ordered the jaguar to leave. Tutu said that his leg was badly torn apart, and by that time he just wanted to die from the pain. But when Natowa picked him up and carried him to a place in the rainforest where Natowa lived, he and a beautiful young woman by the name of Enesa gave him medicine and wrapped his leg in herbs and plants. They also gave him medicine to drink. When he woke the next morning his leg was completely healed and there was no more pain.

"And Natowa took me to the garden too," added Nino. "I was afraid at first but once I saw Tutu, I knew I would be alright. He was very good to us. He fed us and told us a great story. Enesa cooked and she cut and brushed our hair. Doesn't our hair look nice?" smiled Nino.

The men all laughed and were all mesmerized by the boys story but it was time to head back to camp.

When they arrived Davi fed the two young boys and sent them to their sleeping bags for the night. As Allen, Quinn, Yurah and Davi sat around the fire, they talked about if they would ever find Natowa again.

Then a faint whisper came from Tutu as he lay in his sleeping bag. "I know where he lives. I know how to get there. I'll take you there to meet Enesa!"

"She's so beautiful!" smiled Nino.

The men all looked at each other and Quinn spoke out, "Men, I think tomorrow will be our lucky day!"

# Chapter 10

Tutu and Nino were excited about returning to see Enesa again. They couldn't wait to leave camp and get back into the rainforest. So as they walked on the boys kept running ahead of everyone to hurry them along.

Everyone followed along as the boys led them deeper and deeper. This was the first time that Allen and Quinn had been so deep into the rainforest.

As they walked the rainforest started to change. The ferns and plants started to disappear and then it changed to huge tall trees that went straight up and into the sky. The tops of the trees covered the sun and it was much darker. The more they walked the more nervous they got about being so deep into the rainforest.

"Tutu, how far are we from Natowa's camp?" asked Quinn.

"He doesn't have a camp," said Tutu. "He has a beautiful stone house with many rooms and lots of plant houses where he keeps all his plants and medicines."

Allen laughed, "Do you mean greenhouses?"

"Yes,'" smiled Tutu. "That's what they are!"

"How many greenhouses does he have?" asked Quinn.

"Many," Tutu said back. "He has hundreds of plants and flowers growing in them. And he has a big pond of fish. He also has hot springs surrounded by tall stone walls where the natives get their water to bathe."

The men were amazed at what Tutu and Nino were telling them. It sounded like he had his own paradise right in the middle of the Amazon. As they all walked on, they became even more excited to see where Natowa lived.


Four hours later, they all stopped to take a rest and eat. As they sat feasting on breads, fruit and cheese, they could hear a waterfall close by.

After they ate, they all took off their clothes and headed into the water. The water was so nice and cool that they all wanted to stay in as big mosquitoes swarmed around their heads.

As Quinn swam across the water's opening nearing the waterfall, he looked behind it. By his surprise he could see an image of someone behind the drudging downpour of the waterfall. He couldn't believe what he was seeing!

Curiously he moved closer. He could see a faint silhouette of a young woman with long light blonde hair. She was bathing and had no idea that anyone was there.

He yelled out to the young woman, "Hey . . . who are you?" The others by this time took notice of Quinn and what was going on. They all stood behind him as they stared at the young woman too.

"Enesa!" shouted Tutu. "Enesa it's me . . . It's Tutu!"

When she realized someone was there she ran from behind the waterfall and slipped behind some rocks. The men ran out of the water and hurriedly got dressed.

Then she returned dressed in a short linen tight white sundress with spaghetti straps and sandals. She stood on a large rock just looking down at the men in the water.

"Tutu and Nino, what are you doing here?" Enesa surprised to see them!

Tutu said, "We have come to see you and Natowa!"

"We have brought friends!" added Nino.

Enesa looked down at Tutu and Nino while shaking her head in disappointment.

"I have heard about your friends Tutu and Nino, and you must leave with them at once! They're not welcome here. And if Natowa finds you here he'll . . ."

Enesa stopped talking then turned to hear something. She looked back down at the men and then smiled at Tutu and Nino. You could see from her face she was happy to see them. Then she turned and she was gone.

Knowing that Natowa wasn't going to be happy to see the men again, they tried to come up with some ideas. Their time was running out. If they couldn't get to Natowa one more time, it would be the end of Michael's life for sure! No matter what, they needed to try.

They moved closer and closer to Natowa's as they were led by Tutu and Nino.

"We're here!" said Tutu. "It's just over there!"

The men looked on where Tutu was pointing. They could see a beautiful orchard of white, pink and purple Magnolia trees. They entered inside following Tutu and Nino down a dirt path, and then walking a distance through the Magnolias, they came to a slate path with two huge tall stone walls on each side of it. It was as if Natowa planted the Magnolia trees to make a huge barricade around the garden.

At the front of the path, soft green moss grew on the stone walls with hundreds of colorful flowers, ferns and plants growing on its ledges. Allen and Quinn were mesmerized by how beautiful it was.

They could only see down the middle of the path because of the tall stone walls blocked the view of the garden. They stood far behind them so they wouldn't be seen.

At the end of the path they could see a pond surrounded with Banyan trees with a waterfall way in the distance.

Tutu and Nino told them that in the garden on the left was Natowa's home, and on the right side of the garden led to the greenhouses. Tutu and Nino told them it was the most beautiful place they had ever seen.

They decided to head back out into the rainforest to make some space between Natowa's home and their camp. If he saw or smelled their camp it could anger Natowa and who knew what he was capable of doing. They knew from Enesa they were not welcome there, so they made camp about a kilometer away. Everyone headed to bed by dusk to make an early start of it the next morning.

They all woke to Tutu and Nino shoving them under their blankets.

"Wake up . . . wake up!" shouted Nino. "It's time to head back to Natowa's!"

Tutu and Nino had no fear of Natowa. They were too young and inexperienced.

"We want to see Enesa again!" Tutu shouted with elation.

"I fear our young men are falling in love with Enesa," Yurah smiled at Allen and Quinn.

They laughed as they watched the young boys swoop up their sleeping bags and hurried to pack them away. Smiles lit their faces and you could see that they were both smitten for her.

Allen and Quinn think of the two young men as boys. But in the Amazon, many boys marry at the age of fourteen, so Yurah and Davi had to talk to them and let them know that Enesa was off limits to them since she belonged to Natowa.

The boys were sad by the conversation, but they realized that Natowa was their friend and had to respect his woman. But they were still anxious to see her and Natowa again, so they were already back on the trail before everyone else was even ready.

Catching up with Tutu and Nino, they all stood outside of Natowa's paradise garden wondering how they're going to enter and speak to Natowa one more time.

"Did you know that Natowa's sister is an empress?" blurted out Nino.

All the men laughed.

"Yeah right," said Allen.

Nino gave Allen a dirty look. "Enesa told me and she wouldn't lie!" Nino lashed back.

"She was telling you stories," Quinn said back.

"No!" shouted Tutu. "It's true! We saw her pictures! She's beautiful too, just like Enesa. Enesa got her pictures from a society page in Rio de Janeiro and she lives in a palace!"

The men were looking curiously at Tutu and Nino.

"Okay, so tell us more," said Quinn. "How did she become and empress?"

"I don't know," Nino said back. "She just is . . ."

"So you're telling us that Natowa's sister is an empress in Rio de Janeiro." asked Allen.

"Yes," said Nino.

They all looked at each other wondering if Tutu and Nino were telling the truth.

"What does she look like?" asked Allen.

Tutu said, "She looks just like Natowa. But she's prettier than him."

They laughed again.

"I mean they're twins and they both have the same eyes, mouth and color of hair."

"And his father was related to "King Luis the First!" Nino shouted.

"Okay and I suppose Enesa told you that too?"

"No," said Nino. "Natowa did."

Allen looked at Quinn. They both couldn't believe the young men's stories.

"Look Tutu and Nino," said Allen. "This is no time to be telling us stories. Our friend is dying in the hospital and we need Natowa to help us so enough with these fairy tales." Allen laughed at them and then got up and walked away.

"It's true." A woman's voice came from just a few feet from where Allen was standing. He leaped back not expecting someone to be there. It was Enesa standing next to a large tree.

Tutu and Nino jumped up and ran to Enesa's side. She put her arms around them and then pointed for them to go sit down again.

Tutu and Nino were right. Enesa was as beautiful as they said she was.

She was 5'7" tall. She had light green eyes lined with thick black eyelashes. Her brows were never plucked and had a beautiful natural curve around her eyes. Her hair was to her waist. It was light blonde with natural blond sun streaks. Her skin was medium tan and flawless, and her lips were full and lightly pink.

"You scared me!" Allen chuckled.

Enesa was entertained by surprising him as she smiled. "Well, they aren't an emperor or empress, but they are descendants of a royal family," said Enesa. "You have to leave. Natowa will not be happy that you found him."

Allen looked at Enesa with sadness in his eyes. "Enesa, please help us! We're not here to harm anyone. We're here to save our friend's life. We have a friend living in America who is dying of cancer."

"Yes, I know what cancer is, it kills many people. But Natowa will not help you."

"But why?" asked Allen.

"If he gives you the cure for your friend they'll come to the rainforest and take all his plants, venoms and medicines and the Amazon will die. Just like all the trees that others have taken from the Amazon. No, he will not help you."

"That's not right!" He could help the world!" cried out Quinn.

Enesa turned around to look Quinn straight in the face. "Not right?" Enesa fired back at Quinn! "Not right is when your people came to the rainforest and stole the resources from thousands of the rubber trees.

And killed, bred and enslaved thousands of the people of the Amazon!"

Enesa took a deep breath to calm down.

"When my father and mother came here from Denmark twenty years ago, I was only seven years old. My mother and father came here as missionary doctors, and they helped many of the people from the Amazon deal with the loss they suffered when their families and friends were killed, even after one hundred years later. My parents wound up staying here to help heal the natives from their loss and try to rebuild their civilization. But while travelling to a village along the Amazon River, my parents were killed by snipers in the jungle. Their bodies were found six days later."

Allen and Quinn were horrified to hear how her parents died.

"I'm so sorry," said Quinn, "I didn't mean anything by what I said. We just want to help our friend."

"My parents taught Natowa how to read and write in English. So we wrote back and forth to stay in touch when I was sent back to be raised by my aunt and uncle. I was sixteen years old, and after university, I came back to see Natowa, and I decided to stay.

To understand more about Natowa, you must understand his life. My father practically adopted Natowa from the time he came to the Amazon when he was six years old. My parent's also helped Ana, Natowa's keeper. She never had any of her own children and told people that Natowa was the son of a sister that died.

Natowa loved my father too. My father, mother, and Natowa all worked together with the help of the natives. They found many cures that could save the world from disease and sickness.

My father taught Natowa everything he knew before he died. My father believed Natowa was a natural healer being so young when he was taught. He had a gift that couldn't be explained by any professor or scientist. He was very curious and loved to explore, so he came across many antidotes and together they discovered a lot of medicines and cures.

Natowa promised my father that he would never sell or give away his knowledge. And he promised my father to keep the secret cures and antidotes only within the Amazon or outsiders would come back and take all of our resources, and then for sure the rainforest would die!"

Now it all made sense to Allen why Enesa didn't look like a native woman. She was much fairer and her eyes were green. She spoke very fluent English, but had a Danish accent too.

Allen recognized her accent. She came from Denmark which he has visited with Michael and Quinn when they were in Copenhagen on a research trip while attending university.

He could see that she was fairer than the normal Brazilian women.

Allen felt sick inside knowing what his people did to the rainforest. Rubber was one of the most important products to come out of the rainforest.

Though indigenous rainforest dwellers of South America had been using rubber for generations, it wasn't until 1839 it became a demanding product. Charles Goodyear of Connecticut, accidentally dropped rubber and sulfur on a hot stovetop, causing it to char like leather yet remained rubberized and elastic.

Vulcanization, a refined version of this process, transformed the white sap from the bark of the Hevea tree into an essential product. With the invention of the automobile in the late 19th century, the rubber boom began.

As the demand for rubber soared in small river towns like Manaus, they were transformed into overnight bustling centers for business. Manaus, situated on the Amazon where it's met by the Rio Negro, became the heart of the rubber trade.

Big fortunes were made by barons, and wealth was taken for granted and squandered on lavish meals and social gatherings which gave the barons and their wives the chance to flaunt their wealth and possessions.

Their wives detested the muddy waters of the Amazon, so they sent linens to Portugal to be laundered and cleaned. They ate food imported from Europe that was shipped in daily and some costing thousands of dollars.

Men retired to any one of a dozen brothels. They shipped materials like diamonds from Africa, silk from the east, and other riches from faraway places to only have the finest things.

But with the progress that was made from the rubber trees for tires, many of the natives of the rainforest lost their land to the barons. Just to make a profit, barons had to acquire control over huge tracts of land. Most did so by hiring their own private armies to defend their claims, acquire new land, and capture native laborers. Labor was always a problem so barons got creative.

One baron created a stud farm where they enslaved over six hundred native women whom he bred to make more slaves. Young native woman where sold for prostitution.

Other barons simply used terror to acquire and hold on to native slaves. Natives captured usually submitted since resistance only meant more suffering for them and their families.

Production soared but the native population fell from over thirty thousand to less than seven thousand while they exported over four thousand tons of rubber earning over seventy five million dollars. The only thing that stopped the holocaust was the downfall of the Brazilian rubber market.

Allen did a lot of research on the rainforest before their trip. He was ashamed that his country had anything to do with the holocaust of the natives and its resources.

Allen could understand the dislike that Natowa and Enesa had for outsiders of the Amazon. But he knew he had to make her understand that they were not there to take their precious resources. All they wanted to do was to save their friend Michael. But how could they get through to Natowa? Michael's time was running out!

"Enesa," said Allen. "Tell us about Natowa's sister in Rio de Janeiro.

Enesa sighed. "I told the young boys because I never thought they would tell anyone. You must never tell anyone you know about this!"

"We promise we won't," said Quinn.

Enesa sat down on the edge of a large rock. She began to tell Allen and Quinn the story.

"When Natowa was born, he was born into a royal family in Rio de Janeiro. He was born with a twin sister. At birth, Natowa had a bit of a cleft lip. When you're born in Brazil with a cleft it's highly socially unacceptable. Honor was everything to Natowa's mother and father. Miguel's father felt an obligation to the royal family of King Luis the First.

They had doctors perform surgery to correct the cleft and the surgery was quite a success leaving no physical scars. But he was still shunned by the Andre's friends and Henry's colleagues and clients. It was resulting in loss of income for Henry.

Natowa's birth name was Miguel Henry Andre. Henry Andre was afraid it was also affecting Louisa his wife and young daughter Marilyn's lifestyle. So one night when Miguel was sleeping, Henry Andre had Miguel kidnapped from his bed and taken to be raised in the Amazon by Ana.

The family covered everything up by saying that Miguel was kidnapped and killed and found dead three weeks later. It was a high profile kidnapping and murder that reached the world. They staged their son's funeral and hundreds of flowers were sent from royal families, dignitaries and presidents.

Natowa was old enough to remember the events that happened to him for he was six years old. He didn't hate his father or mother for what they did. But as he got older he never wanted to see either of them again. He cried for months for his sister Marilyn. Ana would hold and rock him every night until he was asleep.

After many months he realized that his life and sister were gone. Once he accepted the change, he learned the ways of the people of the Amazon. Everyone loved him and Ana told everyone that he was the son of a sister who died. She feared for her and Natowa's life if the truth ever came out.

On her death bed she told Natowa what happened to him and he was the son of a royal family. But he already knew. And although he never laid eyes on his sister Marilyn again, he never forgot her.

Being born twins, Miguel and Marilyn were very close. They had a special bond and love for one another. Miguel told me that they did everything together and loved to pretend they were agent spies. They spied on people in the palace all the time. They would sneak into their father's office and hide while he had meetings with clients and dignitaries. The maids knew the children were there, and went along with it. He told me that he and Marilyn used to sneak out of the palace at night to catch lightening bugs in the backyard. No one ever knew but them.

Natowa still to this day says that someday he'll return to Rio de Janeiro to see his sister again. But right now he just wasn't ready."

Allen and Quinn had a hard time absorbing the story that Enesa just told them. How could anyone be that cruel as to take a child because of such a minor and correctable malformation as a cleft lip, and to have him taken into a dangerous rainforest to be completely forgotten? It was totally unconscionable to both of them!

After Enesa told them of Natowa's past, they promised again the secret was safe with them. Allen felt sorry for Natowa. To have his life stolen from him was a scandal! How could people be so shallow he questioned over and over again. Knowing what he knows now, how can they ask Natowa to help them to save Michael? He had his own crosses to bear.

Then with that thought in mind, Allen thought to himself, "Maybe we can help Natowa, and in return he can help Michael."

"How bad does Natowa want to see his sister?"

Enesa smiled at Allen, "It's his ultimate dream to see his sister again."

"Then we will help him," Quinn said back.

Enesa looked at Allen and Quinn, "How can you help him?"

"We'll go to Rio and get her," said Allen. "We'll tell her about Natowa and that he's not dead. And we'll bring her to him."

Enesa on several occasions told Natowa that he should go to see his sister. But Natowa always resisted saying the timing was wrong.

Enesa felt that he was afraid he wouldn't be acknowledged by Marilyn. He also feared he may put her life in danger, for it could cause such a scandal again if anyone found he was still alive.

Many people contributed money to his family in condolences and people might think it was a scam. He knew that if he went to see her, he would have to warn her first. But right now the time just wasn't right for him.

"Enesa, you have to trust us. We're doctors just like your mother and father. We love people and we would never do anyone harm to make a personal gain. We can help each other," said Allen.

Enesa thought for a few seconds. "Well, if it's for Natowa, than I guess it's okay. I must go now," as she turned behind some trees and then she was gone.

Back at camp that night, Allen and Quinn told Yurah and Davi about Natowa's life. Yurah stated he remembered hearing about the story and the kidnap years ago. The news went through Brazil like wildfire!

He explained everyone looked for his body for weeks throughout the land and into the rainforest.

Then the news hit that he was found dead. Everyone from all around felt the sorrow for this young royal man. People from all over the world sent gifts and money to the Royal Andre family. Allen and Quinn told Yurah and Davi that they wanted to leave the Amazon and head to Rio de Janeiro to find Marilyn, so the men headed back out to the river. Allen and Quinn were disappointed that they couldn't get Natowa's cooperation. But knowing what they know now they could understand why he wouldn't. Maybe if they can reunite Natowa and Marilyn, maybe then he will help them. It was a chance they had to take!

# Chapter 11

The bell boy took Allen and Quinn's bags up to their hotel rooms in Rio de Janeiro. As soon as Allen and Quinn got to their rooms they both called Michael. He was still in the hospital but his brother John was with him now. Michael asked if they made any progress and if they got to see Natowa. They both filled Michael in on what was going on. They kept their conversation as short as possible since they wanted Michael to rest and stay well until they could return.

Allen told Michael they had to extend their stay for another week. They said to him that they had to find Natowa's sister and reunite them before they could return. They told him to be well and they would check on him in a few days.

Michael told them to be safe and keep him posted. They called their secretaries and told them to keep referring their patients to other doctors for another week.

Falling back on his bed once in his hotel room, Allen fell deeply to sleep. He woke with a knock on the door a few hours later. He sleepily opened the door and Quinn walked in.

"Are you ready to grab something to eat?" asked Quinn.

"Yes, just give me a few minutes to take a quick shower. Make yourself a drink while you're waiting."

Quinn went to the bar and made himself a scotch and water. He sat in the couch and looked at a magazine while Allen got ready. After Allen emerged from the bathroom, Quinn said to him, "So you think we can do this?"

"Do what?"

"Do you think we can get Marilyn to come with us to see Natowa?"

"Yes, if we can prove that he's still alive, I know she'll come with us. They were very close."

Quinn asked, "But how are we going to prove it?"

Allen went to his suitcase and pulled out a little white box. He opened it and pulled out the long hair that they found that belonged to Natowa.

"She'll know if it's his."

Quinn looked at Allen acknowledging what he said. "Okay, then we'll get an early start to the library tomorrow morning."

Allen said, "We'll find the newspaper articles of Natowa's kidnapping and try to piece everything together to find her from there."

The next morning they took a cab to the National Library in Rio de Janeiro where they started their search for newspaper articles regarding Natowa's kidnapping.

They archived over fifty articles that were written. From Henry and Louisa Andre giving birth to Miguel Henry Andre (Natowa's birth name) with his sister Marilyn Louisa Andre, to the first article that was reported when Miguel was kidnapped.

They also found the articles of his funeral and statements made by Henry and Louisa.

They also contacted the American Embassy and they located Marilyn Andre where she lived on the beautiful coastal beach of Icarai in the city of Niteroi. She was engaged to Emmanuel (E • man • u • elle) Sicard, an attorney from Paris, France who was a third generation corporate attorney.

Allen and Quinn even found a newspaper article that announced their engagement.

Marilyn and Emmanuel met at a fund raiser auction in Paris while she was buying some art pieces for some clients. Emmanuel told Marilyn that he took one look at her and he fell madly in love!

Emmanuel flew to see her every other weekend and proposed three months into their relationship. It was fast but he kept reiterating that he knew she was the one.

Marilyn fell in love with Emmanuel because of how true and loyal he was to her. He never once cancelled a weekend with her. He called her every night asking her how her day was and to wish her good night. When he came to see her he always brought her beautiful jewelry, designer clothes, shoes, purses and the best French perfume money could buy!

It wasn't the gifts he brought her that made her love him, but the fact he loved her so much that he would do anything for her.

Emmanuel was temperamental just like his father, except with Marilyn, but he could be very hard on his staff, family and friends. On many occasions she could hear conversations where he raised his voice while talking on his cell phone. Once he realized what he was doing, he would compose himself and apologize to Marilyn for his conduct.

She knew in time she could change that side of him. He was overwhelmed sometimes from everything he had on his plate. He ran a third generation law firm very successfully with sixteen attorneys.

The firm was started by Emmanuel's grandfather. Then after he passed away Emmanuel's father, Joséph (Jo • seff) Sicard took over the firm with his brother, Franck (Fraunk) Sicard. Emmanuel's father was a tyrant. He was known as one of the best defense attorneys in France and would stop at nothing to win a case.

He was not close to his brother Franck who was also an owner in the firm. Joséph tried to buy Franck out many times to no avail. No deal was good enough for Franck. He felt it was his duty to stay in the company for the future of his own sons, and to keep an eye on his brother's crooked undertakings.

During the time they took over the firm, Emmanuel, Joséph, Franck and his two son's grew the company from three attorneys to sixteen, with a staff of paralegals, clerks and secretaries totaling forty-five employees.

Emmanuel was a very busy man, and he lived, ate and drank everything for the firm. He was thirty-two years old, and in his spare time he played polo and soccer.

He was in great shape and he was medium height standing 5'10" tall and thin with black hair. He wore it stylishly tucked behind his ears.

He dressed in the most expensive custom made Italian suits and handmade designer Italian shoes. He had great taste in everything he gave Marilyn. He loved seeing her put on a beautiful evening gown or cocktail length dress with stiletto high heels.

Emmanuel had a thick French accent but always spoke in English to Marilyn who was also very fluent in English. Only in romantic situations would he talk to her in French.

She loved dressing up for him for it was her way of repaying him for his kindness. She thought that once they were married she could work on helping him with his pressing responsibilities. She knew that when he was with her, he was a much different person. She knew she would be good for him.

# Chapter 12

Marilyn remembered the galas and dinner parties her parents would have in the palace. But she also remembered the bad memories of Miguel's death and it took her years to get over it.

After Miguel's death everything changed. Her father took ill years later and her mother would have to take his meals to him in his room every night. It would be days sometimes before Marilyn even got to see him.

She became somewhat reclusive in her own room as well. She was home schooled which left her with very little friends. Other than families coming to visit, she was all alone.

The maids and her mother would encourage her to come out and play. But she had no one to play with once Miguel was gone. So she found herself in her room writing stories and drawing pictures.

She would set her dolls up and pretend they were her family and everyone was happy and Miguel was still alive. She would write stories and draw pictures of the two of them playing.

Once her father passed away suddenly in bed from heart failure, her mother needed her. She was seventeen by then and a young woman. So she put her focus over the next few years to aiding her grieving mother. She took over the household responsibilities, as her mother would just sit at the window in her bedroom and look out into the gardens.

One day her mother called for Marilyn. When she entered her mother's room her mother was sitting in a high back chair staring out the window into the garden. Her mother said, "I want you to go find Miguel."

Marilyn couldn't believe her ears! Her mother from the day he was buried never mentioned his name again. Neither did her father.

"Mother, what are you talking about?" shouted Marilyn!

"Miguel is still alive." Louisa said as she just stared out the window.

"Mother!" yelled Marilyn. Miguel is dead! He died years ago!"

Louisa slowly turned her head to look at Marilyn.

"No, he's not dead. And you must find him and tell him how sorry I am and how much I still love him."

Just as Marilyn was about to respond to her mother again, her mother reached into her pocket and pulled out a gun. She quickly put the gun to her right temple and pulled the trigger. The noise was so loud it made Marilyn's head turn away!

For a few seconds Marilyn couldn't absorb what just happened. She was in shock and by this time their maid Trinity ran into the room grabbing Marilyn by the shoulders.

"What happened?" shouted Trinity!

With no emotion, Marilyn uttered the words, "I don't know, my mother just pulled out a gun and shot herself."

"Oh my Lord!" shouted Trinity. "Marilyn, get out of here! Go as fast as you can!"

By then another maid, Marie entered the room.

"Get Marilyn out of here!" yelled Trinity.

Marie grabbed Marilyn and led her out of the room.

Marilyn woke up the next day in her room. There was a nurse and doctor standing over her.

"What happened?" asked Marilyn, while she was still sleepy from the sedative the doctor gave her.

The doctor and nurse looked at each other. "Marilyn, I'm so sorry to tell you that your mother is dead."

Then the sound of the gun ran through Marilyn's ears one more time. She put her hands over her ears like she was hearing the gunshot for the first time. It was coming back to her what happened. She was still in shock over what her mother had done to herself.

Doctor Favaloro looked down sadly at Marilyn. "Your mother has been sick for many months now, and

I should have told you since you're a young woman now. But your mother pleaded with me not to tell anyone, and I now so wish I did. Your mother was suffering from early dementia. I have been treating her for about a year. I recently gave her some medication and I think it had an adverse reaction on her."

What Dr. Favaloro told Marilyn made much sense to her. She noticed that in the past few months her mother was acting very different. One minute she would be putting on a dress, and then she would put a pair of slacks on underneath her dress.

Another day she found her in the garden on her hands and knees picking a flower in the garden and putting it in her mouth. She ran to her mother and yelled at her for doing such a crazy thing! But her mother just looked up at her and stared.

The next day Marilyn pulled herself together and started to make plans to bury her mother next to her father and brother. A week later the funeral was over and the palace was filled once again with flowers and presents from friends, dignitaries and families that lived all over Brazil.

Many of them offered to have Marilyn come and stay with them, but she felt compelled to stay where she was. She still had workers in the palace that were like family to her. Trinity was like a second mother. There were still many things she had to prepare and get ready.

She stayed in the palace for eight years and kept the same staff her parents had. She completed her university studies in fine arts. She became a wonderful gardener and cook, and entertained friends quite often at the palace that she met at university.

But when Trinity caught influenza and died and Marilyn met Emmanuel, she wanted to make some changes in her life. A few years earlier, a man from the City of Rio de Janeiro offered to lease the palace from her as a historical landmark. Marilyn found his card and she called him. She made arrangements with him for a one year lease and signed the contracts.

She found a pavilion in Niteroi on Icaria Beach. It was one of three beaches that lined the coast of the Guanabara Bay. She moved amongst many very wealthy families. She had a beautiful view of the Santa Cruz Fortress and harbor. She had a beautiful large terrace that spanned the water side of the entire house.

The pavilion was graced with large windows and patio doors that gave the whole house a view of the beaches and mountains that surrounded Niteroi. She loved the sailboats and would sit and watch as they sailed by hoping one day to sail with Emmanuel.

She was happy here and it gave her a chance to put all the bad things that happened in the palace behind her. She was free to move on with her life now. She was about to get married to Emmanuel. She was finally happy again!

# Chapter 13

After Allen and Quinn left the Library, they had their hotel clerk book them a room in Niteroi in case they had an overnight stay.

They rented a Mercedes Benz convertible so they could unwind and enjoy the ride from Rio de Janeiro to Niteroi. Niteroi was also known as the Smile City and Niquiti. It's also known for being the richest city in Brazil. They reached the Rio-Niteroi Bridge located at Guanabara Bay that connects the cities of Rio de Janeiro and the municipality of Niteroi.

The box girder bridge spanned eight miles long. It was two hundred and thirty feet high to allow boats to travel under it.

As they drove over it they admired the beautiful view and boats that passed through. Once they reached Niteroi they felt like they were in another part of the world. The coast was lined with high rise condominiums and hotels as far as the eye could see. The beach went on forever and curved around the natural coastal edge. You could see the beautiful mountain range of Sugarloaf and Corcovado Mountains in the background.

They could understand why Marilyn would want to live there. It was very festive and expensive shops and restaurants lined the streets. The beaches were filled with people basking in the sun, wind surfing, sailing and walking on the beach.

Allen and Quinn had everything to do to remember they were not there for fun. And after a few hours of getting to know the sites, they found a nice little patio restaurant where they could eat out and watch people go by as they went shopping and site seeing along the way.

They each ordered a beer and took in the beautiful sights of the buildings that embanked the bay. Then the waitress came by and took their order for fish dinners and another round of beer.

The sun beat down on their faces and the gentle wind from the ocean cooled their skin. Unlike the Amazon the heat didn't affect them the way it did on the Rio Negro River. The humidity was much less from the breeze coming off of the water. They enjoyed the dinner and the view, but as soon as they ate they headed back to the hotel to plan for the next day.

They had already taken a quick drive past Marilyn's pavilion to see if there was any sign of life. There was a silver Porsche in the driveway that they assumed was Marilyn's. They were happy to see it which meant they would have a good chance tomorrow of catching her in the morning.

They planned on being outside of her pavilion at sunrise. They still didn't know what they were going to say or how to introduce themselves. But they knew that tomorrow would be the day.

When they arrived in front of Marilyn's pavilion the silver Porsche was gone. They were disappointed to see that the Porsche wasn't there. Did that mean that Marilyn wasn't there? Or was it a friend's or lover's car and they had left?

Just as they sat out in front for a little while the Porsche pulled back into the driveway. They could feel someone in the car with sunglasses looking at them as she pulled in. The windows of the Porsche were heavily tinted.

"I think she's suspicious," noted Quinn.

"I know, I saw her look right at us," said Allen.

No one got out of the Porsche. The Porsche backed out again and took off down the road. Allen and Quinn pulled into the driveway and turned around to follow the car. The Porsche sped around the winding road while Allen driving the Mercedes tried to keep up. The faster they went the faster the Porsche sped up. So they decided to slow down and see what she would do.

All of a sudden the car pulled over to the side of the road and a woman about 5'7" tall with black sunglasses, white tight pants and black chiffon sleeveless top got out of the car. Her hair was black just like Natowa's, but it was mid length and very wavy as it blew back and forth from the wind.

She slammed the door and started to walk back towards them shaking her thin hips from side to side. They pulled the Mercedes over. They sat in the car admiring how stylish and beautiful she was in the white skinny jeans and black sleeveless blouse. Then she ripped her sunglasses off her eyes and stuck them in her blouse. As soon as they saw her eyes, Allen and Quinn were amazed at the resemblance between Natowa and her.

Allen looked over at Quinn and said, "Slowly get out of the car."

As they both opened the doors and climbed out, they watched her approaching them stomping her feet in her high heel black sandals towards them. Standing with their hands in their pants pockets, Marilyn walked up to Allen just three feet from his face and started to shout at him.

"What the hell do you think you're doing? I can tell that you're tourists and just being nosey, but that's my home!" as she pointed up the road. "And I don't appreciate being followed! I have a camera inside my car so right now anything that you do is being recorded! So I suggest that you get back in your rental and get out of here!"

Marilyn went to their Mercedes and opened the driver side door and pointed for them to get back in.

Allen and Quinn were taken back by Marilyn's confidence and how she confronted them with no fear.

This woman that stood 5'7" tall could stand up to two men she didn't even know.

Allen asked, "Are you Marilyn Andre?" Not even acknowledging her outburst.

She stared at Allen and Quinn for a few seconds. "What do you want?"

"My name is Allen Greenburg and this is Quinn Adams, and we're doctors from New York. We would just like a few minutes of your time Ms. Andre. We have some information for you. We have some information about something that happened to your brother many years ago."

The first thing that went through Marilyn's mind was that they wanted to extort money from her.

"You get out of here right now before I call the police!"

Marilyn pulled her cell phone out from her hip pocket and started to dial.

Allen put his hand out to her, "I have something for you."

She stopped dialing and looked up at Allen as he opened the door to the Mercedes. He leaned into the car and he pulled out the little white box from a briefcase in the backseat. He walked back up to Marilyn and handed her the box.

"Is this some kind of a joke?" asked Marilyn.

"This is far from a joke!" said Quinn.

She gave them both a long stare, and then she opened the small box and saw a long black hair on white satin lining inside the box. At first she stared at it wondering what it was supposed to mean to her. She sensed that the black hair belonged to someone that she knew. She looked back up at Allen and Quinn.

"Who does this hair belong to?"

Allen and Quinn just stared at her for a long moment.

Allen said back to her, "Its Miguel's."

She looked deep into both their faces again, and looked back down at the hair. Then suddenly she snapped the box closed.

"If you're trying to get money from me, this game is over!" as she began to dial the police again.

"If you make that call you will never know whether we're telling the truth or not," said Quinn. "Just listen to what we have to say, and if you don't believe us, then by all means than make that call."

Marilyn thought that these men didn't fit the characteristics of criminals as she looked them both up and down. She was still not sure what they wanted but decided to at least listen to what they had to say.

Allen asked her, "Can we buy you a drink? This just isn't the place we want to talk to you about what we know about your brother."

Marilyn looked around and realized that they were in a very conspicuous place.

"Okay," she said. "Follow me."

Allen and Quinn got into the Mercedes and followed Marilyn down the coastal road to another road that ran off to the right. As they followed her she came to a stop at a little cabana style bar and restaurant. There were just a few people having lunch outside.

Marilyn took them inside and the bartender came out from the bar and spoke to Marilyn in a whisper. He then walked up to Allen and Quinn and led them to a table that overlooked a large orchard of fruit trees. It was a beautiful setting and private enough to talk to Marilyn. As they waited a few minutes Marilyn joined the two men at the table.

"What do you have to tell me?" asked Marilyn with a scorned look on her face.

Allen and Quinn looked at each other as if to say who is going to start.

Then Allen looked at Marilyn, "You might not believe us when we tell you this. But if you listen and keep your mind open to the possibility we can help solve some things about your brother's disappearance when he was kidnapped."

Marilyn sat across from Allen staring into his eyes. Her dark brown eyes didn't leave his for she wanted to read him to see if he was telling her the truth.

"Marilyn, what I'm about to tell you is going to be a shock to you. But you have to believe us when we tell you this. Your brother is still alive and he's living in the Amazon Rainforest."

He waited for a response from her, but she didn't say a word.

"We met him Marilyn," said Quinn. "And he's alive as the three of us sitting here."

Marilyn still didn't believe a word they were telling her.

"Did you and Miguel sneak out at night and catch lightening bugs?" asked Allen.

Marilyn looked surprised that Allen would know that. "How did you know that?"

"Well, he told the story to one of the native boys who carried our cargo when we were in the Amazon.

"It's a long story," said Quinn.

"What were you doing in the Amazon?"

"The first time we were there we were on a vacation. That's when we met Natowa." said Allen.

"Who is Natowa?" she asked with curious look on her face.

"Miguel's name was changed to Natowa," said Quinn.

The more they spoke the more curious Marilyn became.

"Listen Marilyn, the reason why we're giving you the hair is so that you can have a DNA test on it to prove it's Miguel's. It's just that he's grown up and a man now," said Allen.

"My brother was kidnapped and his body was found in the woods behind our home three weeks after he was kidnapped. He's buried in the Francis De Paula Cemetery with my mother and father."

"No he's not," said Quinn. "Your brother was born with a cleft lip and your parents were out casted because of it. So your father had him taken to the Amazon to be raised."

"My brother had surgery and it was corrected!" Marilyn fired back at them.

"Yes, but people knew. Your father was losing business and he was losing the palace. It was hurting the royal family name."

Marilyn looked down at the table after listening to Allen and Quinn.

"Yes, that's true. I remember my father coming home upset that he lost an account. Or friends or an ambassador had a party and didn't invite my parents. I used to cry for my father because I knew it hurt him. But my father would never do anything to hurt my brother. He loved him!"

"I'm sure he did," said Allen. "But the truth is your father took Miguel into the rainforest to have him raised by a woman by the name of Ana. She became his caretaker until she died."

Marilyn wasn't convinced Allen and Quinn were telling her the truth. She pulled out the white box from her purse. "This little white box is going to tell me the truth. I'll have the DNA test done to see if what you're telling me is the truth. If it is Miguel's hair, I want to see him. But what do you want from me?"

Quinn and Allen stared at her for a moment.

"Your brother is a great medicine man Marilyn. We would like for him to give us the antidote to help us save a very good friend of ours. Our friend Michael has been diagnosed with terminal cancer. Miguel might be the only person who can save him." said Allen.

"I see," Marilyn said back. "Where are you staying?"

Allen pulled out a piece of paper with all their contact information on it. "Please let us know one way or the other Marilyn. We're on borrowed time right now and our friend's life depends on it."

She looked at Allen and Quinn once more and nodded. "You'll hear from me," as she got up from the table and left.

Back in their rooms at their hotel, Allen and Quinn called Michael. He was still in good spirits and he asked how things were going. They told him they were making progress but some things still had to be in place before they would know anything for sure. John was still there with Michael. John also knew it was just a matter of time.

Quinn and Allen were happy to know John was there with Michael. They didn't feel so bad leaving him on his own. But they knew their own practices were going to suffer if they didn't make any headway soon. Time was everything!

They planned on calling Marilyn the following afternoon if they didn't hear back from her by then. They needed for her to get the DNA test done as soon as possible. And then they would tell her that they needed her to come with them to the Amazon.

That evening around 9:00 p.m. there was a knock on Allen's door. When he opened it he was surprised to see Marilyn standing there. She looked as though she had been crying.

"May I come in?"

"Yes, of course! Come in," as Allen was excited to see her.

Marilyn walked by Allen as he closed the door. He could smell the expensive French perfume she was wearing as she walked by him. He could also smell the light scent of Jasmine coming from her hair. He shook his head briefly to jar his thoughts out of his head.

She was a very beautiful woman although Allen could definitely see the strong resemblance between Natowa and Marilyn. In some ways they were exactly alike and in others they were as different as night and day.

"Would you like a drink?" asked Allen.

"Yes please, if you have some brandy that would be fine."

"I do," as he poured them a few ounces of brandy into brandy snifters.

"Please, sit down," as he handed Marilyn one of the glasses.

She sat on the couch and Allen sat down next to her.

"It's Miguel. It's his hair and he's alive." Marilyn's eyes welled up with tears again.

"Why are you crying?" Allen reached for a tissue and handed it to her.

"My brother has been alive all these years and I didn't even know!" I don't know how he has been living, or if he was abused? Did he grow up hungry or sad or lonely?" She broke down crying hysterically. Allen didn't know what to say or do. So he reached over and put his arms around her like she was a piece of fine china.

As she cried into his shoulder he could feel her sadness and pain. He pulled her closer to him as she rested in his arms listlessly. He could tell this news has left her in despair and crushed emotionally and physically.

"Listen Marilyn, you're lucky that you had a chance to find out he's still alive. Many people never get found again."

"By your own father? That's why my mother shot herself. She knew he was still alive and couldn't live with what my father did. My mother's last words to me were to go find Miguel. I thought it was from her dementia.

My mother was a good woman and honored my father's wishes. But she had to live her life with this horrible secret! How could he? How could my father have done this? I feel I have been so betrayed! I can't even imagine what my brother must be feeling!"

Marilyn looked up at Allen. It was all he could do not lean over and gently kiss her on her lips. All he wanted to do was comfort her. He felt so bad he had to burden her with this news that has led her to all the family lies and secrets.

"Can you take me to him?" Marilyn asked anxiously. "I want to see him!"

"You will. That's why we're here. We need to take you to the Amazon to see Miguel. He knows you're alive and he thought you were still in the palace where you grew up."

"I kept the palace but I don't live there. There were just too many bad memories."

Allen felt sorry for Marilyn. She had so many terrible things happen in her life. He could feel her walls as she protects herself from the elements of pain she endured. He admired how she dealt with her life. And instead of caving to her sorrow, she kept her head high and managed her pain. But Allen wondered that when the doors were closed at night, did she feel the emptiness and despair of her past?

Just as Allen stared into Marilyn's eyes, there was a knock on the door. It was Quinn. Allen left her side reluctantly to answer the door. Allen looked at Quinn and then turned his head towards Marilyn. Quinn was surprised to see her.

"Come on in," said Allen.

Quinn walked towards Marilyn as she sat taking a sip of her Brandy. "Hi Marilyn, I'm happy to see you here!"

"I had the hair tested, It's my brother's."

Quinn sat down and sat back in the chair with such relief.

"Yes, we knew it was your brother's."

They all talked for a few minutes and arranged they would leave the next morning for the Amazon.

Allen told Marilyn, "You'll need to dress very comfortably and bring ..."

Marilyn stopped him in mid sentence. "I already know what I need to bring. I have visited the Amazon before. I'll meet you here tomorrow morning at 6:00 a.m. I'll arrange for a charter plane and we will leave at 7:30. Please be ready," as she closed the door behind her.

# Chapter 14

When Marilyn returned home, she called Emmanuel.

He answered his cell phone, "*Bonjour Belle*." How are you? What do I owe this pleasant surprise?"

"Are you free to talk for a minute?" asked Marilyn.

"Yes babe, anytime for you."

Emmanuel was alone in his office. As they talked he stared out his twelfth story office window into the streets of Paris below while seeing the Eiffel Tower in the distance.

"Well, something has come up and I have to go to the Amazon."

"The Amazon!" shouted Emmanuel. "No lady of mine is going to the Amazon!"

"You don't understand Emmanuel. I have to go, and when I tell you why you'll understand."

"Okay, tell me what's going on."

Marilyn said, "My brother's alive!"

Emmanuel stopped talking and sat down in his chair.

"What!" Emmanuel shouted.

"Yes, he's alive!"

"What makes you think he's alive?"

"I had two men from New York City who came to see me. They told me that Miguel was alive and living in the Amazon.

"And you believe them?" Emmanuel retorted in a very stern voice. "Who are these men? Why would you trust strangers you don't even know?"

Marilyn was getting upset with Emmanuel for scolding her. "Listen, Emmanuel. I have no time to fight with you about this. It's a long story. But the men brought me a black hair. I had it tested and it's Miguel's. The DNA test showed a perfect match!"

"This sounds like a set up to me!" yelled Emmanuel. "I forbid you to go with these men!"

"Forbid me?" Marilyn yelled back at him. "No one forbids me to do anything!"

He stopped to get his composure. "I'm not forbidding you Marilyn. It was a bad choice of words. I guess what I'm trying to say is that I don't want you to leave with these strangers. It sounds like a set up. If you're going, I'm coming with you!"

Marilyn smiled as she knew he meant what he was saying. He was very protective. She knew he only had her best interest at heart.

"No babe. You have too much to do, and the time I have is very limited. Just in case of an emergency, we're leaving tomorrow from the Santos Dumont Airport on a chartered plane at 7:30 in the morning for the Tishi Amazon Resort. We'll be heading into Amazon as soon as we can. There's just no time for you to come."

He wrote down everything she told him. He sat back in his chair and he knew if he demanded that he go with her she would get upset. "What can I do, you'll do it no matter what I say!"

Marilyn smiled again and reassured him everything would be Okay. She told him they had experienced tour guides to take them where they needed to go. She told him that her cell phone would not work once in the Amazon, and that she loved him and she would call as soon as she could. Before he could say a word she said, "Good bye my future husband, I love you!" and she hung up.

When Emmanuel got off the phone he yelled for his secretary to come into his office.

"I want you to get me a list of everyone that's on a chartered plane to the Tishi Amazon Resort from Rio Santos Dumont Airport departing at 7:30 tomorrow morning. And I want it as soon as you can get it. And get my father's plane ready. I need it as soon as possible!"

Marilyn pulled up in a limo and motioned for Allen and Quinn to get in. The bus boys loaded the trunk and they pulled away to catch the plane. As they drove Marilyn asked Allen and Quinn, "Can you tell me about my brother?"

They both started talking at once. Then they looked at each other and laughed.

"You first," said Allen to Quinn.

"Marilyn, your brother is a great man. He's a self taught medicine man with a wealth of knowledge in healing. I was bit by a deadly snake and, well, I was dead. Your brother brought me back. Your brother saved my life!"

Her eyes widened as he told her the story.

Allen explained, "Marilyn, we have asked Natowa." Then Allen reminded himself of Natowa's birth name. "I mean Miguel to help us with a cure to save our friend Michael who is dying at home right now from cancer."

Marilyn looked at the both of them sadly, "I'm so sorry to hear that, I have a feeling that this is why you've come for me isn't it?"

"Yes, somewhat," said Quinn.

"But that was before we knew about Natowa and his life," said Allen. "We feel he can help us and we can also help him. It's a win/win situation."

"I see, and just in case I haven't said it before, I do appreciate what you have done for me and Miguel. But one thing I'm curious about."

"What's that?" asked Allen.

"Does my brother know I'm coming?"

Allen and Quinn looked at each other.

"No he doesn't, at least not yet!"

Marilyn took a very deep long breath and stared out the window of the limo. "Should I ask how are we going to tell him?"

"Well," said Quinn, "We haven't figured that out yet. But there's a woman."

"What woman?" Marilyn looked on to them with a curious look in her face.

Allen said, "Her name is Enesa. She lives in the garden where your brother lives. We're not sure if they're lovers or just friends. But she's a beautiful young woman from Denmark. And she cares very much for your brother."

Marilyn was happy to hear that Miguel had someone in his life even if she was a friend. Someone who was looking after him, and he could share his pain and loneliness with.

Allen said, "He has a good life Marilyn. But he also is haunted by his past. And like you he has made the best of his life. He had people who loved and nurtured him. But there was one thing he wanted to do in his life, and that was to find you and see you again."

Marilyn's eyes welled up with tears. She tried to hide it but they finally made their way down her cheeks. She wiped them dry again and said, "We were very close. So close that when he was gone I felt like part of my body and soul were gone too. It took me years to find my heart again. But it just was never the same."

Allen and Quinn could feel her pain. Allen choked back his emotions and sadness he felt for her.

"And now after all these years I find out he was never gone!"

When they arrived at the Tishi Amazon Resort, Marilyn was very familiar with its surroundings. She had been there once as a young girl with her parents. A man came and talked to her father in dark sunglasses, and when she asked her mother who he was her mother just said, "Your father is taking care of some business."

Now she wonders if he was looking for Miguel. Maybe he couldn't live with his conscience and realized what he had done.

She had many questions in her mind since her new discovery that Miguel was still alive. Maybe that's why her father confined himself to his room for years. And maybe that's why her mother lost her mind and shot herself. It was all making sense to her now.

Allen and Quinn introduced Yurah, Davi, Tutu and Nino to Marilyn. The two young boys were quite smitten with her.

"You're Natowa's sister?" asked Tutu.

"Yes I am," said Marilyn with a smile.

"You're beautiful like Enesa," said Nino. "But you also look just like Natowa."

Marilyn gently laughed at the boys. They brought light to the whole menagerie. She was happy to meet people who knew her brother. Nino and Tutu talked on and on about Natowa and what a heroic man he was.

Tutu told her how he saved his life from the jaguar, and how Enesa and Natowa healed him from his mangled leg.

Marilyn listened on to the boys in amazement. Her brother could do all this? She already had such a great admiration for him. He hadn't changed a bit!

When they reached their destination, It was always the old log that protruded from the river that marked the spot. Once they made camp along the river, Allen, Quinn and Marilyn walked along the river's edge talking about how they were going to approach Natowa and tell him that Marilyn was there to see him.

The next morning they rose by dawn and Marilyn was as eager as Tutu and Nino to get started. So Marilyn ran ahead with the two young men and walked with them into the Amazon jungle. Yurah, Davi, Allen and Quinn followed closely behind keeping watch.

A half hour into the walk, Yurah waved for everyone to stop! And everyone stood still while Yurah and Davi listened to the movements and sounds in the jungle. Something was near but they couldn't sense what it was. The animals were all silent including the Spider monkeys. It was too quiet thought Yurah. He motioned for everyone to walk slowly and moved Marilyn and the two boys in between him and Davi.

Allen and Quinn kept a watch also following behind. All the men carried a rifle. They were used to carrying them by now and were ready to use them if needed.

As the sounds of the rainforest jungle came alive again, Yurah motioned to everyone it was safe. But he kept a very watchful eye feeling that something was close by. He was watching to see if it would come out.

Five hours later, they were camped just one kilometer from Natowa's homestead, as they made camp Marilyn slipped down to the waterfall to bathe. Yurah went with her and stood guard for her.

When she was done she slipped back into some clean clothes and returned with Yurah to the camp. She told the men that she would help cook dinner that night, but Yurah and Davi turned her down.

"You will relax and rest for we have much more of the journey to complete," said Yurah.

So she sat down between Quinn and Allen admiring the roaring fire. Allen could smell the scent of Jasmine in her hair again. It was a very soothing and comforting smell.

"I love the smell of your Jasmine," said Allen.

"How did you know it was Jasmine?"

Allen didn't answer her back but smiled at her. Instead he got up and walked away.

Marilyn looked at Quinn. "Is it something I said?"

Quinn shook his head no. "Every time he smells Jasmine it reminds him of Stephanie."

"Who is Stephanie?"

"She was Allen's first and only love. She was killed in a car accident on her way home from university for Thanksgiving weekend. Allen was supposed to go with her, but he stayed behind a day to get some things done for school. He just hasn't gotten over her yet."

"I'm so sorry, he must have loved her very much if it was that long ago."

"Yes, it was quite a few years ago now. He has good days and bad days, but mostly good days. But if something reminds him of her, he closes up."

"I can imagine," said Marilyn as she watched Allen walk to the edge of the river.

Marilyn got up and walked towards him. She didn't know exactly what she would say when she reached him. She walked up next to him staring out at the same spot he was looking.

"Life isn't fair sometimes Allen."

He looked at her and knew Quinn told her about Stephanie. He was silent and then looked back out over the water again.

"All you can do is to keep her alive in your heart like I did with Miguel."

"You get a second chance."

"Yes, and I know you won't, but she was very lucky to have someone like you in her life. I'm sure she was very happy."

"Yes, we were happy."

"Then hold on to that. Don't ever blame yourself, she wouldn't want you to."

"How do you know?"

Marilyn knew he was blaming himself for not going with her that Thanksgiving weekend.

"Because I'm a woman and I know. I know she must have been a wonderful person for you to love her so much. And I'm sure she wants you to be happy. It's hard to let go when we lose someone tragically. Trust me, I know Allen. I know how you feel."

"I know you do," said Allen. "And thanks for the talk," as he smiled at her.

She turned to look at him. For a minute he forgot about Stephanie when he looked into Marilyn's eyes. She stared back into his. They caught each other spending much too long looking at each other. It was quite noticeable to both of them that something was starting to happen between them.

While the men slept on the ground near the fire, Tutu and Nino made Marilyn's bed much more comfortable by building a small platform between two large limbs in a tree to keep her safe. She didn't want them to go through the bother but they both insisted. They were quite proud of the job they did and Marilyn acted like she was being treated like a princess.

Once everyone was settled in for the night, Yurah and Davi took turns watching the camp.

Marilyn had a hard time sleeping. As much as the boys tried to make her comfortable she missed her own bed. But once she got settled into her sleeping bag she made the most of it trying to lie still not to disturb anyone else. It was a very still night and all that could be heard were the tree frogs and buzzing insects all around.

As she was just about to fall asleep, she heard a rustling in the jungle just below and behind her. She turned to see what it could be. The noise stopped! And then she heard it come closer again.

Yurah was too far away to call him and she didn't want to wake and startle everyone. So she watched into the ferns until she could see the top of someone's head coming towards her.

She was just about to call for the men when the man looked up at something in a tree beside him. She looked into the man's face and then she realized it was her brother Miguel! She almost jumped up and then realized she was ten feet off the ground.

Miguel heard her move and turned his head to look up into the tree. He looked at her for a long second, and then turned and walked quickly back into the ferns.

Marilyn wanted to run after him but by the time she got down she was afraid he would be gone. She looked around and everyone was still fast asleep. She hurried down the tree to the ground. She tiptoed away from Yurah as he sat staring into the fire sipping on some coffee. She quickly moved behind the tree then went towards the ferns.

She heard a sound coming from just inside of them and she knew it was Miguel. She moved slowly towards the noise. The noise kept moving farther away. She was reluctant to go any further, but she needed to see him. She knew he came to see her, so when she was far enough into the ferns, she whispered, "Miguel, it's me! It's Marilyn your sister! I've come to see you. Please come out!"

There was a deep silence. She thought maybe he had left. She kept turning around since she knew if anyone saw her missing they would come after her and maybe scare Miguel away.

"Miguel, please don't leave!" she whispered again.

Just as she pulled some ferns apart to look deeper, she gasped and jumped back! It was Miguel standing right in front of her.

Staring into her face he said to her in a soft deep voice. "Hello my sister, you should not be here. The Amazon is no place for you."

She was surprised to hear his voice. It was so much deeper than when they were children. She couldn't believe his size for he had grown a foot taller than her.

"I'm safe," she smiled at Miguel.

He smiled back at her and then moved out of the ferns to stand in front of her.

They both stood for a minute looking into each other's faces mesmerized by the similarity they still had. They could see the strong resemblance and admired how they had grown up.

She softly ran her hand down his face. "Miguel, you're alive!" she said with a very soft voice.

Miguel looked at her with a smile and put his hand on hers, "Yes Marilyn, I'm alive."

She wrapped her arms around him as he did her and they held each other for quite a few moments.

"How are you Miguel? Are you happy?"

"I'm well and I'm happy, and I'm even happier to see you. You're more beautiful than I even imagined!"

Tears filled her eyes again. She couldn`t grasp the thought that she was standing there with her brother. As much as she could feel him and touch him, it still didn't seem real.

"Tell me I'm not dreaming," said Marilyn.

Miguel said with a smile, "You're not dreaming, but I never thought we would meet this way. I wanted to see you again, but I wanted the time to be right."

Marilyn paused for a second. "Mother and Father are dead."

"Yes I know, I'm sorry to hear they passed away. You must miss them."

"You know that I thought you were dead too don't you Miguel?"

Miguel looked into Marilyn`s eyes as they started to well with tears.

"Yes, I know you thought I was dead." He put his arms around her to comfort her.

She put her head into his chest and cried, "I'm so sorry Miguel!" How could our father have done such a horrible thing?" She looked into his face now pushing her own emotions away to comfort him. "You know he loved you don't you?" Marilyn emphasized as she stared hard into his face.

He smiled down at her. "Yes, father was an honorable man. He did what he thought was best for you and mother."

"Did he ever come to see you?" asked Marilyn.

"I think so, once a long time ago some men came into the garden asking Ana, my caretaker some questions. She made me stay in the cliffs with a native friend while she talked to them. When they left she told me I had to leave for a few days.

Dr. Erikson, a missionary doctor took me and Enesa, his daughter, away into a cave while Enesa's mother stayed with Ana just in case they returned. We returned a few days later. I overheard Ana tell Dr. Erikson that they were here to take me home."

"Did you want to come home?"

"No," Miguel said, as he looked sadly into her eyes. "By then I had a new life. I had people around me who mentored me and loved me. I had already started working for a few years with Dr. Erikson and his wife to make medicine, and started researching plants and animals. There was no going back. I was a young man by then. The only one I missed was you. And I knew we would see each other again someday. And here you are, as beautiful as I remembered you."

Then Miguel reached down and pulled out a leather bag he had strapped onto his chest. He opened it and took out a little silver locket pendent with the initials "*m.L.a*". The initials stood for Marilyn Louisa Andre. He handed it to Marilyn.

Marilyn looked at the locket pendant in her hand, and then she realized it was a pendant that her parents gave her on her fifth birthday. Inside of the pendant there was a picture of Miguel dressed in a black velvet suit jacket with matching dress shorts, and Marilyn was dressed in a matching black velvet dress. They were sitting on a large red velvet chair in the palace with a large portrait of their parents hanging above them. They both looked identical only Miguel had short hair and Marilyn had long flowing hair down to her waste.

As she looked at the picture her eyes welled up again. "I remember this picture!" she cried out with pain in her voice. "I wondered what happened to it. I looked everywhere for it. How did you get it?"

"When I was taken to the rainforest to be raised by Ana, two men took me there. They were sad that they had to do what they did. They worked for our father, and they were instructed to take me there and never talk about it to anyone or they would be deported back to their homeland in El Salvador. They were refugees and if they returned to El Salvador they would have been beheaded.

Before they left me with Ana, the one man gave me his address and took my hand and told me to hold on to the pendant, and if ever I was sad or lonely to open it and it would comfort me. So that's what I did. I looked at it every night before going to bed. And when I felt lonely or I missed you, I would pull it out and hold it close. It was my way of staying close to you."

Marilyn's heart was so broken. She missed her brother as much as he missed her. She was so glad that he had the pendant to bring him comfort as she did through her stories and drawings.

Marilyn looked up and Miguel and said, "Well, we're here together now Miguel, and nothing will ever tear us apart again. I promise I'm not going anywhere, and we will be as close as we were when we were children. That I promise you!"

He smiled at her and said, "It's only the beginning. But it's getting late, and the men who brought you here are going to start to realize you're missing. I'll walk you back and then I have to leave. I'll find you again."

She didn't want to leave Miguel. She wanted to go with him, but she realized that this wasn't the time yet. There was so much she had to absorb and understand about his life.

After Miguel made sure she was safe back in her camp, he hugged and kissed her on the forehead. Miguel turned and walked into the ferns and he was gone.

Her heart felt broken again like the day she heard the news Miguel was dead. It was the same emptiness she felt that day. She took a deep breath as she looked towards where he departed and said to herself, "I'll see you again soon my brother."

# Chapter 15

When everyone was up the next morning, Allen made a plate of food for Marilyn as she walked across the camp to the fire.

"Good morning," smiled Allen. "You need to eat."

She looked down at the large tin plate he handed her. He filled her plate with pork, eggs, potatoes and rice.

"I can't eat all this!" Marilyn laughed.

"Try to eat as much as you can. Today we'll have a busy day and not sure when we'll eat again." He then poured her a cup of coffee. "So how did it go with Miguel last night?"

Marilyn looked up at him in surprise!

"How did you know?"

"I followed you. I had a feeling you heard the same thing I heard, and when I saw you get down from the tree I wanted to make sure you were safe."

She smiled at Allen. "Thank you but I was fine, and my reunion with Miguel was simply a dream come true! He's so tall and handsome! He gave me this!"

Marilyn pulled her hair away to show Allen the pendant. Allen looked at it and realized how much Miguel must have missed her to hold on to something that many years. Allen knew he never forgot her.

"That's beautiful!" smiled Allen.

"Yes it is, and when he left he said it was only the beginning," as she smiled up at Allen.

Allen smiled back at her as he put his arm around her waist.

"I'm glad I could share your happiness with you Marilyn. I really am!"

Then there was that feeling again. Their eyes met and she felt tingles all down her spine from his touch. But she couldn't feel this way for Allen. She was engaged to Emmanuel. Thinking of Emmanuel again, she looked at Allen one more time then turned and walked away.

Allen could sense she was fighting back her feelings for him as he fought his feelings for her. He thought there was no sense in starting something since she was already engaged. He also didn't want to complicate anything since he needed to make sure nothing would go wrong that could jeopardize the main reason why they were there, and that was to save Michael.

After their camp was cleaned up and everything packed, they had a meeting in front of the fire before they put it out. Quinn led the meeting saying that they needed Tutu and Nino to try to get a hold of Enesa once they got to Natowa's. They decided to somehow sneak Tutu into the garden to bring Enesa to them. They needed Enesa to talk to Natowa. But then Tutu said he knew a back way in not to be seen.

They knew from the conversation that they had with Enesa that he had discovered a cure. And the only way they could save Michael would be to get the medicine or antidote from him. Time was running out. They only had three more days before they had to return to New York. The time they had invested could not be wasted. No matter what, they had to convince Natowa to help them.

Once they reached Natowa's homestead, they sent Tutu on his own into the garden. They knew that Tutu had befriended Natowa and Enesa and he would be safe.

A half hour later he returned with Enesa. As she walked closer to them Marilyn admired how beautiful Enesa was.

"My brother is a very lucky man," said Marilyn to Allen as she leaned towards him.

Allen smiled, "Yes, and he's about to get even luckier with two beautiful women in his life." Just as he finished talking, Enesa walked up to Marilyn and stood in front of her.

"Hello Marilyn, It's so nice to finally meet Natowa's beautiful sister.

"Hello Enesa, and you're as beautiful as Tutu and Nino said you were."

Nino and Tutu blushed and everyone laughed!

Then Enesa took Marilyn by her hand, "Come with me. I'll take you into the garden, and we can talk and get to know each other. I can also answer any questions you may have."

Enesa looked at Allen and Quinn, "I'll return Marilyn in a few hours."

Allen looked a bit concerned, but then he smiled and nodded his head as they walked close together and talked while Marilyn and Enesa disappeared down the slate path.

As Marilyn entered the garden she was astonished by what she saw. It was the most beautiful botanical garden she had ever seen. The flowers and foliage were way beyond anything she had ever seen before. There were beautiful gardens everywhere.

As Marilyn looked up the sides of the cliffs, she could see hundreds of Tiki lanterns that hung from the walls. Under the lanterns were square holes all different sizes. She could tell they were manmade and wondered what they were for?

"What are all the lanterns for?"

"They light up the whole garden at night," said Enesa. "It's a beautiful sight and sometime soon you will see for yourself."

"And I see square holes underneath. What are they for?"

"You will find out what they're for also. But right now I'll show you the rest of the garden and house."

"How could anyone light all those lanterns? There were hundreds of them!" she thought to herself.

Enesa looked at Marilyn as she wandered through the gardens.

"You're pleased?" asked Enesa.

Marilyn turned and looked at Enesa. "Pleased is an understatement!" And the two women laughed.

She was mesmerized as she looked around to see this paradise that they had built. Marilyn loved to garden and designed all the landscaping at the palace, but never could she have ever envisioned anything like the gardens she was standing in right now.

She was speechless looking around at flowers she had never seen before. There were hundreds of different kinds with vibrant colors everywhere. And although they were in the middle of a botanical rainforest, this was a paradise within a paradise!

On the far side to the right of the garden, there were little round greenhouses with thatched roofs. She could see all kinds of colorful flowers and plants inside of them. Between the cliffs and greenhouses were small hot springs separated by rock boulders and more gardens.

"Hello, and welcome to the garden!" someone called out.

Marilyn wasn't expecting anyone else to be there so she turned in a hurry towards the voice, but no one was there! No one but a large colorful parrot on a bamboo perch.

"Hello! How are you today?"

Then Marilyn realized the voice was coming from the bird.

"I'm sorry," said Enesa. "I should have warned you."

"That's okay," laughed Marilyn. "He's adorable!"

Yes, but he is nothing but a big squawk box," laughed Enesa.

"I heard that!" squawked the bird.

"This is Jaukeu," (Jah•koo) also known as Jack. He keeps everyone in line in the garden."

"Hello Jaukeu, it's my pleasure," as Marilyn ran her hand over his beautiful rainbow colored feathers.

"I'm in love!" Jaukeu called out.

Enesa and Marilyn laughed.

"What kind of bird is he?"

"He's a Scarlet Macaw which is one of the largest and colorful species of parrots. He was given to my father as gift when he saved a village from the fever."

Then Enesa picked up a whicker basket sitting on the ground and handed Marilyn a peanut.

"The best way to Jaukeu's heart is through his stomach," Enesa smiled.

Marilyn put the peanut in front of Jaukeu.

"Yummy!" Jaukeu called out dancing up and down on his perch grabbing the peanut with his beak.

Marilyn and Enesa laughed again.

See you later Jack, said Enesa, as she and Marilyn walked further into the garden.

Marilyn walked towards the pond that had a waterfall in the distance. There were large Banyan trees that surrounded it. It was a fresh water pond and when she looked down inside of the clear aqua colored water she could see hundreds of beautiful fish and plants in the bottom. The fish were every color you could imagine. Some were multi color with stripes and spots and all shapes and sizes. These were fish that she had never seen before. For some reason Marilyn felt that these were extraordinary fish that had been bred for a purpose.

In the middle of the pond was a six foot long very unique large black fish. Its body and texture resembled somewhat of a shark. On top, it had one smaller black eye on the left side of its head, and one larger light green eye on the right side of its head. Marilyn gasped when she saw it! It also had a long tail like a large cat, and when she looked at the fish it gave her goose bumps as the big fish watched and followed her with its big green eye.

"What kind of fish is that?" Marilyn asked in astonishment!

"It's part shark, and bred with another species of animal."

"What other species?"

Enesa just smiled, "It's a cross between an animal and a shark. I'll let Natowa tell you the rest."

When she looked closer at the black fish, she couldn't believe what she was seeing! The fish looked towards her as she stared back at it. She realized its green eye was of a large wild cat like animal.

Everywhere she walked the mammoth fish watched her. As she walked along the pond its body moved slowly to follow her but it never left the center of the pond. And when she stopped, the fish stopped moving still never taking its green eye off of her. The other fish were scurrying around it faster and faster as it moved in a circle to watch her.

"How could a fish have eyes like that?" asked Marilyn dumbfounded by its look and behavior.

"There are many phenomenons in the garden," Enesa said, "But I have to admit, I have never seen it act like this. It keeps watching you. It seems that you have made a new friend!"

All of a sudden a little squirrel monkey went flying out from one of the gardens being playfully chased by a Kinkajou. Marilyn could tell they were pets that lived in the garden.

Enesa said, "You never know what you're going to see around here!"

Marilyn laughed!

They walked towards the house and Marilyn asked, "Where's Miguel?"

"He'll return after nightfall." Unfortunately you won't be able to see him today."

Disappointed, Marilyn asked "Where is he?"

"He's looking for a plant that glows at night. Come with me, I want to show you the house," Enesa added with excitement!

When Marilyn entered, again she was taken by surprise by what she saw. "This is so beautiful!"

"Thank you," Enesa said back."

Marilyn looked around the room as the whole house was open to a thirty foot high cathedral ceiling with log cross beams at the top.

It was made completely out of Mahogany wood throughout. The smell of the wood and flowers were so aromatic that it gave such a sense of comfort when Marilyn walked in.

The floor had mighty wood planks with spikes anchoring the planks throughout. It gave the rooms a rustic look and the house fit perfectly in its botanical setting.

The windows had large beautiful stained glass valances throughout. All the windows were dressed with different scenes of animals of the rainforest. The scenes showed birds, deer, wild cats, monkeys and fish. They were beautifully designed with multi colors and each window told a story of the Amazon Rainforest. Each one was soldered with a pewter medal and there was no need for any curtains.

"These are so beautiful!" Marilyn said as she looked at every window she could see.

"Thank you," said Enesa.

"Who made them?"

"They were made from the Ashuan natives like many of things in the house. Natowa and I will explain to you later."

The furniture was also made of dark Mahogany and beautiful floral multi colored tapestry that were hand sewn with needlepoint. Couches and love seats were all throughout the huge open room.

The far wall was graced with a stone fireplace that went from wall to wall and three quarters high with a large beam that held a mix of Terracotta pottery. The room had large Mahogany posts that supported the second floor balcony.

Amongst the chairs and couches were beautiful tables carved with flowers, animals and birds with panther claw feet. The furniture told the same story as the stained glass valances on the windows.

Everything had a harmonized theme throughout and Marilyn knew they were all hand carved. There were hand woven matching rugs that lay under each couch and chair. Marilyn never saw such a beautiful mix of colors and fabrics. There were beautiful sofa and chair pillows all in different colors and fabrics. On every table were beautiful flowers mixed with ferns and plants.

As they moved through the house they came to a large dining room with a table that could seat at least forty people. It was larger than the table that they had in the formal dining room at the palace.

A large china cabinet sat at the end wall and was packed with a beautiful set of terracotta hand painted pottery. They were all themed with flowers and the edges with black trim.

They came to a large room with a big desk in the middle. All around the room there were book shelves and each shelf sat hundreds of medical and plant books. A large stained glass chandelier that was filled with kerosene lights hung from the middle of the room over a large desk. On each side of the desk were suede and leather chairs and couches. The chandelier lanterns matched the windows telling a story of the rainforest etched with animals, birds and flowers.

As they moved to the back of the house a large room opened up to the kitchen that took Marilyn's breath away! She had never seen such a beautiful kitchen. A long narrow Mahogany table ran almost the length of the kitchen with a large beautiful bouquet of flowers in the middle.

The Mahogany cupboards were built around three walls and at the end was a large walk in pantry filled with jars of preserved jams and canned vegetables, fruits, dried beans and grains.

The floor was made of multi color stones of all shapes and sizes and then mortared into place with Terracotta colored mortar.

The room had a ceiling that vaulted twenty feet high to the middle of the room. Below the ceiling there were large planked Mahogany beams that held a large six foot long fern which draped down from the center of the room.

The windows also had stained glass valances to match the rest of the windows throughout the house and beautiful stain glassed lanterns were mounted all the way around the walls.

The counters were made of multi colored granites and more ferns in beautiful hand painted pottery lined each countertop.

There was a mahogany wine rack on the other side of the walk in pantry. The wine rack was filled with wines that Marilyn could see were all homemade.

Enesa walked up to the wine rack and pulled out a few dusty bottles. On one of the bottles it was finely etched with the word 1985 Pomegranate Chardonnay, and on the other bottle was etched with 1987 Blackberry Shiraz.

"This was my father's private stock of wines he made with some of the native people," as Enesa showed them to Marilyn. "I would like for you to have them."

Marilyn looked at Enesa and smiled.

"Thank you Enesa. I'll keep them for something very special."

Enesa pulled out a few white rags and a cloth bag from a drawer and carefully wrapped the wines in the cloths. Then she put the two bottles of wine in the cloth bag and set them on the counter.

"We'll return to get them later," said Enesa. "Come with me, and I'll show you the upstairs rooms."

They went up a wide spiral staircase. Half way in between was a landing with a large beautiful handmade tapestry on the wall.

The needlework was absolutely beautiful as it made a story of the native people interacting with nature and wildlife. The tapestry represented peace and harmony from the natives and the rainforest. It was a work of art that if sold at an auction would bring thousands of dollars.

Marilyn knew art for she studied it in university. Being an art buyer, she travelled to many museums and knew the value of art. But this was one of the most beautiful tapestry pieces she had ever seen. And she stood for a few minutes studying it and its meaning.

Then she turned to Enesa. "I'm sorry, I was just looking and studying the story this tapestry tells."

Enesa smiled at her. "It's nice to see you appreciate the value of its meaning. It took quite a few years for the native people to complete. They gave it to Natowa for saving their people from a deadly influenza that would have killed their people. It's one of Natowa's most prized possessions. He created this spot on the landing so he could admire it every day."

As the women climbed the stairs Marilyn looked down below to see the remarkable view.

They came to a long open hallway that ran the length of the upstairs and overlooked the great room below.

Enesa came to a room and opened the door and let Marilyn go inside first. In the middle of the room was a king size bed made out of Mahogany dressed with a white hand stitched embroidered duvet and matching shams on the pillows. There was a beautiful mural of colorful birds sitting in a tree behind it.

There was an armoire to the left of the room that shelved a large floral arrangement. The smell of the flowers scented the room with Fuchsia, Magnolias, and Lilies of the Valley.

On the other side of the room was a love seat made in white and yellow satin that matched the bedding.

There were two end tables on each side with a beautiful stained glass kerosene lamp on one and another bouquet of flowers on the other. A long yellow and white floral rug sat over the wood floor, and a white satin mahogany chair sat at the foot of the bed.

"This is my room," said Enesa.

"It's so beautiful!" Marilyn smiled back at Enesa. "This must be a perfect retreat for you."

"I'm sure you have seen many beautiful homes in Rio de Janeiro."

"Yes I have. But nothing decorated as beautiful as this!"

They walked down to a second room and Enesa opened the door. She could tell that this was Miguel's room. The first thing Marilyn noticed was the beautiful built in fish aquarium that was built the whole length of the east wall. It was filled with beautiful tropical fish of all colors, shapes and sizes with beautiful colored coral reef and stones that lay on the floor of the aquarium. She walked over to the wall and just stared into it totally mesmerized by its beautiful colors.

"Did Miguel build this aquarium?"

"Yes, he did." Enesa said back.

"I could stay here all day just looking at it!" laughed Marilyn.

Enesa laughed back at her.

The room was more masculine. It had a large king size bed in the corner on an angle that faced the fish aquarium. On the bed was a beautiful brown suede and lamb's wool blanket.

There was a large stained glass window etched with antelope and ferns in the corners.

He had a spectacular view of the whole garden. At the base of the window was a large leather high back chair and end table. She could tell that the chair had been sat in many times. She imagined her brother sitting there looking down at the garden and probably keeping a watchful eye!

Marilyn turned to Enesa, "He never kept his room this clean."

The women both laughed as Marilyn and Enesa walked to a third room.

"And this will be your room," as Enesa opened the door.

Marilyn was surprised to hear they had a room for her. Marilyn smiled at Enesa as she entered. She gasped when she walked in!

As soon as she walked in she saw a large 3' x 5' black and white painting that hung over the bed. It was the picture of Miguel and her from her pendant. She moved closer and stared at the painting that looked exactly like the two of them.

"Who painted this?" Marilyn said with excitement!

"I did," smiled Enesa.

"I'm so amazed! I don't even know what to say!"

She caught every detail of the picture from the buttons on their clothes to the shadows on their faces to the lights of the backdrop. The only thing that was missing was the portrait of their parent's in the background. It was truly spectacular to see herself with her brother on such a beautiful canvas work of art.

The bed was only dressed with a white sheet and pillows. The only other things that sat in the room were an armoire and a vanity.

"We haven't finished your room. We wanted to see what you wanted in it so you would feel at home."

"It's perfect!" Marilyn commented with excitement.

She was already envisioning what she would do with the room with the painting being the focal point. All of a sudden her mind drifted back to her home in Niteroi. "I cannot live here," she thought to herself. "I'm getting married soon." But she kept her thoughts to herself not wanting to spoil anything for Enesa.

"I'm going to love this room!" said Marilyn smiling at Enesa.

Marilyn wondered why Enesa and Miguel had separate bedrooms. "Are they lovers? Or are they just friends? Or are they like brother and sister?" Marilyn was happy for Miguel that he had such a wonderful woman like Enesa in his life.

When Enesa returned Marilyn back to Allen and Quinn, everyone was anxiously waiting. Marilyn and Enesa hugged and gave each other a smile. Then Enesa disappeared once more down the slate path into the garden. Marilyn walked towards Allen and Quinn.

"So how did everything go?" Allen anxiously asked.

"I'm sorry, but I never got to see Miguel."

Allen and Quinn looked disappointed.

"Enesa is coming back tomorrow for me. I'm to meet her here at the same time. She told me Miguel should return by then and I promise you I'll get an answer for you."

"Marilyn, our time is running out," said Allen. "We only have two days before we have to go back to the resort. Then we fly back to New York the next day."

"Yes, I have to leave no matter what before I get served with divorce papers when I get home," said Quinn.

Quinn looked worried they weren't going to see Natowa again. He was worried the whole time they spent here was all in vain.

"I know how you're feeling. I'm disappointed too. And tomorrow I promise you that if Miguel returns and I get to see him, I'll have an answer for you. I'll try to convince him to help you."

# Chapter 16

They headed back to camp. It was a long day and after dinner everyone was ready to make it an early night to get started early the next day. Once Marilyn was settled into bed she fell fast asleep. She fell asleep so fast and so hard that she woke up a few hours later not knowing exactly where she was. She let out a little shriek and Davi came to her and stood below the tree where she slept.

"Is everything Okay?" asked Davi.

"Yes I'm fine," as she smiled down at him. She lay back down but unable to get back to sleep. Then she felt someone climbing up towards her in the tree. She turned around and there was Allen looking up at her.

"Can't sleep?" asked Allen, as he pulled himself up on the platform sitting right next to her.

She smiled at him, "Well it's not like home."

He chuckled and then looked straight out into the sky.

"Did you see the moon tonight?"

Marilyn turned her body towards the moon and to her astonishment it took up most of the sky!

"No wonder I couldn't sleep, the light from the moon makes the rainforest so bright."

"Yes it does, I've only seen it like this once before."

They both sat from the platform in the tree admiring its beauty.

"You seem worried today Allen. Is something else bothering you?"

"I'm just worried about Michael."

"Tell me about Michael."

"Well, he's a great guy. Quinn, Michael and I have been best friends since university. We do everything together. We would be lost without him."

Marilyn looked into Allen's face and realized that Michael was a very special person in Allen's life. Marilyn understanding how he must feel to lose his friend, as she did her brother, knew she had to do whatever she could to help Allen and Quinn. She laid her hand on his back and gently ran it down the middle to comfort him. Her touch provoked Allen's sexual desire and he pulled his back away from her hand.

She looked at him, "Are you sure you're okay?"

He looked back into Marilyn's face. Then he ran his eyes down her body to rest his eyes on her feet.

"I need to stay focused. I have to go."

He climbed back down the tree and went to his sleeping bag in front of the fire. He laid his head back and put his arm across his forehead and eyes. She couldn't tell if he had fallen back asleep. She lay back down and stared back at the moon.

Before Marilyn knew it, she was awakened by Tutu who was pushing on her feet. "Good morning Marilyn, breakfast is ready!"

After Marilyn went down to the waterfall's to bathe, she and Yurah returned to the fire and Yurah made her some breakfast. She looked around but she couldn't see Allen. She could see Quinn packing for their day with Tutu and Nino in the distance.

"Where's Allen?" asked Marilyn.

"He has gone to bathe in the waterfall," Davi answered back while packing some dishes.

"We didn't see him on the way. When did he leave?"

"He left about fifteen minutes ago."

"Then Yurah and I should have seen him on the way."

Davi looked at her and then realized they should have seen him walking as they came back. They both looked at each other for a long moment.

Davi yelled down to Quinn, Yurah, Tutu and Nino. "Everyone come quickly!"

They all came running!

"What's wrong?" said Quinn.

"Marilyn and Yurah came back from the waterfall and never saw Allen."

Everyone went silent for a moment. Quinn dropped the backpack in his hand and started to run towards the waterfall. Then Yurah, Davi, Tutu and Nino followed. Marilyn was frozen for a moment and then ran to catch up to them.

"Allen! Allen!" Quinn shouted! Everyone was calling out for him but there was no response.

Then Yurah and Davi decided to split everyone up into two groups to cover more territory. Marilyn went with Yurah and Tutu. Quinn, Davi and Nino went in an opposite direction.

"Meet back here in a half an hour no matter what!" shouted Yurah.

Marilyn ran with the men. Fifteen minutes later, they all realized something was wrong if he wasn't responding to their calls.

"What do you think could have happened?" Marilyn frantically called to Yurah!

Yurah looked very worried. "I have no answers for what could have happened," shaking his head back and forth. "We have to go back and see if he returned to camp."

Fifteen minutes later everyone was standing back at camp. Everyone but Allen and Quinn!

"Where is Quinn?" Yurah asked Davi. Davi turned to look around but Quinn was nowhere in sight.

"I'm worried," said Davi. "What could have happened to them?"

Everyone looked at each other totally at a loss for words.

They waited at camp until after dinner for them to return. Yurah and Davi knew time was crucial to find Allen and Quinn. They knew that they had to go find them now before they lost their tracks. They didn't want to take Marilyn with them because of the dangers she might be exposed to.

They decided to take Marilyn back to Natowa's home and leave her there. They left a note under a rock near the fire for Allen and Quinn just in case they returned to camp. The note read they were taking Marilyn to Natowa's. Then they would continue to search for them. The note also read that if they get back to the camp, they're to wait for Yurah and Davi to return.

It was dark by the time they reached Natowa's. They had a hard time finding the exact location in the dark. In the distance they could see a soft light brimming above the cliffs. They followed the light which took them into the garden. As they looked up they could see a beautiful light transmitting up to the sky.

"Those are from the lanterns in the garden," said Tutu.

"Yes," said Marilyn. "I remember all the lanterns. How could anyone light so many?"

Nino laughed at Marilyn. "The natives light them."

"What natives?" Marilyn asked.

Nino looked with bewilderment in his face at Marilyn. "You know, the natives that live in the cliffs."

Yurah, Davi and Marilyn all looked at each other. "The natives live in the cliffs?"

"Yes!" said Tutu laughing at them. "Many families live there!"

Marilyn was astounded! It was all making sense to her now why the grounds and the house were so well taken care of. As she moved towards the light, she entered the garden and walked down the slate path. She could see the lanterns lighting the whole garden from above.

It truly was one of the most beautiful things that Marilyn had ever seen. She slowly walked and twirled herself in a circle to get a full view of the high cliffs on each side of her. As she looked into the square manmade holes she could see silhouettes of people moving around. Now she realized the holes were windows.

Looking into one of the holes she could see children and parents sitting at a table. Then in another hole he watched a man and a woman talking and moving around. She turned to look up the other side of the cliff and she could see an old woman sitting near one of the windows and doing needle point as she rocked in a rocker.

"Marilyn!" he shouted to bring her back to reality! It startled her and she jolted her body around to see Miguel standing behind her.

"Miguel!" Marilyn yelled out as she ran to his side.

He grabbed her and worriedly looked her up and down. "Are you alright?"

"Yes, I'm fine. But my friends Allen and Quinn aren't. We think they've been taken!"

"Who took them?"

"We don't know. First it was Allen and then it was Quinn!"

Miguel pulled his head up from looking at her and turned to look down the path.

"Do you know if you were followed?"

"I don't think so."

"Who brought you here?"

"Allen and Quinn's guides brought me. Tutu and Nino are with them too. They're all waiting for me outside the path."

"Let's go get them. It isn't safe out there!"

"But what about Allen and Quinn?" cried Marilyn!

"There's nothing we can do tonight." We'll set out as soon as day breaks in the morning."

When everyone was safe inside the garden, Natowa, Yurah and Davi kept watch for the night just in case they were followed. Yurah and Davi took guard at the front of the garden, while Natowa, Tutu and Nino waited inside with a few of the native men scattered throughout the gardens. Marilyn and Enesa were inside the house preparing coffee, tea and sandwiches for the men.

"You look very worried," said Enesa.

"I'm very worried. Where could they be?"

Tears filled Marilyn's eyes just thinking about what could have happened to them in a jungle like the Amazon's. They're city men, not rainforest men she thought to herself.

"You seem to be very close to these men. Especially Allen," said Enesa as she handed Marilyn a cup of tea.

Marilyn caught herself sounding too concerned for him. "Well, they did bring me to Miguel," and then she corrected herself, "I mean Natowa."

"It's Okay to call him Miguel. I kind of like the name myself." Enesa smiled at Marilyn.

Marilyn could tell Enesa was deeply in love with Miguel. But how did Miguel feel about her? How could he not be in love with such a wonderful and beautiful woman? Yet he has never talked about her.

The women walked outside with trays in their hands. Enesa asked Marilyn to serve Miguel, Tutu and Nino while she went to the front gate to feed Yurah and Davi and the other native men. She took Jaukeu with her on her shoulder as he beautifully whistled "On Top of Old Smokey" all the way down the path.

Miguel was sitting on the front steps of the house while Tutu and Nino watched out in front of the pond.

Marilyn sat down next to Miguel on the steps. She poured him a tea and handed him a plate of sandwiches. He looked at her and smiled as he took the plate.

Miguel said, "It's so nice to see you again."

"Yes, it's nice to see you again too, "Natowa!" They both laughed!

Tell me about you and Enesa," said Marilyn as she peeked curiously at Miguel from the corner of her eyes.

He knew where she was going with the question.

"There's not much to tell," as he laughed at her curiosity.

"What do you mean? She's beautiful! And I can tell she's madly in love with you."

Just then she could tell she struck a sore nerve with Miguel.

"I'm sorry. I didn't mean to be so nosey."

"No, it's not that," said Miguel. "You have every right to know what's been going on in my life. As I have the right to know what's going on in yours."

He paused for a minute and then said, "I know she's in love with me, and I'm in love with her."

Marilyn was elated to hear he felt the same way for her.

"But there can be no future for us."

"What, but why?" said Marilyn.

"The rainforest is no place for a woman. She's been here for too long. And even though I know she stays because of me, she's missing out on all the wonderful things in this world. That's why her father and mother sent her back to Denmark to complete her schooling.

She's a great scientist now. She has been a big help to me. But she's too educated and curious to stay here forever. And it's very soon I'll send her back to Denmark so she can live her life. She can live the life she deserves, and the life her parents wanted her to have."

"Home is where the heart is Miguel. I cannot see her returning anywhere without you."

Miguel looked deep into Marilyn's eyes. "She'll forget me," as he got up and moved towards the center of the garden.

Marilyn knew it was hard for him to talk about it. Marilyn couldn't even imagine either one of them being with anyone else. By sending Enesa away, Miguel would be making a very big mistake!

As Marilyn lay in the bed Enesa prepared for her in her room, she couldn't sleep thinking of Allen and Quinn out in the rainforest. Not knowing where they were was killing her inside. Especially never seeing Allen again was killing her even more.

Enesa's question about Allen made Marilyn think about her own feelings for him. It has been days since she spoke to Emmanuel. And sometimes she would have to make a conscience effort to think of him when she was around Allen.

She remembers her mother telling her as a teenager, "You will know when you know. And it might not be the person you thought would be the perfect man for you. It comes from the heart. And if you don't follow your heart you will truly be unhappy."

Marilyn knew her mother spoke these words from her own heart for she was a beautiful woman that could have had any choice of man she wanted. But she fell in love with her father and loved him until the day she died.

# Chapter 17

The morning came fast and the first thing she thought of when she woke was Allen and Quinn. She woke very worried for both of them. She jumped into her jeans and tee shirt and quickly washed her face and brushed her hair and teeth.

When she got to the bottom of the stairs there was a set of luggage sitting at the door.

Marilyn thought, "Who was here?"

And then she heard Enesa and Miguel talking in the library. They were talking in a whisper but loud enough that Marilyn could over hear him say to her. "This is best Enesa. You will be much happier living a full life than staying here with me. When my work is done here, then who knows what will happen."

She could hear Enesa say, "I can tell that having Marilyn here is calling you back to Rio de Janeiro."

Miguel stood with his head down, "It's hard for me to say good bye to you, but it just has to be this way. I just can't promise you anything right now."

Marilyn pushed her body against a wall behind some tall plants near the door so they wouldn't know she was there. As they approached the door she was embarrassed that she entered and overheard their very private conversation. Then the door closed and the luggage was gone.

She looked out the window from behind the plants to see Enesa being led by four men down the slate path. Marilyn was heartsick to see Enesa leave. But she couldn't say anything to her brother or he would know she overheard their conversation. The door closed again and Miguel was gone too.

Marilyn made a large breakfast for everyone. She knew the men would be very tired and hungry. It was safe inside the garden during the day for people were moving around and hard at work. But just to be safe, four native men manned the front of the path.

When everyone was done having breakfast they set out to look for Allen and Quinn. Natowa was concerned that a wild cat or wondering boars got them. But it was strange how one went missing and then the other. If someone had them in the rainforest, Natowa would find them.

Back at the garden, Marilyn was getting very worried. Now it seemed they were all missing and she was left alone with the native people. The natives treated Marilyn very kindly, and a few of the native women stopped by the house to see if she needed anything, but she was fine.

Marilyn walked down to the pond. She found looking at the beautiful fish and flowers therapeutic and helped ease her tension and thoughts. By now she had named the large black fish "Eye Spy" for every time she went near the pond it just stared and followed her like it was spying on her with its big green eye.

"Why do you stare at me Eye Spy?" she said as if she was expecting to get an answer. She turned around to look at some flowers planted in one of the gardens. As she walked Eye Spy followed her with its eye.

She started to make a game of it. She walked faster and faster around the pond and ducked in and out of the Banyan trees that surrounded it. No matter how fast she walked, the black fish kept its eye on her turning its body around to follow her. All the fish in the pond scattered around it faster and faster. She laughed at how it controlled the other fish.

After entertaining herself, she turned to walk away with her back to Eye Spy saying, "You seem to follow me wherever I go Eye Spy." And before she could finish her sentence a sharp pain split down the back of her head while something large sent her whirling to the ground!

Blood splattered into her eyes and down her face. She realized she had been struck by a very large object as she lay on the ground unable to move. The pain filled her head as she couldn't even speak. And then everything went black!

When Marilyn woke she was facing the sky. She stared up at it not knowing for a minute what had happened to her. She tried to hear if anyone was there, but the native people must have panicked and fled to the cliffs for safety.

Marilyn reached her hand up to her head and she could feel the cold blood. She tried to get up but the pounding inside her head didn't allow her to. Then she turned her head slowly to the left and there laid two large men with rifles attached in harnesses on their chests just within four feet of her.

She pulled her head up to look deeper at them, and then she realized they were dead. "They had blood everywhere on their bodies with large bite marks and scratches all over their arms, faces and necks. Their clothes were shredded and Marilyn could tell they were attacked by an animal!" Marilyn was frantic inside! She tried to move away as she panicked at the sight of them. But then everything went black again and she was out cold!

When she finally opened her eyes again, she turned to look away from the two men. She wanted to call for help but she was too weak. When she turned, she went panic-stricken when she saw a large black panther laying on her right side staring down at her. She was frozen at the sight of it and she couldn't move.

It had one big light green eye on the right side of its head and one smaller black eye on the left exactly like Eye Spy. Her heart was pounding so hard and she was going into shock from her fear and loss of blood.

She tried to remain composed but the pain and terror she felt was making her black in and out. Everything seemed foggy and distant in her mind as she tried to think of what happened. The two men were obviously dead and she was afraid that if she moved it would attack her too.

The panther got up and went around to the other side of her to stand between her and the two men. When she looked up it was staring down at her into her face with its big green eye. She closed her eyes again in fear it was coming back to finish her.

As Marilyn felt her tears come down her face as she thought it was over. It was coming back to kill her like the men lying beside her.

Then voices started coming from the garden. It was some of the native men shouting at the panther to "Get away!" Just then the panther turned to look around at them. Then it looked down at her again and she was thinking this was it, it was going to kill her!

She closed her eyes as tight as she could and began to cry. And then she heard it turn and it walked away from her. She slowly opened her eyes and she couldn't see where it was going since she was too afraid to move for it might return.

Then she heard two large roars coming from the cat and then she heard it lunge into the pond. She could hear the other fish flopping and jumping around as it entered the water.

Then after a few minutes all the noise stopped. Still reluctant to move she lifted her head a bit and the panther was nowhere to be seen.

"Oh boy!" she heard Jaukeu say from a distance.

Then she started to hear voices coming closer towards her. It was some of the native people running to her side. When they got to her they started working on her head wounds right away. The two men who lay next to her were carried away by some of the native men. Marilyn couldn't believe what just happened and how she just escaped the jaws of death!

Later, after she was taken into the house she was given something dark green to drink. It tasted like herbal plants and something else she couldn't distinguish.

She amazingly felt one hundred percent better. A native woman washed her hair and face.

She felt so good that she got up and walked over to a mirror to see what damage was done to her. She was reluctant to look at first, but when she looked into the mirror she couldn't believe her eyes! She didn't have a scratch on her face.

"How could this be? Was it a nightmare?" No, thought Marilyn. What happened wasn't a nightmare. It was as real as could be.

She started to understand the power of the medicines that her brother, Dr. Erikson and native people had discovered.

Now she understood why Allen and Quinn want Miguel to help them. They have healing powers way beyond what has ever been discovered in the medical world. As Marilyn touched her face she thought to herself, "This is truly a miracle!"

The native woman made Marilyn a tea as Marilyn laid down on her bed. She heard footsteps coming up the stairs. Just as she looked up there was Miguel.

"Miguel, you're okay!" Marilyn cried out while she ran to his side. "I was so worried about you! Did you find Allen and Quinn?"

Just as she uttered the words Miguel stepped aside and in walked Quinn and then Allen.

When she saw all of them she let out a little elated scream. "Where have you two been?"

"Are you alright Marilyn? The natives told us what happened!" said Miguel as he looked at her happy to see she was okay.

"Yes, everything is fine. I'm just fine."

Allen held on to her and gave her a hard long kiss on her neck as he squeezed her tight into his arms. Miguel and Allen looked at each other with concern in their faces.

"What's wrong?" What's going on?" as she looked into all three of their faces.

No one wanted to tell her, and then Allen reluctantly said, "We have something to tell you Marilyn. You had better sit down."

Marilyn sat on the corner of her bed looking up at the three of them.

Allen stood in the middle and said, "Quinn and I were being held hostage. We were tied up and left in the rainforest to die. They didn't want to take us because they told us we would slow them down. We were told if we weren't dead by the time they returned they were going to kill us. Miguel and the natives found us."

Quinn shook his head to confirm what Allen told her.

"What! Who would do such a terrible thing?" Marilyn uttered with disgust in her voice. All three men looked at each other again.

"It was Emmanuel and one of his men," said Quinn.

Marilyn remained speechless for a minute. "How do you know it was Emmanuel?"

Allen looked sadly down at her, "He told us who he was and he said he was coming to get you."

Then she looked up at them with contempt for Emmanuel in her face. "I hate him for what he's done!"

Marilyn started to feel sick to her stomach. She raced to the bathroom and hung down over the toilet. She felt a tearing feeling in the pit of her stomach. She began to feel numb and weak.

Allen and Miguel ran to her side and Miguel picked her up and carried her back to her bed.

"I'll stay with her," said Miguel. "You two go get something to eat and rest. I need to talk to Marilyn. I need to find out what happened in the garden and then I'll come and get you."

When Marilyn woke up a few minutes later Miguel had a warm wash cloth on her forehead.

She sat up and said, "I'm Okay Miguel," as she pulled the washcloth off.

He smiled at her and said back to her, "You'll be fine. I shouldn't have left you alone. Marilyn, I need to know what happened today in the garden."

"I was knocked out cold by something. When I woke up the." then Marilyn's words stopped, "The men were already dead. They were killed by the panther."

"Did you see the panther kill them?"

"No, I couldn't have been able to take it. Just seeing the men was enough for me." Marilyn started to weep.

Miguel held her close and told her everything would be okay.

"All I remember is the panther coming over the top of me. I was frozen with fear. Then it turned away and jumped into the pond. That's the last thing I remember."

Miguel put his head down in great concern.

"Is the panther gone?"

Miguel looked up at her.

"What's wrong Miguel? Is there something you aren't telling me?"

"The panther was protecting you."

"Protecting me? Why? I have never seen it before!"

Miguel slowly said, "Yes you have."

"I don't understand Miguel, what's going on?"

"The panther and Eye Spy are one animal. The panther was cross bred with a shark and it took Dr. Erikson years to develop him. There's supposed to be an exact balance between the shark and the panther. They both share the same immune system. They even share parts of each other's DNA that was supposed to alter the panther's characteristics. Our next step was to transform the panther back to its original anatomy but only with the immune system of the shark."

"But why would you breed a shark and panther?"

"Sharks very rarely develop cancer or disease," said Miguel," so by altering the panther's immune cells with the shark's, we can alter his immune system so he will have a very low chance of developing cancer or any other diseases.

We've also found a way to administer this into humans as well. And we have discovered a way of reversing cancer once a human has developed it. But we need the pond and the panther for our antidotes. But somehow the panther is showing dominance, and that's not good. Not for you and not for the pond.

It's the most vital element. The other fish share parts of its DNA and immune system. Now that he has killed I don't know if he'll ever be the same. He may kill again. He may also kill anyone who comes near you."

"Do you mean like you and Allen?"

"Yes, and if I have to put him down the other fish, animals and plants we use for healing are going to die too. Now that he's killed, I'm not sure what will happen.

One without the other will be devastating to our work and research."

"But why is he protecting me?" Just as Marilyn asked the question, she realized that Eye Spy was watching her from the pond and he must have seen the men approach her from behind and he transformed himself into the panther. Then he lunged from the water and knocked her out of the way.

"That's what hit me from behind, and then he killed the two men. He was protecting me, wasn't he?"

Miguel shook his head yes.

Marilyn took a deep breath. "What are we going to do?"

"I don't know Marilyn, I really don't know."

When Marilyn fell back asleep, Miguel returned back downstairs to talk to Allen and Quinn. They were sitting in the kitchen and finished eating.

"Can I make you a plate of food Natowa?" asked one of the native women.

"No," he said, "Later please." Right now I need some time with these men."

The two native women quickly left and he sat down across from Allen and Quinn.

"Why did you come back?"

Allen and Quinn just looked at Miguel with deep sad eyes and despair.

"Natowa, the first time we came to the Amazon, we had a friend with us. He was one of the men who were there when you healed Quinn when he got bit by your snake," said Allen.

"I remember three men," said Miguel.

"He's our best friend. He's dying in the hospital right now with cancer."

Natowa looked sorry to hear he was dying.

"Natowa, you can help him!" Quinn said desperately.

"I cannot come with you to save your friend," said Natowa.

"Why?" asked Allen. "You could save millions of people who are dying with cancer and other diseases!"

"I do have the cure to heal cancer. Someday I'll discover a way to use the antidotes from the pond to share with the world. I'm almost there. But right now there's more research and studies to do. Dr. Erikson mastered sharing the immune systems of fish, plants and animals to combat deadly viruses and disease. The pond's habitat cannot only replace each other's immune cells but also replace human's immune cells to cure them from cancer and other diseases. But without the pond I cannot cure him. I'm very sorry I cannot help you."

"But you have to help them Miguel! I promised I would make sure in return for what they did for us you would help them!" The voice came from Marilyn who was standing at the opening into the kitchen. She was weak from the trauma her mind and body had taken from the day.

Allen got up and went to Marilyn's side to help her sit down at the table.

"I'm Okay," said Marilyn, as she sat down. "Miguel. Why don't you want to share it with Allen and Quinn so they can help them save his life?"

Miguel looked sad as he looked at his sister's desperate attempt to get him to help.

"I can't help them because I cannot leave the rainforest and our research. The only way I could cure him if he was to come here. I also promised Dr. Erikson that I would never give our antidotes to people outside the Amazon because they will come and steal our valuable botanicals and animals, like they did with the Rubber and Mahogany trees. We need them to keep the Amazon alive!"

"I understand your concerns," said Quinn. "And we're not here to bring any harm or take anything from you or the rainforest. We're here for one reason and one reason only, and that reason is to cure Michael. If that means you only give us what it will take to save him, then that's all we need!"

"But I cannot heal Michael unless he's in the garden."

"Why?" asked Marilyn.

"There's a natural balance between the rainforest, animals and plants that make our antidotes work. Without one or the other they're useless."

Allen asked, "Can't you give us enough to take back with us?" You can show us what we need to do."

"I cannot give you a certain amount to take with you. It's all based on his own immune system. Then we administer the antidote to fight what he needs. It needs to be a perfect science for his body and where his body needs to fight the cancer to make it work. I need the pond as my research center to administer what he needs to cure him."

It was in some small way making sense to Allen and Quinn. But they were still very disappointed that their trip was going to come up empty and that they had to return to tell Michael they had no hope. He had no chance to survive without Natowa's help.

"Then bring Michael here," said Marilyn.

Allen and Quinn looked at her like she had lost her mind!

"Bring him here?" He's almost dead!" cried out Quinn.

"Yes almost," Marilyn said back. "But he still has a chance. It's seems to me it's the only chance he has."

Allen and Quinn looked at each other. How could they ever get Michael in his condition to agree to come to the Amazon? He hardly believed their story when they told him they were coming to get Natowa. Now how could they ask him on his death bed to travel all this way to find a cure that might not even save him? Or worse, kill him on the way!

# Chapter 18

Michael lay in his bed as the nurses at his side administered some morphine for his pain.

"Has anyone heard from Allen and Quinn?" asked Michael.

"No," said one of the nurses. "I'm sure we will be hearing from them very soon. They usually call us every other day to see how you're doing, but they haven't contacted anyone in a few days."

Michael started to become worried. Just then the phone rang. He was hoping it would be Allen or Quinn. He picked up the receiver. "Hello," said Michael.

There was a pause on the phone. Then a woman's voice said, "Hello Michael, how are you doing?"

He didn't know who it was for at first, but then he realized it was Alex. She took him by surprise!

"Hello Alex, he said with a weak voice.

"I was devastated to hear that you're ill Michael. I never ever would wish that on you. I really am so sorry!"

Then he heard her voice break into a cry.

"Oh babe, I know that," he said to comfort her. Things just happen in life. I'm just glad you called."

The nurses looked at Michael with a smile on their faces. He looked so happy to hear from the person on the phone. He looked up at them and asked them if he could have a few minutes alone.

The nurse said, "Yes we're all done," as they left the room.

"How are you Alex?" It's been quite awhile."

"I'm doing well, I guess, until I heard the news."

"Where are you?"

"I'm in New York. I flew in last night. I want to come and see you."

Michael couldn't believe Alex was in New York!

"Are you on a flight?"

"No, I flew in to see you."

Michael was happy she flew all the way from Amsterdam to see him.

"I'm flattered," said Michael.

"Michael, you know I still care about you. Before I flew here I called Cindy. When I told her about you, she told me everything that happened. She told me to say hello and to get well soon."

He really didn't want to hear Cindy's name but he said, "Tell her thanks," and left it at that.

"When can I come to see you?"

"If you're ready to see me look the way I do, then anytime will be good. I wish we were getting together under better circumstances, but it is what it is."

"Yes, but I'm still looking so forward to seeing you."

"Can I ask you something Alex? How did you know I was sick?"

"Quinn contacted me a through the airlines. I was so glad he did. I couldn't have lived with myself if I hadn't come."

Of course he would," thought Michael. He just can't mind his own business!" as he laughed and thought to himself.

When Alex knocked on the door Michael was laying in his bed.

"Come in," said Michael.

Alex entered and turned her eyes right to him as he lay in his bed so frail and weak. She promised herself that she wouldn't cry when she saw him. No matter what he looked like she would be strong. Not just for her, but for Michael too.

"Hello gorgeous," Michael said to her as she went to his side and knelt down to kiss him on his lips. He couldn't believe how beautiful she looked. He felt a rush of embarrassment as he looked so pale and fragile next to her.

She was still in such good shape and her hair was a bit longer to her mid back. She wore a black leather rain coat and leather boots that went just below her knees.

"Let me look at you." He pushed her back for a minute to see her body. "You still are the most beautiful woman I have ever seen. And if you're the last thing I ever see . . ."

She stopped him from continuing his sentence.

"Don't ever say that again!" She fired back in a stern voice.

Michael laughed at how she pounced on what he said. "So come here and sit next to me so I can touch you."

She sat at the side of his bed looking down at him. Even though he was frail and weak he was still so very handsome with his dark looks, eyes and hair. He was clean shaven and smelled like he did the first time she met him.

He was wearing a white tee shirt and a cotton checker red and black robe with matching pajama bottoms.

She reached into his robe and rubbed his chest and she kissed him softly on his lips. Michael moaned as she continued to kiss him. When she stopped he looked up at her, "I never thought I would ever see you again."

They both smiled and he pulled her coat off of her. He looked up and down her body one more time taking in her curvy shape before he pulled her down on top of him.

"We can't do this!" laughed Alex.

"Try to stop me!" as he kissed her neck and chest.

When he stopped he returned his eyes to look deeply into hers.

"I never stopped loving you."

"And you never will since I won't let you!"

He smiled at her comeback. "How long are you here for?"

"I'm here for as long as you need me. I have weeks of vacation owed to me. I can stay as long as you want me here."

"Forever?" he asked her.

"Forever," she said back!


Later Alex left Michael to rest while she went to her hotel room to get settled. Her cell phone rang and it was Quinn.

"Hi Alex, It's Quinn, "I heard that you got to see Michael today."

"Yes, I'm here in my hotel room and I just got back from seeing him."

"I just called him and he seems to be in very good spirits. You were good medicine for him Alex. Thanks for going to see him."

"Nothing could have stopped me!"

"Alex, we need your help. You better be sitting down when I ask you this."

"Where are you?" asked Alex.

"Allen and I are at the Tishi Amazon Resort. We just got in our rooms a little while ago. We've been in the rainforest."

Alex was confused. "I thought you would never want to go back there after what happened to you."

"I know," said Quinn. "And this is not a pleasure trip at all! We're here for Michael. And we need you to do something that will save Michael's life."

Alex said, "Anything!"

"We need you to bring Michael to the Amazon."

She stopped for a few long seconds before she answered him not believing what he just said. "What! You're joking right?"

"No Alex, I'm not joking. We're here with Natowa."

"Natowa, Isn't that the man in the rainforest that saved your life? The man that Yurah said was a spirit?"

"Yes, that's him. But he's not a spirit. He's real, and we need for you to bring Michael here so that Natowa can save him the same way he saved me. He has an antidote that can cure his cancer."

"Why don't you bring the antidote to him? He's too weak to travel Quinn. I don't think it's a good idea."

"It's all we have Alex. He's terminal. There's nothing that anyone can do for him there. They'll make him comfortable for the rest of his days, but nothing is going to save him."

Quinn's words cut through Alex's heart. She started to cry softly as it struck her for the first time the man she loved was going to die!

She took a deep breath, and said. "I don't know if I can do this Quinn. What if something happens on the way? I would never forgive any of us for making him do this!"

"Alex, I would never ask you to put Michael in danger. This is all that we have to save his life!"

"But what if he doesn't want to go? What do I do?"

"You have to convince him that it's his last chance. It's all he has left."

Alex was so confused. She didn't know what to do. Quinn was right in a lot of ways. This could be the only chance that Michael has to live, but what if they're wrong?

"I need to think about this Quinn," This is not a decision I can make this quickly. I'll get back to you."

"I'll call you again tonight Alex. Please say yes." And then he hung up.

Alex returned to the hospital to see Michael a few hours later. He was sitting up and she could tell he was anxious to see her. His coloring was coming back a bit and he had a gleam in his eye as she walked towards him.

"Alex, you have made me so happy, and I love having you near me at this time in my life. I love you, but I ask myself if this is fair to you?"

"I don't want to hear any more of this talk Michael! I'm here and that's all there's to it! So just suck it up and kiss me!"

He looked into her eyes and knew he was defeated. Just as he kissed her Dr. Richardson walked in. He smiled as he caught them pulling away from each other.

"Don't let me disturb you," said the doctor.

They laughed at him as Michael said, "This is Alex, the love of my life." She walked up to him and shook Dr. Richardson's hand.

He took Michael's vitals and then pulled a chair up for Alex to sit as he sat down on the bed.

"Well Michael, your ultra sound show's that there was some more movement in the cancer." Alex looked so sad to hear the words from the doctor. "I'm not going to suggest any chemo therapy Michael. The cancer has spread and there's nothing more that we can do." The doctor put his head down like he was defeated in saving Michael.

"It's okay," said Michael to comfort his doctor. "I already knew that," as Michael smiled at him.

Alex did everything she could not to break down. But she couldn't hold back her tears as they ran down her cheeks. Michael put his hand on her leg to comfort her.

Michael said, "Then I would like to go home."

The doctor nodded his head sadly and promised he would make sure Michael had a nurse twenty four/seven with him as long as he needed. Michael thanked the doctor as he left the room.

Alex's thoughts were exhausting her. She rubbed her temples trying to know what to do.

"What are you thinking beautiful?" asked Michael.

She turned and looked at him. "I'm going to do whatever it takes to save you!"

He looked at her with despair. He put his arms around her waist. "Alex, you heard the doctor. I'm terminal. There's nothing that anyone can do. Please don't put this kind of pressure on yourself. It's time to accept it. I know this isn't fair to you Alex. But now that you have been dealt with it, you have to accept it. I know it's hard. It's hard for me too. Knowing I'll not be with you is tearing me up inside. But we have to accept it!"

She looked up at him with a straight face. "No Michael, I'm not going to accept it. Quinn called me today. He wants me to bring you to the Amazon. He told me that Natowa can save you!"

Michael threw his hands up in the air. "I'm going kick his ass when I see him! Look Alex, I can't go anywhere. I don't know if I even have tomorrow!"

"You will make it, I promise!" she cried out to him and grabbed his arm. "I have a friend who is a doctor. He flies on my plane with patients all the time. He takes patients from one country to another who are sick and in need of hospital care for alternative healing. I'm going to call him and arrange that he take you to the Amazon. He'll make you comfortable. I'm going to also arrange a chartered plane to take us there. I'm going to get your things ready. I'll be back for you in a few hours!"

Just then John walked in looking horribly sad after talking to the doctor in the hallway. "I'm so sorry Michael," as he put his head down to cry.

Michael slapped John on the back, "Well, don't count me out yet. I'm going to the Amazon to see someone. Someone who might be able to help me."

Michael sat up on the edge of the bed. He felt he owed everyone the chance to do this for him. Even if it meant his life, death was inevitable anyways. If this would give Alex, John, Allen and Quinn the closure they needed than he would do it for them.

# Chapter 19

When they arrived at LaGuardia Airport, they met Dr. Anthony Miles at their terminal. He pulled up a wheelchair for Michael to sit in and once he sat down Anthony reached down to shake Michael's hand.

"Hi Michael, I'm Anthony."

"It's nice to meet you Anthony."

"Well, it looks like we're in for quite a long ride. How are you feeling right now Michael?"

"I feel pretty good right now."

"Alex told me about your prognosis and I'm very sorry to hear. Let's hope this trip finds a cure for you. I fly a lot of people to different countries for alternative healing and medicines. Some are successful and some aren't. But from what Alex told me, this man who is a healer can help you. You look fit enough to make the trip so I'll ride along and make sure you're comfortable."

"Thanks Anthony," said Alex. "I owe you big time for this!"

He put his hand on Alex's shoulder and said, "No Alex, you don't owe me anything. Look at all the times you upgraded me and my patients to first class. You don't owe me anything at all. Not only that I've always wanted to see the Amazon," as he smiled at her.

She patted him on his back as he took Michael and loaded him into the plane.

The plane was also being flown by one of Alex's best friend's husband who has his own charter plane. He walked onto the Tarmac to greet Alex.

"Thanks for doing this Robert. I know it was short notice."

"Hey, I was only going to be watching a football game anyways."

Alex laughed at him as they all bordered the plane. When the plane took off Michael reached over and took Alex's hand into his.

"Thank you for doing this for me. And no matter what happens I want you to know that I love you and I appreciate what you're doing."

Alex looked into his eyes wondering if she was doing the right thing. "Time is going to tell Michael. All we have right now is hope. And no matter what I want you to know that I love you too, and I hope I'm doing what's best for you."

"It doesn't matter what the outcome is," said Michael. "You did this out of love. And that's all that matters to me."

When they landed in Manaus, Quinn, Allen, Yurah and Davi were waiting for them. As soon as they saw Michael get off the plane, Allen and Quinn were so excited to see him! They jumped into the air as they ran towards him.

"Easy! Easy!" said Alex as she laughed at their excitement.

As they neared they could see Michael had gotten weaker since the last time they saw him.

"Hey guys!" cried out Michael when he saw them running to him.

They all gave each other a high five and then Allen and Quinn bent over and playfully gave Michael a kiss on his cheek. Everyone laughed as they all reunited.

Once they were in the resort, they got Michael into his room and by now he looked like he was feeling some pain and weak from the trip. He didn't sleep very much since he was excited just being with Alex and returning to where they had first met. Anthony took Michael's blood pressure and heart beat as Alex, Allen and Quinn looked on.

"How's he doing?" asked Quinn.

Anthony said, "Well, he's tired and he's feeling a bit of pain, aren't you Michael?"

Michael hated to admit it but shook his head yes.

"Why don't all of you leave Michael with me for a bit and I'll make him comfortable."

Alex hated to leave his side.

"You go too Alex. Go get something to eat."

"Okay, and when I return I'll take over for you and you can have dinner too."

"Sounds like a plan,'" said Anthony as he smiled and administered some morphine into Michael.

The next day they prepared Michael for the trip into the Amazon. They had a larger boat this time so they could lay Michael down and make him as comfortable as possible. Tutu and Nino were left at Natowa's to keep an eye on Marilyn while they were gone. Natowa spent a lot of his time researching the pond after the episode with the two men and Marilyn.

Once they reached the destination of the log in the water, they pulled the boat in and got Michael onto a stretcher. Allen, Quinn, Yurah and Davi carried Michael into the rainforest jungle on a stretcher. Alex and Anthony walked along side of Michael. Anthony held the Intravenous drip of morphine to make Michael sleep most of the journey.

About four hours later they were outside the garden. When they walked in Tutu and Nino saw them coming and ran shouting in excitement to see them all. Marilyn was inside with two of the native women making breads and dinner when she heard the commotion. She looked out the window and saw them coming up the slate path. She wiped her hands clean on a towel and ran outside to greet them.

The first person she looked at was Allen. He was smiling at her as he got closer and closer. Then he broke away from the others and ran towards her. He picked her up by her waist and he pulled her into his arms. "I missed you!" he whispered in her ear.

"I missed you too," she said back smiling.

After he put her down, Marilyn looked down the path and spotted Alex as she smiled from Allen's excitement. Marilyn walked up to Alex.

"Hello Alex, I've heard so much about you and Michael," as Marilyn looked down at him on the stretcher. Marilyn reached down and grabbed Michael's hand. "I know my brother can help you."

"Thank you Marilyn, I have heard a lot about you too," as he looked over at Allen smiling.

Alex introduced Anthony to Marilyn. They all walked to the house. Marilyn told the men to take Michael into the house and up to her room.

"Thank you so much for letting us stay with you," said Alex. "Natowa's home is just beautiful!"

"Thank you," said Marilyn. "I'll let him know what you said. Let's get Michael into his room. We want to make him as comfortable as possible. You must be tired too. You can sleep in Enesa's room, and Anthony can sleep on the sofa bed that we put in Michael's room. Yurah and Davi can sleep in the cliff with Tutu and Nino."

"The cliffs?"

"Yes, that's where the natives live. Would you like to come and see it?"

"I would love to," said Alex. Alex checked on Michael and Anthony assured her that he would be sleeping for a few hours.

Alex left with Marilyn to help her make up a room in one of the cliffs. Marilyn took a basket of eggs and some butter with her to leave in the room. They walked across the slate path and entered onto another path. The path was lined on each side with fuchsia bushes as far as the eye could see.

"This is so beautiful!" said Alex.

"Yes it is, and this path leads to the opening into the cliff."

They walked for a few minutes and then they were standing at the base of the tall stone doorway that led them inside.

When they entered, just above them were lanterns that lit up a stone stairway which led inside the cliff.

"This is so incredible!" as Alex looked up the stairs. The stone walls were marbled with multi colors and were etched in calligraphy drawings of animals, natives and other scenes of the rainforest.

As they climbed the stairs it twisted and turned from one landing to another. Each landing had its own calligraphy drawing to represent what landing they were on. Then off the landings were stone hallways that led to Mahogany doors with iron straps and rounded at the tops. They came to a landing with a leopard and fern carved into it.

"This is the landing we need to stop at," said Marilyn. "Now we need to find the door."

They turned down the hallway and walked to the last door on the left. There was a symbol carved into the door of a deer and a fern.

"This is it!" Then Marilyn took out a skeleton key and opened the door.

When Alex walked inside she was astonished! They walked inside a 14' x 16' room with wood floors. A Teak wooden table and four chairs sat in the middle of it. On the table sat a stack of dishes, cups, wooden spoons and forks with cloth napkins. Along the wall on the right was a built in shelf with canning jars filled with preserved vegetables and fruits. On the floor on the far right hand corner was a big white cloth bag of flour. In the other corner hung dried beef jerky and hard cheeses wrapped in mesh strung off of a wood pole mounted to the wall. On the opposite wall was a cast iron stove with a cast iron pot, pan and kettle sitting on top of it.

Around the corner was another room. The room had four beds with feather down mattresses. On top of each bed was a folded handmade quilt with a pillow and sheet. A rocker and an end table sat under the window with a lantern on top of the table.

"This is amazing!" said Alex. "Are all the rooms like this?"

Marilyn laughed. "I asked Miguel the same question. He said some are larger for families, but this room is just for guest. The natives made their homes here over

150 years ago during the invasion for the rubber trees. The only way they could survive and escape being enslaved was to barricade themselves inside the cliffs for protection."

"How sad they lost their homes and land!"

"Yes it is," said Marilyn.

"How many homes are there in the cliffs?"

"I tried to figure it out but there are homes all throughout the cliffs."

When they left and while walking down a landing of stairs, a door opened slowly from one of the rooms. They could see a little girl's big eyes peeping out the door looking at them.

Marilyn looked at her and smiled. Then all of a sudden a mother's voice called to the child and bellowed, "Close the door before your eyes fall out!" The little girl's eyes popped open and then she slammed the door shut!

Marilyn and Alex both laughed as they walked back down and out back onto the path.

It was dark now and everyone was concerned for Natowa since he hadn't returned to the garden yet. Marilyn thought he had never been so late since she had been there. Allen and Quinn paced the floor waiting for him to return. Even though Michael was resting comfortably, they knew his days were nearing the end.

"What could be holding him up for so long?" thought Allen. He walked out on the porch and looked all around to see if he might be in the garden. He then looked down the path and he was nowhere to be seen. Quinn met Allen on the porch.

"Do you think something's happened to him?"

"I'm getting worried," said Quinn. "He should be back by now. My worst fear is that Emmanuel has him."

Allen shook his head confirming what Quinn said. "What are we going to do?" asked Allen.

Quinn said, "We have to go find him. We'll have to take Yurah and some of the Natives with us. We'll leave Davi, Tutu and Nino here to watch over everyone."

That night Allen told Marilyn they had to go find Natowa. They told her they felt he had been taken by Emmanuel and his men. Marilyn agreed something was wrong, and knowing what Emmanuel was capable of doing she agreed they needed to go find him.

That night the search for Natowa started out. They took seven native men with them who were highly skilled in tracking and hunting. Yurah led the way and had enough food and water to last two days.

Hours later they found some tracks that made them think Natowa had headed that direction. He wasn't alone. There were tracks of two other men. But they had travelled enough for one night and made camp to get up at day break to find some more tracks.

The next day after they packed up and descended from the camp, one of the native men ran ahead. He returned a few hours later saying he could hear men talking just up ahead of them. Yurah waved to everyone to get down and be very still and quiet.

Yurah, Allen, Quinn and the native who heard the men walked into some Laurel bushes. They could hear two men talking back and forth. Yurah opened a small patch of brush to expose the men and they could see the two men sitting in front of a fire as they were sipping on a cup of coffee.

The one man turned to look over his shoulder at something. They followed his eyes. They could see a tent just on the other side of the camp.

The native man snuck away from everyone to see what was in the tent. He went in the bush behind the tent. He lifted the back of the tent from the ground and then he put it back down and returned back to Yurah, Allen and Quinn.

"Natowa is in the tent."

"That's Emmanuel and one of his men," said Quinn.

Is Natowa Okay?" asked Allen.

"He has been beaten, but he saw me. He knows we are here. He'll follow our lead. So when we are ready to get him he'll be prepared."

The men returned back to the other natives who sat very quietly on the ground until everyone returned. They huddled around each other to set up a strategy to get Natowa out of the camp. They all quietly snuck up and all around the men's camp.

A few minutes later the man with Emmanuel jumped up! "*Someone's here!*" he yelled out in French. He grabbed his rifle and ran towards the tent and entered inside.

Emmanuel was standing by now and holding a pistol pointing it all around him.

The man returned with Natowa. Natowa was beaten up and drugged. He swerved back and forth as the man pushed him forward holding on to him.

Natowa said to the man, "You will die before this is over!"

The man just kept shoving Natowa to keep walking. The two men stood behind Natowa like he was a human shield.

Just then a gunshot came from behind. It struck the man who was holding on to Natowa in the side of the head and he fell to the ground like a rock!

Emmanuel grabbed on to Natowa and put his pistol to Natowa's head and cocked the gun. Emmanuel was very nervous. He was screaming into the bush, "I'll kill him!"

Then all of a sudden Natowa forced his body back with his brutal strength and knocked Emmanuel to the ground!

Yurah, Allen, Quinn and two other natives stormed in with their rifles pointed at Emmanuel as he lay on the ground. Yurah grabbed Emmanuel by his collar and dragged him back up to his feet.

Allen said to Emmanuel, "You sent two men to try and capture Marilyn in the garden. What the hell do you think you're doing?"

"I came to take Marilyn back home. Take me to her!" demanded Emmanuel.

"Take you to her?" Allen said angrily. "Are you fucking crazy? She would never want anything to do with you again! You tried to have her kidnapped and now you beat and drugged her brother! You must be out of your mind!"

All of a sudden Allen went towards Emmanuel but Natowa grabbed Allen and pushed him back.

"We'll take him back to the garden. We'll get them on a plane back to France. Unfortunately his men will return in wooden boxes!"

"What do you mean my men?" asked Emmanuel confused by Natowa's comment.

"Two of your men were killed in the garden, and now this one," as Natowa pointed to the man on the ground. "Now it's only you!" Natowa lashed out at Emmanuel. "If you ever return to the Amazon again, I'll feed you to my panther the same way he killed your two men!"

Emmanuel didn't know what happened to his two other men. They went off to search and never returned back to the camp. He was shocked to hear how they died!

They walked up the path to the garden with Emmanuel in the center as two native men kept a rifle on his back while his hands were tied behind his back. Marilyn heard Tutu and Nino shouting Natowa's name.

She ran to the porch and there she saw the men walking up towards her. Then her eyes moved to the center and she could not believe what she was seeing! Emmanuel was with them.

She started to run towards them not knowing what was going on. Allen could tell she was angry and was headed right for Emmanuel. Allen ran up beside her and grabbed her arm to stop her.

Natowa walked up next to Marilyn and told her to go back into the house. "Marilyn, come with me. I need to talk to you."

"What happened to you Miguel?" She cried as she could see how badly beaten he was. Her eyes went back to Emmanuel as he looked back at her.

Emmanuel yelled to her with his thick French accent, "Your brother showed up at our camp and we thought he was going to hurt us! Marilyn, please believe me when I tell you this, I didn't know he was your brother! I did everything for you and want what's best for you because I love you! I'll take you home with me and marry you as soon as we get back to France." Please Marilyn say yes!"

As Allen gently pushed her back into the house she was getting upset that he wouldn't let her go face Emmanuel.

"What's going on?" she yelled at Allen!

"I have to tend to the pond right away said Natowa. You talk to her and I'll be back in a little while."

Marilyn was so angry by then she wanted to beat Emmanuel herself. "I feel so responsible for this! How could I have ever trusted such an evil man?"

Don't blame yourself Marilyn. He's devious and that's how he gets what he wants."

Allen looked at Marilyn feeling sorry for her. Even though he was in love with her he knew it still broke her heart to love someone and that deceived her so badly.

"I have to talk to him!" she protested.

Allen gave in to her plea, "Okay, but not alone."

They took Emmanuel to one of the greenhouses and locked him inside. They gave him some food and water, and made him a bed on the floor.

Marilyn needed to compose herself and it took her a few hours before she could stomach going to talk to him. But finally she was ready. Allen and Yurah went with her.

"You go in with her Yurah," said Allen. You need some space without me," as he looked at Marilyn empathetically.

Yurah entered the greenhouse with Marilyn. Emmanuel jumped to his feet and rushed to grab Marilyn in his arms but she pushed him back and away from her. He knew she was very upset and stayed back.

"How could you have done this to my brother?" she yelled!

"You don't understand Marilyn. I didn't know it was him. It wasn't until after we captured him that we found out who he was. He came into our camp and we didn't know what he was capable of doing. So one of my men jumped him and beat him so we could drug him. I'm so sorry all this has happened!

My only intentions were to come and bring you back with me to France. I wanted us to get married right away. I realized after you left how much I loved you. So why delay the inevitable. Marilyn, come back to France with me. Leave this place and be my wife. You will never want for anything again!"

Marilyn's eyes filled with tears. "Why did you send the two men?"

"I didn't send them. They went off on their own. I just found out about their horrible death by your friend Allen. I only brought them with me to make sure we got out of the Amazon safely. You have to believe me Marilyn. I just wanted to make sure you were safe!"

After hearing Emmanuel, she didn't know what to believe. But she knew no matter what she couldn't fix what had happened. It was over for her.

"Emmanuel, you have to leave right away. This was all a bad mistake for you to come here. You have caused a lot of trouble and you have to go. I cannot marry you. It's over between us!"

Emmanuel stood and looked at Marilyn knowing already what she was going to say. He looked defeated.

He silently looked down at the ground trying to find something to say to change her mind. But then he realized it was over.

"Okay, I'll leave as soon as I can. I need to get to the airport. But I have one request. I need to return with my men. My father will make arrangements for their clearance out of Brazil so I can return them back to France."

Marilyn sadly looked at Emmanuel knowing he was frustrated. "I'll arrange to have your men sent with you." She walked out of the greenhouse past Allen and then disappeared into the garden.

The next morning as she looked out the window from the kitchen, Emmanuel was leaving with Yurah and twelve native men that carried the three wooden caskets down the path.

Miguel sent Yuri to make sure he boarded the plane and left Brazil. Her heart was wrenched as she saw him leave. She couldn't forgive him for what he did to Miguel, Allen and Quinn. How they beat Miguel and drugged him. How he left Allen and Quinn to die in the rainforest. She realized he wasn't the man she fell in love with.

She was glad she found out what he was before it was too late. She thought to herself, "He's lucky Miguel is letting him leave alive!"

# Chapter 20

When Natowa returned to see Michael, there was not one bruise or cut on his face or body. There was no indication that he was beaten by Emmanuel and the other man. Everyone looked at him astounded that he didn't have any cuts, bruises or scratches on him. They knew Natowa had taken something to make the bruises and cuts disappear. It was way beyond what any of them could comprehend!

Natowa stood at the edge of the bed next to Michael. Michael was sound asleep resting comfortably from the last dosage of morphine.

Anthony stood next to Natowa, "Do you really think you can help him?"

"Yes, I can help him. Where's his cancer?"

Anthony pulled out some medical records and x-rays of Michael's cancer and he showed Natowa where the spots were.

Allen and Quinn sat outside the room nervously waiting. Marilyn took Alex downstairs into the kitchen to make her some tea. When Natowa walked out he told Allen and Quinn he would be back in a few hours.

Allen, Alex, and Quinn then returned to Michael's bed and sat next to him waiting for Natowa to come back. About an hour and a half later Natowa returned with a large square metal box. He carried it in from a handle that was attached to the top.

He put the box on the bed next to Michael. Then Natowa opened the box and pulled out some test tubes with surgical instruments and a microscope. He set up a small laboratory on the end table. He then pulled out a purplish grey fluid in a vile.

Natowa said, "All of you must leave now."

"Even me?" called out Anthony in surprise! "But he's my patient!"

"You can sit over there," Natowa pointed to a chair in the corner of the room.

Quinn asked nervously, "Is he going to be okay?"

"You asked me to save your friend and that's what I'm going to do."

Allen and Quinn left the room wondering what was going to happen to Michael. They felt so responsible for what was going to happen. They waited outside the room for a half an hour. Then they heard a large moan come from Michael.

"What's happening?" as Quinn jumped up at the sound of the moan. Allen buried his head into his hands worried sick about what was happening to Michael inside the room.

They heard Anthony say, "You can't do that!" And then there was silence.

The silence went on for over an hour. Allen and Quinn by now were pacing back and forth passing each other. Alex sat with her hands folded across her stomach while Marilyn sat next to her for moral support. Then the door opened and it was Anthony. He was dampened in sweat on his forehead, chest and underarms.

"What's going on in there?" asked Allen.

"I don't quite know what's going on. He has hundreds of microscopic fish like animals. I can't explain what they are. He showed me under a microscope when I asked him what he was doing. He's mixing them with plants in a bluish colored fluid. I have no idea what he's going to do with it and I don't want to know! I need to get some air. I hope you people know what you're doing!" as he walked down the stairs.

"I don't know what we're doing!" said Alex as she sat lifeless in the chair not knowing if she would ever see Michael alive again.

Then another moan came from Michael. "I know it hurts but it will be over soon," they could hear Natowa say.

Michael moaned again and then he screamed out loud! Natowa locked the door from the inside not allowing anyone to enter.

Everyone was panicking wondering if Michael was alright!

Quinn shouted from the outside of the door, "Is everything okay in there?"

Marilyn held on to Alex as she cried in Marilyn's arms. And then there was silence that went on in Michael's room for over two hours.

Anthony already returned upstairs and paced the floor with Allen and Quinn. Then the door opened and Natowa stood there motioning for everyone to come in.

Anthony rushed to Michael's side. "He has a heartbeat! His heart actually sounds pretty good! And his blood pressure is normal!"

Natowa smirked at Anthony while he scampered around taking all of Michal's vitals and examining him. As they all looked at Michael, they could see color coming back into his face.

"I can't believe how good he looks!" remarked Alex with elation in her voice.

Then Michael opened his eyes.

Natowa smiled down at Michael, "You're healed Michael and there's no more cancer."

Michael lay in bed feeling no pain at all! Michael smiled, "Have I died and gone to heaven?" as he looked at Natowa.

"No, you're not in heaven. You're alive and you're cancer free."

Allen said, "You look great Michael! Then jokingly he said, Maybe even better than before!"

Everyone laughed!

They all stood around Michael knowing he was going to be okay.

Michael turned and looked at Allen and Quinn with a smile and said, "I've never felt better!

Quinn asked, "Do you remember what happened?"

"I had a lot of pain at first, but then it changed into like this Euphoria. It felt like something was travelling through my body and everywhere it went it was healing me. I can't explain it but I had no fear at all. It felt great! I felt like it was helping me so I just laid there while it took over my body. It's like the most wonderful feeling I ever had!"

Everyone looked on to Michael smiling so happy to see him well again.

What did you do to me?" Michael asked Natowa.

Natowa walked up to Michael and sat next to him on the bed. "What entered your body is apart of you now Michael. You and microscopic organs that entered your body share each other's DNA and immune system. They were bred in the pond, and everything in the pond takes care of each other. It's because without each other they can't survive. I added your DNA and immune system to the pond and the fish had to alter your cancerous immune cells in order to combat the cancer so they could live. And then it was administered back into your body to fight the cancer and return your destroyed cells and damaged tissue back to normal."

"Are they still in my body?"

Natowa smiled, "Yes, they have become part of your DNA and immune system and will stay in your body forever. And you will never have cancer again."

"This is a miracle!" shouted Quinn. "Natowa, do you know what you have here?" You can save the world from cancer and other diseases!"

"Not yet. I need to do much more to save the world. But I'm working on it," as he smiled at Quinn.

Natowa insisted that Michael still rest for the night. While Alex and Anthony stayed with Michael in his room, the rest of them went downstairs to get something to eat. Marilyn by now returned to the kitchen and was heating up a large pot of soup for everyone. Natowa walked up to her and looked down into her face.

"You're sad Marilyn, I can tell."

She tried to change the subject by saying, "You have a great gift Miguel. Thank you for helping Michael. It means so much to everyone."

"I was happy to do it. If it wasn't for them you wouldn't be here right now. So what will happen from here?"

"Well, I guess we'll all go back to our normal lives. Miguel, I would like for you to return to Rio de Janeiro with me. Will you consider coming home?"

He looked at her and smiled. "No Marilyn, this is my home now. It's where my heart is. I have been in the rainforest longer than in society. I have made this my home."

Marilyn knew what his answer was going to be. She was sad knowing she would have to return to Rio without him. She didn't want to go now. Her Pavilion would seem even emptier for her now than it was before.

"Then maybe I'll stay with you."

"No Marilyn, You need to go back and live the life you're accustomed to. I want you to find a wonderful man and get married and have children someday. There's nothing the rainforest can offer you."

"It offers me peace Miguel. Something I haven't had in many years. Home is where the heart is and my heart is here with you."

"Marilyn, there's another reason you can't stay."

"I don't understand. What is it?"

"The panther," said Miguel. "He'll eventually put you in danger."

"What do you mean?"

"He has become possessive. If he see's you with anyone he may kill again. And if he feels that you're in danger, he'll kill anyone in the way. He's an animal with animal instincts. Trust me when I tell you this, you cannot stay for your own safety. He may kill even you!"

"I don't want anything bad to happen to him, but isn't there some way to alter him by turning him back into the shark?"

"No, we need him. We need his DNA and immune system to keep the pond alive. Every time he uses his animal instincts he upsets the balance. The pond is our research base and where we get our cures and antidotes. If we lose him, we will lose the cures."

"I know your work is very important to you Miguel. I don't want to do anything to upset that."

"My work is for all mankind Marilyn. This isn't about me. I need to finish what Dr. Erikson started."

"Speaking of Dr. Erikson, have you heard from Enesa?"

Miguel put his head down, "I'm sure she arrived in Denmark, but I haven't heard from her.

"Do you miss her?"

"She's better off where she is."

"That isn't what I asked you."

"It doesn't matter if I miss her or not. She'll have a better life without me."

"Miguel, why don't you let her be the judge of that? I know she loves you. I don't want to see you live for the rest of your life in the Amazon with no one to love. Your life will be empty!"

Miguel looked at Marilyn and smiled. "I have spent most of my life on my own. I'm used to it."

"Please consider what I'm telling you," pleaded Marilyn. "I don't think Enesa will find happiness without you. You're the man she loves. Please reconsider and contact her. Tell her to come back. I know it will be one of the best decisions you'll ever make."

"I'll consider it," said Miguel. He smiled at Marilyn and then walked away.

Marilyn went up to check on Michael and see if anyone needed anything. When she knocked, Allen opened the door.

"Hi beautiful, I was just coming down to find you."

"Do any of you need anything?"

"Yes I do," Allen smiled.

"What can I get you?"

He walked her out into the hallway. "Can you spend some time with me in the garden tonight? We'll be leaving in the morning to take Michael back so we can get him back on his feet."

Marilyn's heart fell thinking of Allen leaving. She thought this might be the last time she would ever see him again.

"I would love to spend some time with you."

"Great!" Allen hated the thought of leaving Marilyn also. Tomorrow was going to be a very hard day for him. He hadn't felt this way for anyone since Stephanie. Now he has to say good bye to the woman he loves again. Their worlds were far apart and he knew it would be a long time before he would see her again.

That night they walked through the garden admiring the cliffs all lit up.

Marilyn avoided going near the pond because of what Miguel had told her about the panther. She didn't want to provoke him anymore and they walked down the slate pathway that entered into the Fuchsia bushes.

"Hello, how are you!" called out Jaukeu as they walked by his perch.

Marilyn smiled and said, "Have a nice evening Jack!"

"Thanks, you too!" squawked Jaukeu.

Marilyn and Allen stopped and looked at each other. Then laughed!

As they walked they talked about what their plans were after tomorrow. Allen then stopped Marilyn and moved his body in front of hers. He looked down at her as she looked up into his eyes.

"I don't want to say good bye."

"I know," said Marilyn. "And neither do I, it just has to be this way for now."

"We have to get Michael back to New York *as* soon as we can. Quinn and I are taking over as his doctors. And Catherine, Quinn's wife is going to be his nurse at home. Alex is going to stay with him also. Once we have him stabilized I want to come and see you again. I also have to get back to my practice and get things in order. Is that going to be okay with you?"

"Yes, I would love to see you as soon as you can get away."

His eyes started to fill with tears and he moved his head back to stop them from rolling down his cheeks.

Marilyn was surprised to see him show his emotions that way. She reached up and ran her hand down the side of his face.

"We'll see each other again Allen."

He grabbed and kissed the palm of her hand.

"The last time I said good bye to someone I never saw her again."

Marilyn knew he was talking about Stephanie. Marilyn's eyes filled with tears knowing how he must have felt getting the news of her accident. She pulled herself into him and rested the side of her face on his chest.

"I promise I'm not going anywhere." He pulled her into his arms as close as he could without hurting her. She could feel the strength of his muscles under his shirt from his arms and chest. Marilyn felt so comfortable in his arms and dreaded him leaving again.

When Marilyn woke the next morning she went downstairs to the kitchen to make coffee and breakfast for everyone. The sun was already high in the air and she knew she had over slept a bit.

Miguel entered the kitchen and stood under the threshold of the door as he said good morning to Marilyn.

"Good morning," she smiled back at him. "I hope you're hungry. I'm going to make my famous pancakes for you. Remember we used to make them with Trinity every Sunday morning."

Miguel smiled back at her and shook his head.

"What's the matter? Why are you looking at me like that?"

"Marilyn," said Miguel. "Allen left this morning."

As his words sunk in it felt like someone plunged a knife through her heart.

"He just couldn't say good bye. He couldn't stand the thought of leaving you behind. So he asked me to give this to you." Miguel handed Marilyn a white envelope and then sadly walked out of the kitchen. The letter read:

*Dear Marilyn,*

*Please forgive me for not saying good bye to you. I was up all night wondering how I could say the words as I left you to head back to New York. I just didn't have the heart. I think you know by now how much I love you. And I haven't felt this way for many years. Saying good bye is not easy for me. So I will not say good bye. I will say I love you. I'll call you when you get back to Rio and I'll see you very soon. Stay safe!"*

*Love always,*
*Allen xoxoxo*

Marilyn ran to the porch to see if she could catch him before he left the garden. He was nowhere to be seen. Then she ran down the slate path to the entrance. But there was no sight of him.

Her eyes filled with tears, and the loneliness in her heart returned. She was alone again. All but Miguel remained in her life. Her father, her mother, and Emmanuel were all gone, and now Allen was gone too!

# Chapter 21

A few days after Allen left, Marilyn returned to her pavilion in Niteroi. She planned to visit Miguel in a few months. She missed him already just after a few days and it was like they had never been apart. She could tell he really didn't want her to leave but she knew he made her go for her own sake. So she honored his wishes and returned home.

Marilyn had just sat down on her terrace overlooking the beaches and water. Her phone rang.

"Hello!"

"Hello Marilyn, this is Enesa, how are you?"

Marilyn was thrilled to hear her voice!

"I'm great Enesa, and how are you? I was going to try to contact you. I'm so glad you called and I miss you!"

Enesa laughed, "And I miss you too.

"How are things going for you in Denmark?"

"Well, I'm not in Denmark."

"Where are you?"

"I decided to go back to school and take some extra studies. I'm in Montreal Canada. I love it here!"

"I'm so happy for you!" said Marilyn. But there was a sense of sadness that Marilyn felt that Enesa had seemed to have moved on with her life.

"How is Miguel?" asked Enesa.

"He's doing alright. He's very busy. He's still working on his research in the pond. You know the drill."

Enesa laughed again and said, "Oh yes. I know it quite well!"

They both joined in laughing.

"Did Miguel ever get a chance to help Michael for Allen and Quinn?"

"Yes, and he's doing great! He's up and walking and seems to be making a full recovery."

"That's so good to hear!" said Enesa.

"I'm so glad things are going well for you Enesa. I really am. But I need to ask you something. Were you and Miguel lovers? I'm sorry to pry, but I need to know what has happened in my brother's life."

"I understand," said Enesa. "We were lovers towards the end. It was very beautiful and meaningful to me. I guess he just didn't feel the same way. Then he told me to leave."

"I don't believe that to be true Enesa," I'm quite sure he's in love with you. I think he just denies his feelings to protect himself and to protect you too."

"Why would he protect me?" asked Enesa.

"Because he doesn't think the rainforest is any place for you. He told me he wants you have a much better life than what he can offer you."

"There was a silence on the other side of the phone.

"Are you still there Enesa?"

"Yes, I'm here. I just wanted to say hello and see how you were. But I have to go now and get ready for my classes. It was nice talking to you and please take care of yourself!"

Before Marilyn could say another word, Enesa was gone. Marilyn had a very bad feeling about the conversation. She felt that Enesa was hiding something from her. Something seemed to be wrong. She looked at her call display to get Enesa's phone number. But the display showed the phone number was unknown. How could she get a hold of her? She would have to wait for Enesa to call her again.

The next day, and after taking a hot bath, Marilyn's phone rang and she answered.

"Hello beautiful!" As Allen's voice made Marilyn's face light up with a smile.

"Hi honey!" she said elated to hear from him.

"How are you doing baby?" he asked.

"How could you have left me without saying good bye?" Marilyn yelled at him in a joking voice!

"Whoa!" he said. "I left you a letter. Did you get it?"

"Yes, but that isn't good enough. I miss you like crazy!"

"I'm so glad to hear you say that," said Allen. "But I miss you even more! And if you were here with me right now I would have you on my bed making mad, crazy and passionate love to you."

"I can only imagine," she said with a smile. "Baby, how is Michael doing?"

"He's doing so well that he doesn't need Catherine to help him anymore. And guess what, he and Alex are getting married!"

"What!" She yelled out in excitement.

"He asked her to marry him and she said yes."

"That's such good news Allen, I'm so happy for them!"

"And you're coming to the wedding!"

"Really? I can't wait! When is it?"

"Are you ready for this?"

"Yes!" she laughed.

"It's in three weeks!"

"What!" Marilyn said in disbelief.

"And guess where they're getting married?"

"I'm waiting," she said laughing.

Allen laughed at her. They're going back to get married in Natowa's garden!"

"Are you serious?"

"Yes, they feel that's where their lives began together, so they want to go back and get married. We sent a message to Yurah to get a hold of Natowa, I mean Miguel. It's all arranged, and he can't wait to see you!"

Marilyn was so excited that she was going to be with everyone again, especially Allen and Miguel. "I can't wait to see you Allen, I miss you so much!"

"And I miss you too babe, It will be here before we know it. I'm getting beeped on my pager honey. "I'll call you tomorrow!"

"I love you!" she shouted before Allen hung up the phone.

Marilyn arrived on the Thursday before the wedding at the Tishi Amazon Resort. When the plane landed Allen was already on the Tarmac waiting for her. She was so excited to see him and everyone else. As soon as she got off Allen was at the base of the stairs with a beautiful bouquet of white African daisies.

When she approached him he grabbed her into his arms and kissed her so hard her lips went numb for a second. She laughed at how excited he was!

"Hi baby, you have no idea how much I have missed you!" Allen said as he looked deep into Marilyn's eyes. Almost forgetting he had the flowers in his hand he held them out to her. She lifted them to smell the beautiful aroma. The aroma she missed from the Amazon.

Michael and Alex were already there. They were waiting for Quinn and Catherine to fly in around 5:00 p.m. since Catherine had to finish her shift that morning and planned to sleep on the plane.

Everyone waited until Quinn and Catherine arrived before they headed down to dinner. As soon as they got there everyone else joined them at the Tishi Cabana Bar before they got seated. They were all so excited to be together again, especially Michael, Allen and Quinn.

Once they were all seated for dinner, Michael stood up and spoke, "I would like to propose a toast!" I want to say something to my best friends, Allen and Quinn. If it wasn't for your love and dedication, I wouldn't be standing here right now. I would have never had a chance to marry the woman I love. And I would not be here with my two best friends and the beautiful women in their lives. So I want to say thank you and I love you all, and may we all grow old and happy together!"

"I'll toast to that!" Boasted Quinn, as they all raised their glasses to Michael and Alex.

Allen stood up, "And I just want to say that if it wasn't for Natowa, none of us would be here today. He's a man of great heroism, and he lives to make the Amazon a better place. Here's to Natowa!"

They all toasted as tears of joy filled Marilyn's eyes. She missed her brother so much she couldn't wait to see him again.

The next day they all met at the two boats to leave for the rainforest. Catherine was a bit nervous since it was her first trip into the Amazon. Everyone assured her that it was going to be okay and that she would love the rainforest once she saw how beautiful it was.

She clung to Quinn as they journeyed down the Amazon River. He pointed out to her some of the splendors of the river. She marveled at all the beautiful flowers and birds as they waded down. He warned her that she might get alarmed by some of the animals but not to worry since they were all safe.

Just as Tutu and Nino were getting ready to pull out some lunch for everyone, a large twenty foot long Anaconda slithered by them in the water. It was so close to the boats that they could have reached out and touch it. It created a wave that made the boats rock which made Catherine turn around and look into the water. When she saw the Anaconda she jumped up and let out a horrifying scream! She was terrified of snakes and it was her worst fear to see one on the trip into the Amazon.

Just as she screamed and jumped up, about ten crocodiles ran from land and leaped into the water creating even a bigger wave. They were leaping into the water for safety from the loud cry that Catherine let out. The two boats instantly rocked heavily back and forth almost throwing everyone into the water. The water started to fill the boats. Everyone tried to hang on to the sides as they were being thrown from the seats onto the floors.

Quinn took his hand and covered Catherine's mouth and told her to stop screaming! She looked at him with terror in her eyes!

Everyone was fighting to steady themselves as the crocodiles thrashed around them in the water.

The crocodiles were moving with a fast furry as not knowing what was happening or if they were in danger. As the boats rocked back and forth it almost tipped some of their gear over.

Tutu and Nino grabbed the gear and threw it to the middle of the boats so that nothing would fall over board.

Yurah and Davi's worst fear was that the boats would fill with water and sink. If they wound up in the water they would be a feeding frenzy for the crocodiles. So they jumped up and started to bale the water out as fast as they could! Then Allen, Quinn and Marilyn joined in. Alex held on to Catherine to keep her calm.

After a while of baling, most of the water was gone and the crocodiles were starting to swim away. Then within in a few minutes everything started to return to normal.

"I'm so sorry!" cried Catherine.

"It's okay honey," Quinn added, "You didn't know."

Everyone told her everything was okay now. She was still very shaken by what happened and she blamed herself. She realized the danger she could have put everyone in. She swore to Quinn it wouldn't happen again.

Quinn kept his arm around her. He knew she was traumatized by what happened. He didn't blame her. He was worried for her. He thought he was wrong for bringing her here. But now that they were, he would do whatever it took to protect her from her fears. Once they reached their destination on land, everyone started to regain their composure. They even joked about what happened and prided themselves how they all took control of the situation.

Michael, Allen and Quinn felt they were beginning to master the perils of the Amazon. In such a short time of being in the rainforest jungle they had many encounters being in danger. But yet they were still alive. At least for now!

Alex and Michael led everyone into the jungle. They were so happy to be together again that no matter where they were it was okay, for all they cared about was being in each other's company.

Yurah, Davi, Tutu and Nino walked behind everyone watching and listening for any abnormal sounds.

As they walked they could hear the sound of the waterfall's getting nearer.

"What is that noise?" asked Catherine curiously.

"It's a surprise!" Quinn said as they all looked back at her with a smile. Then he took her hand and ran in front of everyone. When he stopped, he opened up a thick patch of ferns and said to her, "Look!"

She looked inside the ferns and she saw the most beautiful waterfall she had ever seen.

"That is so beautiful!" she said as her big blue eyes widened open.

By then everyone was standing behind her laughing. Alex ran towards the waterfall ripping off her shirt and cargo shorts to expose her bathing suit. "Last one in is a rotten egg!"

Everyone laughed and followed suit into the water. Michael laughed at Alex's playfulness and it was what he loved about her more than anything. She loved life just like Michael. He looked at her and thought to himself, "Michael, you met your match!" and then plunged into the water after her.

A few hours later after they feasted on some food and wine, then Alex asked Marilyn and Catherine to come with her. So they followed her behind a big boulder rock and while they all leaned against trees, Marilyn and Catherine were waiting to hear what Alex had to say.

"Well ladies, I need a maid of honor and a bridesmaid, and I would like to ask you both if you could help me out. Marilyn, would you be my maid of honor, and Catherine, would you be my bridesmaid?"

Marilyn and Catherine laughed with joy! They both wrapped their arms around her and told her yes.

Back with the men, Michael, Allen and Quinn sat leaning against a few large rocks while sipping on some red wine. Michael looked at Allen and Quinn and just stared at them.

"What are you staring at?" asked Quinn.

"Well, I guess I have to ask both of you something.

"Ask us what?" Allen said while taking a sip of his wine.

"I guess I'm stuck way out here in the middle of a rainforest without a best man. So I guess one of you will have to be it."

Allen and Quinn laughed.

"But the problem is I don't know which one of you to ask, so I guess you both have to be my best man."

Quinn joked, "Yeah, I had the same problem."

They all laughed and Allen and Quinn leaned over and gave Michael a pat on his back.

Allen said, "We would be happy to be your best man."

"Here here!" said Quinn. As they all clinked their glasses together.

Just as they were finished with their toast, Catherine came running at the men jumping up and down in terror!

The men saw her face and jumped to their feet.

"What's wrong?" yelled Quinn shaking her gently.

Catherine wouldn't talk in fear she would start screaming.

Quinn shook her again and said, "Cath, tell us what's wrong!"

Catherine caught her breath and grabbed Quinn and Michael's hand and quickly ran them with her.

When Catherine stopped and pointed they looked over and Alex was sitting on the ground leaning up against a tree. To their horror a large banana spider was crawling up Alex's shoulder as she sat there with tears in her eyes looking up at Michael.

Michael's heart sank and he didn't know what to do while one of the world's most deadly spiders crawled up her shoulder almost onto her neck.

"Don't move babe," Michael said in a calm voice to hopefully comfort her.

Alex squeezed her eyes shut and didn't move a muscle.

As the massive hairy spider crawled up, a hand with a thick leather glove came out from behind the tree and plucked the spider off of Alex's shoulder.

Alex was still afraid to move and then Yurah walked out from behind the tree with the leather glove still on his hand and said, "It's okay now, It's gone."

Michael by then was standing at Alex's side and pulled her up and right into his arms as he hugged her tight. "Are you okay baby?" he said to her with fear still in his face.

"Yes, I'm fine," as she held on to him too. She turned to Yurah and said, "Thank you Yurah. I think you just saved my life!"

Yurah smiled at her and said to her in a joking way, "Remember what I told you in the survival course? Don't lean against any trees or stand under them for too long or things can slither or walk down onto you?"

Alex remembered learning that from their survival course the first trek into the rainforest. She nodded to Yurah in a sheepish way and said, "A lesson well learned!"

# Chapter 22

Two hours later they were standing in front of Natowa's garden. They were all so happy to get there. Catherine marveled at the sight of the Magnolia trees as they stood at the front of the slate path.

"If you think this is something, wait until you get inside." said Alex.

"Yes, it is quite the paradise of all paradises." said Marilyn as she smiled at Catherine.

Just then they heard something behind them and they turned and there stood Natowa. Marilyn was so happy to see him she ran and threw her arms around his neck. He laughed as he lifted her up with excitement to see her too.

"Come!" he said, "I have to show you what the natives have done to prepare for your wedding," as he grabbed Michael and Alex and ushered them along.

Everyone was so happy to return to the garden. And Catherine was now beginning to feel safe now that they were in the confines of Natowa's garden.

Quinn walked up and introduced Catherine and Natowa as they walked down the path. She looked around in astonishment at the sight of the huge stone walls with all the lanterns."

This is the most beautiful place I have ever seen!" Catherine commented to Natowa.

"Hello, and welcome to the garden!" squawked Jaukeu while standing on his perch.

Catharine swung around and was looking to see someone.

This is Jaukeu, said Marilyn. Or you can call him Jack.

Catharine went up to Jaukeu, "Well hello there you cute little thing!"

"I'm in love!' said Jaukeu while bouncing up and down on his perch.

Everyone laughed!

Marilyn reached into the whicker basket and handed Catharine a peanut. "I learned that the best way to Jack's heart is through his stomach."

Everyone laughed again!

As they moved into the garden, they couldn't believe what the natives did to prepare for the wedding. It was simply spectacular! Tiki lights were all throughout the gardens and banners of white linen with multi colored flowers hung between each one. In front of one of the gardens was a bamboo threshold laced with white and pink Magnolias and roses, with large white bows.

Michael was the happiest man in the world right now. To think that if it wasn't for Natowa, he wouldn't be standing there. And then to have Natowa make tomorrow the most special day of his life was just too overwhelming.

Michael walked up to Natowa and put his arm on his shoulder and said, "I owe you my life. And I mean that literally!" as they both laughed. "And I don't know how to repay you for all that you have done."

"And I could say the same for you Michael. If it wasn't for you, Allen and Quinn, I may not have ever had my sister back in my life."

"We have a lot to celebrate tomorrow said Michael.

"I agree," said Natowa, as they looked back at the beautiful garden and threshold.

Alex, Marilyn and Catherine got ready for the wedding the next morning. A few native women came to help them. A little five year old native girl came with them to be Alex's flower girl. Her name was Alahee (Al • ah • hee). She was the cutest little thing that Alex, Catharine and Marilyn had ever seen!

"I wasn't expecting to stand up in a wedding said Marilyn. I hope the dress I brought is going to be suitable enough."

"Neither was I," said Catherine. "I just brought a strapless summer dress. I wasn't expecting something this elegant, and I certainly wasn't expecting to stand up in a wedding!" as she laughed.

"My dress isn't anything elegant either, so I'm sure your dresses will be just fine," said Alex.

"We can make you dresses," said one of the native women.

"But we have no time to make dresses," Catherine said smiling from the woman's statement while putting on her lipstick.

"Yes we do," as the native woman brushed Alex's hair.

When she was done she left and returned with six other women. They brought two large wooden boxes and put them in the middle of the floor. They pulled out a few yards of white, light pink and fuchsia satin material.

The women walked up to Marilyn, Catherine and the little native girl and put their arms around them as if to see what size they wore. The women reached into one of the boxes and pulled out some needles and thread, and from the other box they pulled out satin white and pink Magnolias, Lilies of the Valley and Baby's Breath.

They held the cloth up to Alex, Marilyn, Catherine and Alahee and started to cut and sew the material onto their bodies. Alex, Marilyn and Catherine were looking on in amazement as the native women lifted and tucked and sewed the material around their bodies.

In just less than two hours the women backed away and Alex, Marilyn, Catherine and Alahee were standing there in beautiful dresses!

Alex's bridal dress was designed in a toga style and was satin that draped straight to the floor with a long train that dragged behind her.

Beautiful white satin Orchids ran up from her waist and over her left shoulder leaving her right shoulder completely bare. Her train had satin Lilies of the Valley and Baby's Breath that lined the hem of her train.

"This is beautiful!" said Alex. "I feel like Cinderella!"

Marilyn and Catherine looked at Alex admiring how beautiful she looked, "You look like Cinderella!" said Marilyn.

Then Alex looked over at Marilyn and Catherine. She caught her breath as she saw their dresses. Marilyn's dress was Fuchsia and Catherine's dress was pink. The little girl's dress was white like Alex's but a ballerina length with a sweetheart neckline like Marilyn and Catharine's. Their dresses were ballerina length and the tops were a sweetheart neckline. On the right side of their chest was a large corsage of white and pink Magnolias. Around their waists ran a small bead of pearls intertwined with satin Baby's Breath and Lilies of the Valley.

"You both look so beautiful!" cried Alex.

"We all look beautiful!" as Catherine smiled at Alex, Marilyn and Alahee.

They thanked the native women while they gave them all hugs. The native women smiled and looked so proud of their masterpieces.

One of the women went back to the wooden box and pulled out another smaller box. She walked up to Alex and told her to turn around. She latched a strand of pearls around Alex's neck and clipped on a matching pearl on each ear.

Then she took a beautiful bouquet that matched the flowers of Marilyn and Catherine's dress and put it into her hands. Then two other women walked over to Marilyn, Catherine and Alahee and put matching pearl necklaces and earrings on them also. She then handed them a small bouquet that matched Alex's larger bouquet.

The women then twisted the three women's hair into a twist and tied their hair up with pearl edged clips and Baby's Breath and one large white magnolia. They braided Alahee's hair around her head and added Baby's Breath all around the braid.

Within two hours the women were completely dressed and ready to walk down the aisle. Alex cried out to Marilyn, Catherine and the native women. "I can't believe I'm getting married!"

As Alex stood inside the house, Natowa came in to tell her that Michael was ready to begin. He looked at the four beautiful women and smiled. "You all look beautiful!" He especially looked at his sister standing there looking like she was a bride herself. He walked up to her and said, "Someday it will be your turn."

She smiled and gave him a hug.

As Alex took a deep breath and turned to look at her friends and native women, she said, "Well I guess this is it!"

They all smiled at her as Natowa opened the door for them. She walked out onto the porch and Michael stood at the altar anxiously waiting for her.

As she walked down the stairs and onto the path, he couldn't believe how beautiful she looked! He would never forget this moment as she looked more beautiful today then she ever had looked before.

Allen and Quinn looked on to admire their women and smiled at Alahee as they walked slowly behind Alex. Marilyn looked up at Allen while he looked so handsome in his black suit. She could see the men were all wearing a white Lily in their lapel. The native women had this all planned!

When Alex reached the alter Michael helped Alex up the stairs to stand in front of the beautiful garden. He looked at her and smiled.

"You look even more beautiful than I could have even imagined."

She smiled at him and put her hands up to straighten his tie.

"And you look so handsome!"

In the background, two native young men played wooden flutes. It was such beautiful music for this most beautiful moment in their lives.

John couldn't make it on such short notice and being football season. But Michael promised they would have a small reception when they returned for everyone to meet Alex. Michael knew everyone would love her!

The man conducting the ceremony was a Baptist minister and was a good friend of Dr. Erikson's. He married most of the natives in the garden and was a known to be a healer himself. He held a silver goblet with a handle on each side of it holding it out in front of Alex and Michael.

He said, "Alexandria and Michael, how blessed are you both for God has brought you here to celebrate your love for each other. I hope that your love for each other is as beautiful as the garden that you stand in. The garden represents love and respect for all things. It takes time to make a garden as beautiful as this," as he waved his hand for everyone to look through the garden.

"Marriage is very much the same way. It is not something you can neglect for it will die. It is something that you must care for to keep it alive. You need to tend to it even when you're tired and weary. You need to find water even when there's a drought. Like a garden, a marriage needs the same attention. I hope you grow many beautiful things in your garden of love. And I hope it blooms and flourishes and brings you much happiness for the rest of your life. Alexandria and Michael, I now pronounce you man and wife!"

Michelle Dubois

Alex and Michael's eyes were filled with tears. Then Michael turned to Alex and put her hands in his. "Our love has already stood the test of time. Alex, you have already gotten me threw the drought, and now it's my turn bring you the happiness that you deserve. Alex, I'll love you for eternity."

Alex returned his words by saying. "I hope your sickness was the worst challenge that we will ever have to face. But if not, whatever we're faced with, I know that what will not kill us will only make us stronger. We're one now. We're stronger and nothing will ever come between us. I love you too Michael, and I too will love you for eternity."

The words tore through everyone's hearts for all their friends knew how much Michael's cancer brought Alex back into his life. It was a challenge in their lives that bonded them even closer.

As the night went on, everyone celebrated after the ceremony. The natives put on a huge spread of food. Everyone drank champagne to toast the marriage and drank wine at dinner.

The natives put on a beautiful wedding ritual dancing near a bomb fire. They grabbed everyone's hands and before you knew it everyone was up and dancing including Natowa with a beautiful young native girl who obviously had an eye for him.

Then Alahee walked up to the young native girl and tugged on the back of her long black hair. Alahee said to her, "I want to dance with Natowa too!"

Everyone laughed including Natowa as he reached down and swept her into his arms to dance. Alahee was in love!

Tutu and Nino were eyeing the pretty young native girls as they were waiting for Tutu and Nino to ask them to dance. Then Tutu shoved Nino towards one of them. He backed up giving Tutu a dirty look. Then Nino shoved Tutu towards the other girl. They both looked at each other and said, "Let's go together!" And then they both walked up to the two young ladies and grabbed their hands so fast that the girls just laughed!

When the night ended, a native man and woman escorted Michael and Alex to a secret place for their honeymoon night. It was a total surprise to them and when they got there the honeymoon room was inside one of the cliffs.

When Michael carried Alex over the threshold and into the room, they were taken back by what was inside. In the middle of the room was a beautiful large wooden bathtub filled with steaming hot water. There were scented oils, a bottle of red and white wine with two silver goblets sitting on the floor. Candles were lit all around the bathtub, and a large white feather down mattress with pillows and duvet sat in the corner of the room, and white netting was strung all around it. A large bouquet of flowers sat at the foot of the mattress with bottles of massage oils, fruits, breads and cheese.

After the man and woman left, Michael walked up to Alex. He put his arm around her waist and told her just how beautiful she was.

Alex looked into Michael's dark eyes and she couldn't believe she just married this very tall and most handsome man she had ever seen.

He leaned down to kiss her and while gently kissing her lips he slipped her out of her wedding gown. The gown fell to the floor to expose Alex in a white lace corset.

At the reception he had a chance to take Alex's garter off of her and put it on his arm. He then removed it again and knelt down to slowly slip it back onto Alex's thigh.

She could feel the sexual arousal mount in her body as his hands went up her leg and gently touched her thigh.

He then kissed her all over until she couldn't take the anticipation of him inside of her. She pulled him back up to her and she kissed his chest working her way down until he couldn't take anymore.

He then pulled her up and carried her over to the bed and put her down on her back. He looked down at her body and slowly removed her corset exposing her naked body. Then Michael got undressed and dropped his clothes to the floor.

She had the most beautiful body which was the first attraction when Michael met her. She had lost some weight during the episode of him being sick, and her rib cage and hip bones protruded out from her body. Her breasts were very firm and the perfect size for him.

He kissed her again and then ran his mouth slowly down her body stopping at her breast.

He moved his mouth slowly all over her body again. She moaned and gasped as he gently kissed her until she couldn't take anymore.

He pulled her down on the bed and moved his body on top of her. He plunged himself deep inside of her while she moaned and she described to him how she was feeling.

He loved hearing he was pleasing her and was fulfilling her desires. They kissed and grasped each other's bodies and it seemed like an eternity before they couldn't take anymore. Then in the same moment they both looked deep into each other's eyes and each let out a long moan and then went limp in each others arms.

Michael moaned again from the pleasure into her ear. He then held her in his arms for a long while then pulled himself off her body and lay on his back to catch his breath.

Alex lay like she was completely exhausted while she pulled the sheet up on top of her. They turned to look at each other and smiled. He held her in his arms while they lay next to each other.

A half hour later he got up and pulled the sheet from her body. He looked down at her taking her in once more and removed the garter from her leg. He then picked her up off the bed and carried her over to the bathtub.

He put her on her feet and reached down and picked up the scented oil from the floor and poured some into his hands. He massaged Alex's shoulders and down her back and she moaned from the feeling of his soft firm hands.

He moved his hands down her body and he could feel she was ready again. He picked her up and put her in the bathtub and then crawled in after her.

They sat inside the bath facing each other. Michael poured them each a glass of red wine and then he pulled her up to him as she turned around so they were both facing the window staring out at the full moon.

They sipped their wine and Michael said, "This was the most amazing day of my life."

As they clicked their goblets together, Alex smiled and said, "And here's to the beginning of a long life together!"

# Chapter 23

The next evening after the wedding Marilyn and Miguel took a walk in the garden. Miguel purposely avoided the pond since he didn't want Marilyn near the panther. They walked along the garden to enter towards the greenhouses.

As they came to a resting area, they both sat down to talk.

"I heard from Enesa," said Marilyn. Marilyn wanted to wait until the right time to tell Miguel.

Miguel looked at her in surprise!

"Did she call you?"

"Yes, she's in Montreal."

"What is she doing there?" Miguel asked very curiously.

"She's taking some courses at a university."

"I see, is she okay?"

"I don't know?"

"What do you mean you don't know?"

"She seemed uneasy. She just seemed to be evasive about you."

Miguel put his head down, "She's probably mad at me."

"No," said Marilyn. "It didn't seem that way at all. It was just something. I'm not sure what it was, but something in her voice and the way she had to hang up the phone. I felt that something was wrong."

"I think you're over analyzing things," smiled Miguel.

"I tried to call her back but it said caller was unknown on my call display. Before I could get her number she hung up."

"Can we change the subject?" asked Miguel.

Marilyn smiled at him knowing Enesa was a sore subject for him. She knew he still loved her, and if anything was wrong in her life he would be the first one there for her. Marilyn just knew it.

"How is Eye Spy doing?" Marilyn asked smirking at him.

"He seems to be returning to normal. That's why I have to keep you away from the pond. If he sees you it might stir something again."

"What do you think it is about me that provokes him?"

"I have thought of that question many times. I'm not quite sure, I think it's because you somehow made a connection with him."

"I didn't mean to. I was just playing around."

"I know you were. But now I have to make sure he doesn't over dominate the others in the pond. Anything that lives in the pond has to be obedient and complacent so it doesn't upset the balance. He's an animal and if he keeps killing he'll upset the pond. They're supposed to be in harmony with each other. That's what the pond is all about."

"And how will you stop him in the future if he has already killed?"

Miguel looked concerned. "I don't know. I fear I might have to put him down. I have been watching and examining him and right now everything seems to be fine. But if he shows anymore signs of dominance or aggression I don't know what will happen. I'm hoping it was an isolated case. But if it continues he'll be no use to our research anymore. If anything, he'll destroy it!"

"What will happen to your research without him?"

"Without him our research is over. "He's the most vital part of pond. It took us years to breed him. He shares the same DNA and immune system with everything in the pond. He's the one that sustains all of the life inside the pond. Without him everything will die."

After they talked they walked back to the house and said good night. Miguel went back to the garden to do one last check. It was a long day and everyone was leaving early tomorrow morning to head back to the resort. Then the day after that they were all flying out.

Allen was still up and sitting on the porch when Marilyn got to the house. She was happy to see he was still awake.

"Hi baby, did you and Miguel have a nice visit?"

"Yes, and I'm glad to see you're still up.

"I couldn't go to bed without saying good night." He leaned over and gave her a nice soft kiss on her lips.

Her emotions for Allen were getting deeper and deeper. The thought of their separation again after they left the garden left her feeling lonely already.

"Hey, what's the matter?" Allen asked.

"I just hate the thought of not seeing you for a while. Who knows how long it will be before I even see you again?"

He pulled her chin up so that he could look in her eyes," No matter how far apart we are, we're still together. Do you understand me?"

She smiled up at him. "Yes, I understand."

"Good," he said as he gave her a small slap on her butt.

She laughed at his playfulness.

"Now it's time for all of us to get some sleep. We have to be up at the crack of dawn to head back to the resort." Allen gave Marilyn one last long kiss before saying good night.

The next morning they all were up early saying good bye to Natowa and the natives. They walked down the path and disappeared.

Miguel felt empty as he saw his sister leave once more. But he knew it was for the best. He was beginning to worry about her safety in the garden. He didn't know anymore if the panther could ever be trusted again.

# Chapter 24

Once back at the resort, they all had one last night together. They had dinner and then they all said good night. Michael and Alex were the first to leave, and then Quinn and Catherine retired a little while after and left Allen and Marilyn together at the table.

"Come on," said Allen, "Let's take a walk."

They disappeared into the resort to a wooden bridge that spanned over a beautiful stream with lily pads and goldfish. The bridge was lit on each side with Tiki torches and the light of moon glimmered on the ripples of the water.

"It's so beautiful and peaceful here," said Marilyn. "I can totally understand why Miguel doesn't want to leave."

"I can see why too, but there are too many dangers here. I feel much better knowing you're in Rio. I couldn't sleep at night leaving you here."

She smiled at him realizing he was right. Under the right circumstances it was a great place to visit. But in the real world the Amazon had its challenges. She started to feel like she was missing her pavilion and the comforts it offered. But she hated leaving Miguel and Allen again.

"I'll come to see you as soon as I can," said Allen. "And then I want you to come to New York."

"I would love to come to New York again."

"Again?" asked Allen.

"Yes, I was there a few times. I was there on a few art gallery excursions. My job is very rewarding for me when I find a masterpiece. My biggest find was a Monet that was owned by a woman in Monaco. She had an affair with a very wealthy Roman man who gave her the Monet as a gift. When she passed away her daughter who hated the lover called me and asked me to sell it for her. I love what I do and I hope to open a gallery someday."

Allen was very impressed with her accomplishments. He had a love for art also which was another thing that he knew they would share.

"Then if you ever come to New York to live, I guess what I'm saying is that I hope someday if we ever make a commitment to each other, I hope that you would be happy to live in New York. I'll buy you a gallery so you can continue your passion for art. You and I can travel the world looking for art pieces."

Marilyn smiled at Allen. "I thought we were already committed to each other."

Allen smiled at her. "Yes, but I mean if we ever get married."

"Why Allen, I didn't know you were thinking of marriage!"

"I would marry you in a heartbeat Marilyn. But I know there are still a lot of things to consider because of our distance. But I hope someday that can change."

Marilyn knew he was right. There were many things to consider, and even though her feelings changed for Emmanuel, she still needed time to get over what happened.

Back at home in Niteroi, Marilyn walked into her pavilion and listened to her voicemail. She had messages. She scrambled to listen to them since there were so many of them. She was worried something happened to someone. When she listened to the first message she was shocked to hear it was from Emmanuel!

"Marilyn, I want to come and see you as soon as you're home. Please call me!" said his first message.

Marilyn's heart fell to her feet. She felt a chill run down her spine just hearing his voice. She deleted the message and listened to the next one. It was Emmanuel again.

"Marilyn, I don't know if you're home yet? Can you please call me back? It's very important!"

Each message she deleted was from Emmanuel. By the time she listened to the last message his voice and attitude changed. He was threatening her that if she didn't call him back that he was going to come to her house. She locked her doors and windows.

A few hours past and she made herself a cup of tea and her phone rang. She was afraid to answer it. Then over the speaker she heard, "Hi babe, it's me, Allen. I wanted to make sure you got home safely."

Marilyn quickly lifted the receiver and said, "Hi honey, I'm so happy to hear from you!"

"Hi babe, did you get home okay?"

She swallowed hard and choked down her words. "Yes, I'm home," and then she paused."

"Is everything alright?" asked Allen curiously.

"Yes, everything is fine."

But Allen could sense something was wrong.

"What's going on Marilyn? Did Emmanuel try to contact you?" Allen picked up on her silence.

Not wanting to lie to him, she hesitated to say anything.

"Was he there?" He fired his words out with contempt in his voice.

"No!" snapped Marilyn. "He wasn't here! He called and left a few messages."

"What did he say?"

"It first started out that he wanted me to call to talk to him about something urgent. But by the time I listened to the last message, I realized he's very bitter and angry."

"Marilyn, you need to call the police!"

"I need to let him just calm down. That's how he is. His temper blows up and then he's fine. I don't want to start anything. I just want him to go away!"

"That's dangerous Marilyn. He could snap and do something to hurt you. Please call the police!"

"If he comes to my house I'll call, but let me just see what he's going to do. I don't want to provoke him. He can have a nasty temper!"

Yes, I know, I'm so worried about you. I'll stay on the phone with you for the night. Do you have a web camera on your computer?"

"Yes," said Marilyn. She used to use it to talk and see Emmanuel on occasions.

"Then I want you to turn it on and connect me. I'll send you my video message account and I'll be able to watch you and make sure you're going to be alright."

"Okay," said Marilyn. "I would love to see you anyways."

"I can't wait to see you either babe," said Allen.

A few minutes later, Marilyn and Allen were connected online and seeing each other on a web camera.

"You look as beautiful as always," Allen smiled.

Marilyn loved knowing she could see Allen again. Even if it wasn't up close and personal, just being able to talk and see him was good enough for her.

"Has he tried to contact you again?"

"No, I think he gave up."

"I don't think so. I want you to keep the web camera on for the night. I want to see you even in your sleep.

I don't trust him and I know he's capable of anything. As a matter of fact I can almost assure you he'll call again."

That night she lay in her bed and blew Allen a kiss good night. They were both exhausted from the long trip and events, but Allen was determined to stay awake and watch over Marilyn.

He relaxed back in his bed wearing flannel pajama bottoms and tee shirt with his lap top on his end table. He looked at her while she slept in her pink sleeveless satin pajama top and pajama bottoms.

He imagined being wrapped around her and holding her tight. Someday soon, thought Allen. As she slept her short breaths in and out made him want her more. She looked so at peace and deep into sleep.

He was so tired but he just couldn't fall asleep knowing what Emmanuel was capable of doing. The light from the outside terrace lights lit Marilyn's room and it cast a shadow on everything outside.

Allen was having a hard time keeping his eyes open and thought to take something to keep him awake.

He went to his medicine cabinet and returned to his room with a few caffeine pills that would take the edge off of his sleepiness.

As he walked back into his room while downing the pills with a glass of water he looked at his laptop to see Marilyn. His blood instantly went cold! There was a man walking in front of Marilyn's patio doors.

He went to shout for her to wake her but he knew
if he did he would alert the prowler. He hit the mute
button on his computer so she couldn't hear him. He
rushed to the phone and connected with the police
in Niteroi through the operator.

"My name is Dr. Allen Greenburg. I need a police
officer at 1189 Coastal Boulevard immediately!"

"And what is the problem sir?" the female dispatcher
asked.

Allen was panicking since he couldn't see the man
anymore.

"There's a prowler outside the window of my
girlfriend's house. I need for you to get the police there
right now!"

"Okay sir, but where are you calling from?"

"I'm calling you from New York City."

"Did your girlfriend tell you there's a prowler?"

"No, I can see him through my web camera on my
computer. She was getting disturbing phone calls from
her ex fiancée. I was worried about her so I made her
keep her web camera on. She's still sleeping and I'm
afraid to wake her because I don't know what the man
will do!"

"Okay sir," said the dispatcher. "I'll send someone
right away. What is your girlfriend's name?"

"Her name is Marilyn Louisa Andre."

The dispatcher paused for a moment.

"Isn't she engaged to a French attorney? Is this
some kind of prank?"

Just then Allen could see the man enter Marilyn's room. Allen had no choice but to scream to wake her. He hit the mute button off on his computer. "Marilyn, get up and run! There's someone in your room!"

Marilyn jumped out of her sleep and immediately saw the man standing over her bed. She screamed and then jumped out the other side and ran for the door.

Allen was frantic as he saw the man run after her and they both disappeared from the room. He could hear Marilyn screaming and things being broken all over the house. The man never uttered a word. Allen screamed out for her to get out of the house! His heart was pounding out of his chest as he listened to her terrifying screams!

"Get out of the house Marilyn and run! I called the police and they're on their way! They'll be there any second now! Marilyn, I love you!"

He screamed back into the phone to the dispatcher "Get someone there now!"

The dispatcher answered back, "They're on their way!"

Allen broke down into tears. He was trying to give Marilyn some hope knowing the police were on their way. Just then the police cars with sirens went racing up into the driveway.

Five police cars and ten policemen jumped out of their vehicles and broke down the front door and ran inside the house. Marilyn was on the floor in the kitchen looking like a broken doll curled up in a ball next to the refrigerator.

Two the policemen ran to her side and lifted her to her feet. The other police ran through the house while some went out to look outside. One officer helped her to the couch and one of the officer's went into the bedroom.

He looked around the room and saw Marilyn's computer. He walked up and sat down in front of it to talk to Allen on the computer.

"Your girlfriend is alright. She has a few minor scratches but she's going to be fine. It's good you called when you did. The dispatcher heard her screams and sent us right away. We're going to transfer her to the hospital to have her checked over and the hospital will probably give her a rape concoction just in case anything happened."

Allen was mortified to hear the word "rape!" Could he have raped her in that short time? Allen started to weep silently knowing he couldn't be there to comfort her.

"Take care of her until I get there."

The officer nodded to Allen and then left the room.

Allen got back on the computer and booked a flight to Rio de Janeiro."

# Chapter 25

Within thirteen hours, Allen got off the plane in Rio. He caught a few hours of sleep on the way. He rented a silver BMW and drove to the hospital. When he walked into her room she looked like she had been through a war.

As soon as she saw him it brought a big smile. Her eyes lit up and she jumped from her bed and threw her arms around his neck. He held her tight and kissed her neck and lips.

"I'm so happy to see you!" as she threw her arms around him again.

He hugged and kissed her and then pulled her gently away to look at her wounds.

"Where are you hurt?"

"I just have a few cuts and scratches on my legs and back."

"Do you have any idea what he wanted?"

"No he never said a word. He just kept walking towards me. He grabbed for me a few times but I got away. He didn't seem like he wanted to hurt me. I have no idea what he wanted?"

"I know what he wanted," blurted out Allen in a hatred voice. "He wanted to take you to Emmanuel. I called Emmanuel's office and got his voicemail. The recording said he would be gone until Thursday and to leave a message and he would return the call. He's in Rio. I know that man works for him and he was sent to get you!"

Marilyn was worried about Allen and how upset and angry he was.

"Allen, if it was him I'm sure by now he heard what happened. He would be too afraid to come near me now. I'm sure he and his men are on their way back to France."

Just as Allen was getting ready to say something the door opened and in walked Miguel.

Marilyn cried out, "Miguel, I can't believe you're here!" Then just as she uttered the words she knew why he had come.

He looked at her and Allen. "Are you alright?" as he hugged her.

"I'm fine. I just have a few scratches. How did you know what happened?"

"Allen contacted Yurah and he came and told me you were hurt. Allen arranged for me to get here on a chartered plane."

Marilyn looked at Allen.

Allen smiled at Marilyn. "How could I not tell him you were hurt?"

"Emmanuel is in Rio," Allen told Miguel. "I just know he had something to do with this."

"Yes, I know, and I'm going return him back to Paris dead or alive!"

Marilyn was worried that Allen and Miguel were going to do something to retaliate against Emmanuel. She didn't want to see them get into trouble. The law was very stringent in Rio and she didn't want them to get charged with anything.

Marilyn said, "First we don't know it was him. We need to be sure first."

Just then the doctor walked into the room. "You can go home now Ms. Andre," If you have any other problems just call me."

"Thank you," said Marilyn. Now will you both take me home?" as she grabbed onto each one of their arms.

When they walked into Marilyn's house, her things were broken in every room. Miguel and Allen looked at each other knowing the struggle Marilyn put up to save herself. Allen walked over to her and put his arms around her. "I'm so happy you're okay!" as he looked around the room.

Miguel stood just looking with sadness in his face as he observed what went on between the intruder and his sister. Marilyn could tell he was plotting out the events that happened.

Miguel walked into the kitchen and saw her blood on the floor. He shouted out loud, "I'm going to kill him! I'm going to kill whoever did this to you!"

Marilyn and Allen ran into the kitchen. Allen felt sick knowing what went on seeing her blood. She went to the sink and grabbed a rag and went to wipe the floor up. Miguel walked up to Marilyn to take the rag from her.

"I'm fine Miguel. I really am okay!" as she smiled at him.

"You're safe now, said Allen smiling at Marilyn.

Miguel looked at Marilyn and was very concerned for her life. He knew what Emmanuel and his men were capable of doing. He was beaten and kicked badly by Emmanuel and his hit man himself. He was drugged and beaten again so he couldn't fight back. He knew that Emmanuel had to be stopped!

Allen received a phone call from his secretary. He was needed to fly home to take care of a baby who was going through congestive heart failure in the hospital being born three months premature. He had been trying to save the baby for three months and she was doing quite well until she just took a turn for the worse. "I don't want to go but I have to get back to the hospital," said Allen. "I'll come back as soon as I can. Can you stay with her until then Miguel?"

"Yes, I'll stay until you get back."

Allen got into his rented BMW and waved good bye to Marilyn as she stood in the driveway with Miguel.

He started to head down Coastal Boulevard headed for the airport to catch his plane. It was dark and he drove along the winding coastal cliff that weaved downwards. A few minutes later a car came up behind him with the bright lights on. Allen adjusted his rear view mirror to night view and kept driving. All of a sudden his car was struck from behind! It forced his car to lunge forward and he almost skidded off the road.

"What the hell!" Allen shouted out loud.

He turned to look in the rear view mirror when he was struck again. It was a black Mercedes Benz. He slammed on his brakes to warn the driver to get off his bumper, and then the car struck him again! As the car hit him it came with a heavier force this time.

By now Allen knew the driver was trying to run him off the road. He was probably the same man who broke into Marilyn's house. Allen's blood was boiling with anger and contempt for the man. There was no shoulder of the road to pull over. One wrong move and he was going down the cliff and plunge into the rocks below!

The faster Allen sped up the faster he shifted from third into fourth, and then into fifth gear. The other car followed right behind him. All of a sudden the car sped up and pulled right up to the driver's side of Allen's car. Allen looked over to see a man wearing a beret and sunglasses. He could tell he was a large sized man but couldn't get a good look at his face.

The man slammed into Allen and broadsided him. Allen's back wheels flew over to the edge of the cliff almost going over, but he hit the gas and wound back up on the road. By now Allen was furious! Again the car slammed back into Allen and this time even harder.

Allen knew he was in big danger and the man was trying to kill him. He had to do whatever had to be done to stay on the road and fight for his life!

Allen slowed his car down quickly not giving the man any time to think about what happened. Then Allen placed the BMW right behind the man and sped up and slammed into the back of him.

Then Allen came to a dead stop! The man also hit his brakes, and then backing up as fast as he could he was getting ready to slam into the front of Allen's car. Then Allen hit the gas to the floor and sped forward and smashed into the back of the man's car!

Allen was stunned from the impact for a second. He then pushed the other car forward towards the cliff. The man hit his brakes to stop from hurling over the cliff, but it was too late! Allen could hear the man scream as his car went over the cliff and tumbled as it slammed into the rocks all the way down!

Then the car landed on its top and rocked back and forth a few seconds on the rocks fifty feet below. The man seemed to still be barely alive. He struggled very slowly to get out of the car and Allen could hear him as he tried to call for help. Just then the car exploded and there was one last scream!

Allen's heart was pounding out of his chest. He could hardly breathe. The experience sapped every inch of strength from his body. He heard sirens coming from the top of the hill. Three police cars pulled in behind Allen as he stood looking over the cliff at the car. It was the same police officer that Allen talked to on the computer. He ran to Allen's side and put his hand on his shoulder.

"Are you okay?"

"I'm fine. But I'm afraid he's not," as Allen looked on to the car burning on fire below. "How did you know I was in trouble?"

"We received a call from Marilyn. She told us she saw a car go down the boulevard right after you. She was afraid you were being followed. And she was right," frowned the officer.

The police officer drove Allen back to Marilyn's house. The BMW was totaled and towed away. Allen was on his cell phone in the police car to another pediatrician asking him to see after his baby patient.

Marilyn ran out the door when she saw Allen climb out of the back seat. He could tell she was crying. She ran and put her arms around his waist and laid her head on his chest.

"What's going on?" she cried out to him.

"Emmanuel is a ruthless son of a bitch who isn't going to stop until he gets what he wants. And that's not going to happen!" Allen said with vengeance in his voice.

They walked into the house and Marilyn went to the bar to pour everyone a Brandy.

"Where's Miguel?" asked Allen.

"He's here someplace." Then Marilyn looked around the house for him. But he was nowhere to be found. Marilyn thought the worst. And she was right. Miguel went to find Emmanuel.

Marilyn and Allen waited up for Miguel, and just about when they were about to fall asleep on the couch, Miguel knocked on the door to let him in.

Marilyn asked, "Miguel, where did you go?"

"I went to see someone."

"Who did you go see?"

"It's not important," he answered with a smile.

A few hours later there was a knock on the door and Miguel answered it.

"Are you Miguel Andre?"

"Yes I am."

"Can you come with me? My father sent me. My name is Jose Hernandez. You came to see my father today."

"Yes," said Miguel. Do you have any information where Emmanuel is?"

"I know where Emmanuel is staying. I have contacts in every hotel in Rio. He has some men with him. You need to be very careful! But we'll be backing you."

Allen jumped up! "I'm coming with you!"

"No!" said Miguel. "You need to stay here with Marilyn."

Allen knew he was right and stayed behind. He was very worried about her safety and knew that Emmanuel would do anything to revenge her. Marilyn was falling asleep in Allen's arms by now. He was totally exhausted himself. He had only a few hours of sleep in the last twenty-four hours. They both nodded off in each other's arms.

They were fast asleep arm in arm and on the sofa. Allen suddenly woke with something wrapping around his mouth. He then realized someone was gagging him. He was startled and tried to leap up but was hit by something from behind numbing his body.

He went to grab Marilyn but she was gone. He started to panic knowing someone had taken her. He started to feel anger at himself for falling asleep. The man from behind the couch grabbed him to his feet and tied his hands behind his back. Allen struggled to free himself but couldn't. The man was so much bigger and stronger.

Allen looked across the room and saw a man sitting in the dark in a corner chair. He kept his eyes on the man until his eyes could focus.

Then out of the corner of his eye he could see two people walking past him in the dark. It was Marilyn being led gagged and her hands tied behind her back as a man walked behind her. She looked at Allen as she passed him with fear in her eyes.

The man led Marilyn to the man sitting in the chair. It was Emmanuel.

Allen tried to jump up but was pushed back down on the couch. He looked over and Marilyn was standing about five feet in front of Emmanuel.

"*Bonjour Bébé*," said Emmanuel. Long time no see. How are you doing? Are you happy to see me?" he said with sarcasm in his voice. "And you thought I would just go away didn't you?"

Emmanuel waved his hand to the man holding on to Marilyn. He then took the gag off of Marilyn and untied her hands. He moved Marilyn right in front of Emmanuel while Emmanuel still sat in his chair.

"I thought after what happened in the garden and with my brother it was over between us Emmanuel. Why are you here?"

"I missed you," he said back laughing.

Allen watched on so angry he wanted to kill Emmanuel. He knew that Emmanuel would stop at nothing. He was afraid for Marilyn and yet he couldn't do anything to help her.

Emmanuel said to her, "*Viens ici mon amour*," in English means, "Come here my love."

As Marilyn tried to back away, Emmanuel grabbed her and threw her on his lap. She let out a cry and he covered her mouth with his hand.

"Now that would not be a good idea my *mon amour*. You don't want to bring any attention or I'll have to kill you and your lover."

Marilyn looked down at Emmanuel as he removed his hand off of her mouth.

"No Emmanuel, Allen and I are not lovers. You're mistaking!"

Marilyn feared for Allen's life. Emmanuel laughed at her.

"It's true Emmanuel. I swear to you he's not my lover!"

Marilyn tried to look back at Allen but Emmanuel grabbed her head and spun it back to look at him.

"Don't take your eyes off of me while I'm talking to you," Emmanuel continued to say with hatred in his voice.

She closed her eyes for a minute while tears welled up inside of them. She had never been so afraid of anyone in her life! Now she knew what he was capable of doing. She knew this wasn't going to have a good ending.

"Do you still love me?" He demanded her to answer.

She looked at him and lied, "Yes. Yes I still love you."

Her blood went cold saying the words but she knew that if she didn't play the game he would kill Allen and her. "I was mad at you Emmanuel. I was mad at you for what you did to my brother."

"I tried to tell you that I was sorry but you didn't listen!" Then he started to laugh.

Then Marilyn realized he was playing a game with her. He wasn't interested if Marilyn still loved him. He was there to finish Allen and her. She started to softly cry, not for herself but for Allen. She tried to look back at Allen again but Emmanuel grabbed her hair and pulled her face towards him with a harsh jolt.

"If you look at him again I'll kill you!"

Allen sat on the couch trying everything to stay composed. He knew if he showed any kind of aggression they would kill Marilyn, and him too. Emmanuel lifted Marilyn off of his lap. He got up and grabbed her hand.

*"Venir mon Amour,"* as he walked with her towards the bedroom. He said to the man in French, "We need some privacy. I'll call you when I'm done with her." He looked back at Allen and smiled, then led Marilyn crying to her room and shut the door.

Allen was weeping thinking what was going to happen to her. He heard her scream and being thrown all around the bedroom. Allen wanted to die for her. He tried to struggle out of the rope that tied his hands while the man laughed at him and watched on.

Then there was silence in the bedroom, and then a loud gunshot came from Marilyn's room and the man ran after Emmanuel into the bedroom with his gun pointing in front of him. Then many more bullets were fired. All of a sudden there was silence again.

Allen jumped up and ran to the bedroom door. Just when he was ready to kick it open the front door broke open and three other men ran in.

They ran to Allen and started to untie him. Allen didn't know what was going on. He didn't know if these men were with Emmanuel so tried to struggle from them. And then one man cried out! "It's alright, we're undercover police officers!"

The man held up his badge to show Allen. We have Marilyn and Miguel outside in one of our police cars.

Just then Marilyn ran back into the house and ran to Allen. He grabbed her in his arms and he cried as he held on to her for dear life!

"I'm so sorry Marilyn!" he cried out. "I couldn't help you. I'm so sorry!" He felt like he failed her.

She wiped his tears and said, "I know how you must have felt. I know you wanted to help me, and you did. You didn't do anything to provoke him. That's why I'm still alive! Nothing happened. The police shot through the windows and injured the man and took Emmanuel in a police car.

Miguel cut in, "They have Emmanuel in custody. Mr. Hernandez is an undercover police officer. He led his undercover unit here.

Mr. Hernandez smiled at Marilyn and Miguel. Then he walked up to Miguel and said, "My father told me years ago the story of being forced to take you to the rainforest. He didn't want to do it. If we would have been sent back to El Salvador, we would have all been beheaded. My father only did it to save our family. He is so happy to know you reunited with your sister again. If you need anything just come to see me or my father."

"Thank you, and thank your father for me," said Miguel. He shook Officer Hernandez' hand before he left.

Miguel stood at the door looking on at Marilyn and Allen happy to see them together. He was happy that Marilyn had someone in her life that loved her enough he would die for her. They were both taken to the hospital to be checked over and then released.

They all returned to Marilyn's pavilion. She looked around the house and realized she couldn't stay there anymore. There were too many bad memories in this house also, and as time went on it seemed that the palace started to feel like home again. She missed it and the memories she had of her family and friends, especially with Miguel still being alive. She also hoped that Miguel would return one day to marry and raise a family in the palace.

Marilyn and Miguel were sitting outside on the terrace having a coffee the next morning.

"Miguel, I want you to come to the palace with me. There's a big gala at the palace this Saturday. I was invited to come. It's still your home as much as it's mine."

"I'm not ready," said Miguel. "I still think about the day I was kidnapped. It still haunts me."

"I know," said Marilyn. "It must have been so hard for you. I cried for you every night. I drew pictures of us still playing in the garden and catching lightning bugs. And I used to pretend you were with me when I snuck up on the maids in the kitchen. They knew I pretended that you were with me and they would play along and say, "Miguel and Marilyn, what are you two up to?" They knew how lonely I was without you."

Miguel never really thought about how Marilyn must have felt when he was kidnapped. He was too young to analyze it. He felt sad knowing she was just as lost as he was.

He looked at her and said, "If it means that much to you then I'll go with you."

Marilyn was so elated she jumped up and threw her arms around his neck as he laughed at her. Just then Allen joined them on the terrace.

"Did I miss something?" Allen asked groggily while still wiping his eyes open.

"Yes!" shouted Marilyn excitedly! "Miguel is going to the gala at the palace with me!" She ran to Allen and threw a kiss on his cheek, and then ran to get ready for the day.

"Gee," Allen joked. "I thought I was invited!" as he smiled at Miguel. Miguel laughed at him. Then Allen laughed looking back over his shoulder watching her run with excitement. He was happy to see her so alive again. Allen sat down and poured himself a cup of coffee and then turned to Miguel and said, "She has you wrapped around her baby finger."

Miguel looked at Allen and countered, "Yes, and you're next!"

# Chapter 26

It was the Tuesday before the gala and Miguel returned to the garden to catch up on his research and prepare again for the weekend away from the garden. The natives were well trained in what had to be done in the pond while he was gone.

He returned to Marilyn's house on the Friday. Allen waited for Miguel to return before he would head back to New York. Marilyn took Allen to the airport and then returned to visit with Miguel.

Marilyn and Miguel were sitting on the terrace planning the gala event when the front door bell rang. Marilyn got up and opened the door. To her surprise Enesa stood there looking like she didn't know whether she was imposing or not.

"Enesa, come in!" Marilyn shouted with elation to see her. She ran to Enesa and threw her arms around her. When she squeezed her tight she felt a bulge in

Enesa's stomach she had never noticed before. She pulled away and looked down at Enesa's stomach.

Enesa looked up at Marilyn, "Yes, I'm going to have a baby."

Marilyn didn't know what to think for a minute.

"And it's Miguel's baby."

Marilyn took Enesa by the hand and brought her into the house. By then Miguel heard the commotion and walked inside and saw Enesa standing there. Enesa looked so surprised to see him!

"I'm sorry!" she reacted as she looked at Marilyn. "I didn't know anyone was here. I'll leave and come back another time," as she went to turn for the door.

"No, don't go!" Miguel pleaded to her. "You just got here. I'm so happy to see you!"

Enesa looked over again at Miguel. He smiled at her as he walked towards her.

"Hello Enesa," said Miguel. Miguel noticed she looked different. She was wearing a sun dress to her ankles with wedged heel sandals. He couldn't tell what it was. And then he walked up to her and she grabbed on to her stomach as he approached her.

He looked down and he could see the small round bulge on her stomach. At first he thought something was wrong with her, and then he realized she was carrying a baby. He paused for a minute just looking at her. She looked back at him not knowing what to say.

"Yes, I'm going to have a baby."

Marilyn just stood there looking at the both of them wondering how Miguel was going to react. Then he reached down and touched Enesa's stomach. "Is this my baby?"

She took Miguel's hand and placed it on her stomach over the baby and said, "Yes. He's your baby."

"He?" Miguel said back in surprise!

"Yes, he's a boy."

Miguel looked back down at her stomach with a big smile on his face. Then he looked back up at Enesa and pulled her into his arms, "I've missed you."

"I missed you too," as she broke into tears and held on to him like she never wanted to let go.

Marilyn stood watching at this miraculous moment she had so hoped to see someday. Never did she think it would have such a happy ending. Marilyn cried out, "This is wonderful! I'm going to be an aunt!"

Enesa was going to return to the garden with Miguel. She had lots of new research she had discovered through her new studies she took in Montreal. She and Miguel went back to her hotel and gathered her things to come to stay at Marilyn's.

After they returned back to Marilyn's, Marilyn took Miguel into town to be fitted for a tuxedo while Enesa rested.

"I can't wait to see you in a tuxedo!" Marilyn teased him. The women are going to be falling over you!"

He laughed at her and flattery. "And I'm sure you have turned some heads in Rio yourself," he commented jokingly to her.

"I've turned a few," she laughed back at him.

They walked inside of the tuxedo store and as soon as they walked in they were greeted by a saleswoman.

"Hello, my name is Sarah and I'll be assisting you today." She looked at Marilyn and then she turned to look at Miguel. "Your husband is such a big man. You're lucky we carry larger sizes."

"Oh no," said Marilyn. "He isn't my husband, he's my brother."

Then the woman returned her eyes on Miguel and smiled at him. "Oh really, well in that case I'm very happy to assist you," she said in a flirty voice.

Marilyn blushed for Miguel because he was clueless of what was going on. She knew that since Enesa came back he only had eyes for her and no one else. Miguel walked over and saw a little white tuxedo so small it would fit a baby. He laughed and looked over at Marilyn and said, "Someday my son will wear a suit like this!"

Marilyn smiled at him. He was already so proud to be a father. She walked over to him and said, "You're going to be a wonderful father."

He looked down at Marilyn, "I hope I'm a better father than our father was to us."

Marilyn realized Miguel had much animosity for their father and rightly so.

"Miguel, our father was raised differently. It was all about honor. We're not our parents. You'll be a great father. You'll teach him so much." Miguel grew quiet.

"What's wrong Miguel?"

He looked at her, "I don't want to raise my son in the Amazon. It's a hard life."

Marilyn could see Miguel was struggling for where he belonged. Being out of the rainforest and in civilization made him realize there was so much more to life. When Miguel was young he loved to travel. He would show Marilyn books of faraway places and tell her they would go there someday. But instead, his life was spent being hidden away. Away from society and everything he wanted to be.

"Miguel, you have spent your life in the Amazon, and you made a wonderful home for yourself. But it's time to come back. Back to the life you were born to live."

"I can't talk about this anymore," said Miguel, "Let's get the tuxedo and get out of here!"

Marilyn was in her room putting on her evening gown and make up. She brushed her hair after it was set in curlers. The dark curls fell passed her shoulders and down her back.

She wore a black sequence dress that was so tight she could hardly sit down in it. The dress was sleeveless and the back of it plunged down until it hit the small of her back. It had a slit up the side to the top of her left leg.

She wore black satin stiletto high heels and carried a white sequence cocktail purse and white faux fur stole over her dress. She had on black satin gloves that went to her elbows. She had on chandelier crystal earrings and matching necklace. She turned around in the mirror a few times quite proud of her accomplishments.

Miguel had left for a while with Enesa to do some shopping for the baby. When they returned Marilyn had to catch her breath. Miguel had cut his hair all off!

"I found a barber and had him trim my hair. What do you think?"

Marilyn laughed as this was no trim! The barber took all Miguel's hair off up to his ears. It was slicked back to expose his high cheek bones and chiseled face. His dark skin made him look like something out of a high fashion men's magazine.

After he got dressed, he looked absolutely spectacular in his black tuxedo, and she just knew as soon as he walked in every eye was going to be on him. Enesa was fixing his tie and looking so proud of how he looked.

Marilyn walked over to him and smiled. "You look so handsome Miguel. Just like a prince!"

He smiled at her, "And you my dear look like a Princess!"

They all laughed at the flattery and then Marilyn and Miguel headed outside where the black shiny limo was waiting. Miguel looked back at Enesa standing in the doorway throwing him a kiss with her protruding tummy. She never looked as beautiful to him as she did that day!

When they pulled up in front of the palace, Miguel's eyes widened. He looked out the limo window at the palace he once called home. It was exactly the way he remembered it. He could see inside the large chandelier that hung in the middle of the grand foyer.

"We're here," said Marilyn as she smiled at Miguel. The door of the limo opened and the chauffer reached in to help Marilyn out.

"Sir, can I help you out?" asked the chauffer.

Then Miguel climbed out of the seat and stood next to the chauffer who was a foot shorter than Miguel. Miguel smiled and said looking down at him, "No, it's okay. I think I can handle it," as he patted him on the shoulder.

Miguel took Marilyn by the arm and started walking her up the twelve step grand entranceway into the palace. Large floral pots lined the concrete staircase going up.

Miguel looked at Marilyn and commented, "Nothing has changed since I left," as he smiled at her.

As they were walking up the staircase a woman came up to Marilyn and asked, "Are you Marilyn Louisa Andre?"

Marilyn smiled at her and said, "Yes I am, can I help you?"

The lady smiled back and then looked at Miguel admiring his tall dark handsome looks. "Ms. Andre, my name is Lara Perez from the Rio de Janeiro Historical Society. You and your guest are our guest of honor this evening. Would you come with me so I can sit you at the royal table for dinner?"

"Thank you," said Marilyn as she looked up and winked at Miguel.

She led them up the stairs and into the grand foyer of the palace. Miguel's eyes looked all around as he turned in a circle.

Miguel remembered the large grand foyer with the black marble floor and crystal chandelier. Marilyn and he used to run into the palace skidding across the floor before running up the staircase to their rooms.

"Mother kept it exactly the way it was when we were kids," said Marilyn. I stipulated in the rental agreement that the grounds had to be maintained exactly in its original state."

"Not only are you a beautiful woman, but you're a smart one too."

Marilyn laughed.

People were starting to enter the foyer and valets were scurrying around to take peoples coats. After about twenty minutes everyone was led into the State Room. Marilyn and Miguel were led in first. It was a large grand room that their parents used to entertain in.

The State Room was large enough to hold three hundred people. The color of the room was oxen blood red with Mahogany trim. In the middle of the room hung a beautiful large chandelier that was the highlight of the room. Large pillars anchored the dome ceiling all around the room. Patio doors lined the exterior wall that gave a panoramic view of the garden.

Round tables were set throughout the room with white tablecloths. The chairs had white toppers with red bows that tied at the back. The tables were set with white china, polished silverware, red napkins and gold edged wine and water glasses. In the middle of each table was a bouquet of red roses with white Baby's Breath set in crystal vases.

There was a podium set up in the front of the room, so Marilyn knew there was going to be a guest speaker. She didn't know too much about the gala and the invitation. It only read that she and a guest were invited to attend a Gala at the Andre Palace, with the date, and it was going to be a black tie event. She was going to try to find out more but with everything going on in her life she didn't have any time to find out.

Miguel excused himself from Marilyn and told her he would be back in a few minutes. The caterers walked around the room with platters of appetizers and glasses of champagne. Marilyn was hoping Miguel would make it back in time to sample some of the wonderful food and mingle before they sat down for dinner. She wanted him to enjoy the evening and feel part of the festivities.

All of a sudden there was a commotion coming from the hallway and people were starting to gather around the door. Marilyn knew something was wrong and excused herself through the crowd and stood at the entranceway looking up the balcony stairs. Miguel was standing at the top with three men in white tuxedos standing around him.

"Excuse me sir!" One man shouted. "You cannot come up here! This area is off limits!"

Miguel stood there somewhat embarrassed that he drew a crowd.

"I'm sorry," said Miguel. "I wasn't going to do anything. I just wanted to take a look to see if everything was still the same."

Just as Miguel uttered the words he realized what he said. The men looked at him confused. "I mean I just wanted to take a look."

Marilyn knew that Miguel yearned to see the palace. He wanted to revisit his childhood and there wasn't anything wrong with what he wanted to do. The problem was no one in the room knew who he was.

"Excuse me gentlemen!" Marilyn said as she made her way to the grand foyer to look up at the men. "I'm Marilyn Louisa Andre," she yelled up at them. "I'm the guest of honor here tonight and my father was Henry Luis Andre. If you don't mind I would like to give my guest a personal tour of the palace."

She climbed the stairs to meet Miguel at the top. The three men let Marilyn through and apologized to Miguel for the intrusion. Everyone stood below watching Marilyn and Miguel as they walked down the balcony hallway, and then everyone returned back into the State Room. Miguel and Marilyn laughed at everyone's attention.

"I think they were getting ready for a fist fight," Miguel laughed.

"And they almost got one if those men wouldn't have cooperated," said Marilyn.

Miguel laughed again at Marilyn. "You haven't changed a bit. You're still the spitfire you used to be!"

Marilyn and Miguel walked through the second floor of the palace. He stopped at his parent's room and opened the door. The large king size bed with the red velvet blanket was still on the bed. Miguel marveled at how the palace hadn't changed a bit. He thought when he returned everything would be different.

"Father didn't like change," said Marilyn. "Mother wanted to update the decor but father always fought and resisted her. Father always insisted, "It's home to me and it's going to stay this way!" She said in voice mimicking her father.

Miguel laughed!

"Christmas was the same way. He hung all of our stockings, including yours on the fireplace in the family room. He had everything the same way on the Christmas tree every single year. Mother would roll her eyes for it looked outdated. Mother always wanted to add some new decor but father wouldn't let her. Mother was very fussy and kept everything like it was brand new. That's why everything is the same."

Miguel remembered his father always having the last word. He was stubborn and he always won.

Then Miguel came to his own room and opened the door. He walked in and felt like he had never left. Everything sat exactly the same as the day Miguel was taken. All his toys, furniture and shift robe were exactly the same. His green slippers sat at the side of his bed and his green plaid robe lay at the foot of the bed. His library of books he loved to read were still on the shelves exactly how he had them. He knew exactly where every one of his books were. He walked over and took a book from the shelf. It was a book called "In the Night." It was about a young man who snuck out of his house one night and had the journey of his life. His mother read the book over and over to him.

He had lots of toys but his favorite was a stuffed monkey that was made out of a grey wool sock that Trinity had made him for his fourth birthday. She sewed two black button eyes and the red heel of the sock was the monkey's mouth. It had two arms and legs made out of the same material. He slept with it every night. It felt nice and soft and warm on his cheek as he laid on it while he went to sleep.

Marilyn had one exactly like it only hers had yellow yarn for hair for a girl. He sat down on the edge of his bed and picked the monkey up touching it softly and stared at it. He took in everything that he remembered about his childhood.

"How are you feeling about seeing all this?" asked Marilyn.

He looked into her eyes and said, "I thought returning here it would bring back a lot of bad memories. But the only bad memory I really have is the night I was kidnapped. I feel like I have never left. It's still home to me."

Marilyn's eyes welled up with tears. "It's still your home Miguel. It will always be your home. Father didn't take you into the Amazon because he didn't love you. He suffered tremendously after you were gone. And I know he went back and tried to find you. When he realized how he failed you." Marilyn paused for a few seconds. "It killed him inside. He couldn't live with what he did, and neither could mother."

"Mother?" said Miguel. "Mother died of dementia."

"No Miguel," said Marilyn. "She had dementia, but that's not what killed her."

"Then what did she die from?"

"Mother shot herself in the head."

Miguel jumped up from the bed. "Please Marilyn, don't tell me that!"

"I'm sorry to tell you Miguel, but it's true. And just before she shot herself she turned to me and said, "Go to find Miguel."

"You were there when mother shot herself?"

She looked down at the floor. "Yes, I was there."

Miguel pulled Marilyn up off the bed and put his arms around her.

"It's okay. I cried for months. And after everything happened in the palace, I just couldn't live here anymore. I didn't want to sell it since I also still hung on to the good memories. I kept it in memory of you."

Miguel knew that talking about everything was bringing back bad memories for Marilyn. He respected her for how strong she was and all she had to handle on her own. He looked at the door and said, "Let's get out of here. We have a gala to attend!"

They walked back downstairs and into the State Room. Everyone was having a great evening admiring all the beautiful evening gowns and listening to the orchestra playing. Everyone was sipping champagne and feasting on the appetizers. As Miguel entered the room people were turning around and looking at him as he heard someone say, "He looks familiar, where do we know him from?" They could hear people whisper as he walked by them. Some people moved out of his way as he walked through.

Then Lara who approached them outside walked up to the podium and spoke into the microphone, "Everyone may I have your attention!" Everyone turned towards her and stopped talking.

"We're going to be seated for dinner in a few minutes, but first we have a very special guest speaker tonight. He got here a bit late so we are sorry for making you wait. He's the brother of Henry Luis Andre and he has come from Portugal to share with us this evening about the Andre royal family. He's going to tell us a little about the Andre Palace and its history."

Marilyn's mouth dropped open! She had not seen her uncle since she was twelve years old when he and her father had a falling out. Her uncle argued with her father about the estate of the Andre family.

Henry was the oldest son of three boys and was the executor of their parent's estate. Alfred felt his brother Henry was taking liberties of the money and shares in the royal family. There was no truth to the accusations but Alfred was a gambler and always had his hands out for money.

Henry used to say his brother Alfred was getting desperate, and because he was desperate, he started to use desperate measures. It got to be so bad that Henry decided when their parents died and split the estate that Alfred could only be given an allowance each month or he would gamble the whole amount away.

Alfred was very jaded about the arrangement. It made him live a very humble life since he never got the whole one and a half million dollars at once which was his portion of the estate.

Seeing her uncle was a sheer surprise to her. As he walked up to the podium she could tell he had not been kind to himself over the years. His face had leathered and he looked as if he had drunk his life away.

He cleared his voice then spoke, "Thank you all for coming to the gala this evening. My name is Alfred Philip Andre and my brother was Henry Luis Andre. Henry would have been truly honored to have you here this evening."

Marilyn could tell he was working the room with his eyes. In his days he was very handsome, and he had many women who fell for his cunning charm. Then he would use them to get what he wanted for gambling money. She could tell he hadn't changed and was still looking for a hand out.

"As you know my brother and I are descendants of King Luis the First, who was King of Portugal between 1861 and 1889. My brother's middle name was Luis named after the king. His full name was the Henry Luis Andre.

My brother was loved and respected as a savvy manufacturer of textiles. He employed hundreds of people and had great friends and colleagues. When his business became very successful, he and his wife Louisa bought the palace from a Spanish business colleague who returned to Spain with his family.

Henry and Louisa bought it and spent years restoring the palace. Within a few years their twin children, daughter Marilyn Louisa and their son, Miguel Henry were born.

My brother's life changed when his son Miguel was kidnapped at the age of six and found dead three weeks later in the woods behind the palace . . . right out there!"

He pointed out the large patio windows and everyone gasped and whispered back and forth as they looked out the windows and into the woods.

"He never really recovered from the loss of his son. Within ten years he sold his textile company and became very reclusive."

Marilyn was furious when she heard Alfred talking about her father, and Miguel's kidnap and death. She knew he was trying to profit from the family pain and she was angry with him as he continued to talk and pretended he was there for his brother through the whole tragedy. She had to stop him before he discredited her family. Marilyn shouted out from the middle of the crowd. "And what's the name of the cemetery your brother is buried in?"

Everyone turned around to look at Marilyn then they turned back to look at Alfred waiting for him to answer. Alfred heard the voice and was stretching his neck up to look inside the crowd to see who was talking.

"I . . ." he stuttered" I don't remember?"

The voice came closer and closer to him while Marilyn walked through the crowd, "He's buried in Francis De Paula Cemetery!" Then she walked out of the crowd and stood in front of him.

He was shocked to see Marilyn there!

"You never even attended your own brother's funeral and yet you stand there talking about him like you knew what happened in his life! You don't know anything about my father!" she fired at him.

"Hello Marilyn," he stuttered. "How nice it is to see you. I thought you sold the palace?"

"I didn't sell it!" I will never sell it!" she reacted back sharply.

"Then I was misinformed," said Alfred.

Lara walked back up to the podium and nervously spoke into the microphone embarrassed of the confusion. "Mr. Andre, I didn't say that Ms. Andre sold us the palace. I just informed you that the city had taken it over as a historical landmark for the city of Rio de Janeiro. I just assumed you knew she still owned it!"

Alfred looked embarrassed also. "Well, I guess since my niece is here, she can tell you all about the royal Andre family and the history of the palace. It was nice to see you my dear," as he looked at Marilyn.

He excused himself and started to walk out of the room to leave. Just as he passed Miguel he looked up at him and said "Excuse me sir, I just want to get through here."

Miguel moved out of his way. Then just behind Miguel, Alfred stopped cold! He turned around and backed up to look at Miguel staring into his face. He stared at him for a few seconds while he narrowed his eyes at him, and then he turned and looked across the room as Marilyn still stood at the podium. Then he walked back up to her, "And let's hear the real story my dear Marilyn!"

Marilyn looked at him with contempt. She knew he recognized Miguel. She couldn't figure out what he was thinking but he stood there looking back at Miguel with a smile on his face. He knew he had her on the spot. She didn't say a word. She was afraid her uncle was going to expose the family secret.

"We're waiting!" as he pressured her to talk.

Marilyn looked up at her uncle with a long deep hatred stare. Then she leaned into the microphone and quietly said, "Ladies and gentlemen, my family suffered a lot of pain, especially my father. He was a very honorable man. He did everything he could to honor the family name and to protect the royal family's reputation. But my father was of the old school, and he believed that sometimes you had to suffer a loss to do what was right to protect the family. But what my father thought was right finally destroyed him. He and my mother were very much in love. My mother never questioned what my father did. She was a very loyal woman."

People looked on and smiled as she talked so eloquently. Miguel moved in front of her for moral support. She looked into his eyes knowing that any minute the secret would be out. She put her head down as tears filled her eyes. Her uncle was now staring right at Miguel with his arms folded in front of him.

Miguel was certain he was basking in the pleasure of putting Marilyn on the spot. Miguel couldn't stand seeing her in pain anymore so he walked up to her and pulled her away from the microphone, "This is enough!" Then he turned and looked at his uncle. "You know who I am! You came here to exploit our family and you're not going to get away with it!"

His uncle just looked at him.

"Ladies and gentlemen, my name is Miguel Henry Andre!"

The whole room when silent for a few seconds, and then everyone gasped! Everyone just stared at him. Then people turned to each other and started to talk. He could hear people saying, "I heard it was all a hoax."

"They did it for the money!"

He heard a group of people talking, "The kidnap was a scam!"

Miguel shouted out, "No! I was taken and raised in the Amazon! I never saw my parents or my sister again!"

Everyone stopped talking and turned to listen to Miguel speak.

"When I was born, I was born with a malformation, and even though my parents had it corrected they were still out casted by other families and friends.

My father was losing business and the family name was suffering. My father was losing the palace when he sent me to the rainforest to be raised by a wonderful woman by the name of Ana. He knew it was best for my mother and my sister so they could have the life they were accustomed to.

I was too young to understand then, but now I don't hate him for what he did. He did it out of honor. He didn't have me killed as he could have. Instead he gave me a different life. A good life! I was loved by my caretaker, but my father couldn't live with himself and what he did. He even tried to find me, but it was too late. It eventually killed him. And my mother, my poor mother eventually shot herself in the head in front of my sister!"

Everyone in the room gasped!

"No, there was no profit here. It was a complete tragedy to my parents, my sister and to me. And it was all in the name of honor!"

People stood quietly in disbelief. Some people started to cry as they heard the horrible truth. Their hearts went out to Marilyn and Miguel for what they went through. Photographers who attended the gala ran up and started snapping pictures of him.

Miguel walked from the podium to Marilyn. He took her through the crowd of people while photographers took pictures of them as they walked outside and down the stairs. Miguel put Marilyn into the limo as she cried in his arms. Lights were flashing at them from the windows of the limo.

He said to her, "Marilyn, the pain is over. It's no secret anymore. Now we are free."

She looked up at Miguel, "Yes, you and I and mother and father are free!"

# Chapter 27

Miguel and Enesa returned to the Garden the next day and Marilyn called Allen that night to tell him how much she missed him and what happened at the gala.

He was happy to hear that the truth was out and she didn't have to bottle up any secrets and family skeletons anymore. He told her he had some good news for her too.

"Guess what! Alex is pregnant!"

"Are you serious?" she cried out with elation! "How far along is she?"

"They think a few months or so. They think it happened on their honeymoon."

They both laughed!

"I would like for you to come to New York next month. Can you get away?"

"Yes, I think I can. I have an art gallery I would like to visit there also."

"Great babe, I can't wait to see you."

"I can't wait to see you either. It seems empty around here now that you and Miguel have left."

"I'm here anytime you want to talk. I'll call you tomorrow. Good night and I love you!" as he hung up the phone.

When she left for New York and landed at La Guardia Airport, Allen met her at the terminal. They were both so happy to see each other. It seemed like months to one another. Each time they were together it got harder to say good bye.

She arrived on Friday morning and planned to fly back out on Monday afternoon. They met up with Michael, Alex, Quinn and Catherine for dinner at the country club. Everyone was so happy to see her.

Marilyn patted Alex on her stomach as soon as she saw her. "I think I can feel something."

Alex laughed. "I think it's a boy!" said Alex excitedly!

"I'm so happy for you, he'll have a playmate with Miguel's son!"

They sat and talked and Marilyn marveled at how well Michael looked. She couldn't believe he was the same man that she met at Miguel's.

"I would like to propose a toast!" boasted Allen. "To all my very close friends and my beautiful soon to be wife, thank you for having dinner with us tonight. Cheers!" He took a sip of his wine and placed it on the table. Everyone laughed at him.

"Well, don't you think you're being a little presumptuous?" said Quinn, "You haven't even asked Marilyn to marry you yet!"

Allen looked at Quinn, "I haven't? Well, I guess I better do it right now!" Allen reached into his jacket to his shirt pocket and pulled out a little black box and placed it on the table in front of Marilyn.

Marilyn froze when she saw the box in front of her. She looked at Allen as everyone sat around the table and smiled at her.

She picked it up and slowly opened it. Inside the box sat a beautiful platinum two and a half karat round solitude diamond ring in a cathedral setting.

She gasped when she saw just how beautiful it was! Her eyes filled with tears of happiness as she slipped it onto her finger.

"It's so beautiful!" as she looked into Allen's eyes.

"Just like you," Allen smiled. "Marilyn, will you marry me?"

Marilyn got up and kissed Allen on the lips. "Yes, I will marry you, I would be very happy to be Mrs. Allen Greenburg."

The whole table smiled and clapped their hands. Before they knew it everyone in the country club joined in.

That night they arrived at Allen's house. He parked the car in the large driveway in back of the brownstone he bought on 70th West and 69th Street in Manhattan. He occupied the main living space of the brownstone which featured 2,000 sq. ft. on the main level with commercial space on the ground floor, and two bachelor apartments on the third level that he had rented out to interns.

Allen's main floor studio had a kitchen and living room that was open concept with oak hardwood floors throughout. His kitchen was state of the art and featured stainless steel appliances and black granite countertops, and metal bar stools and granite counter that separated the kitchen from the living room.

The living room had a black leather sofa and chair with a red leather love seat with white and black suede pillows. In the middle sat a glass and black marble coffee table with a white soapstone statue of the Twin World Trade Centers. At the base of the sculpture it was etched "World Center Nine Eleven." There was a large 62 inch flat screen TV above a large black marble gas fireplace in the middle of the room.

"You did a beautiful job remodeling your home," Marilyn said looking around.

He smiled at her. "Thank you honey, I'm glad you like it." I want you to be comfortable. It's going to be your home too, and once you move in we can decorate to your taste too," as he poured them both a glass of Beaujolais.

She moved around the room admiring his art collection. "You told me you collected art. I love your collection," as she admired a set of Honoré Daumier collection he had on the east wall of the room.

"Yes, I do too. It all started with my grandfather, Allen Greenberg who I was named after. He had these in his library. When he became successful in the jewelry business, he invested some of his money in art pieces."

"Your grandfather had good taste," she commented as she smiled at him.

"He would have loved you," Allen said as he put his arm around her waist. "Come with me and bring your glass of wine. I want to show you around."

She followed Allen down a hall to an office on the right. It was also state of the art and had another leather black couch and oak desk with a computer. She could tell when he was in his office it was all business for there wasn't much in it.

At the end of the hallway was an oak double door that led to the master bedroom. The walls were painted a soft taupe grey with one red brick original wall that ran down the outside of the length of the room. In the left corner was an oak gas fireplace.

On the wall facing the bed was another 42" flat screen TV. The bed was king size and it had a full white down duvet with black, red, grey and white striped sheets, and two oak end tables with pewter lamps on each one. A large matted white rug lay at the foot of the bed with a black leather bench on an angle on top of it.

Off of the bedroom was a large en suite bath with black porcelain tile flooring, black marble countertops with oak vanity and two black under mounted round sinks with pewter faucets.

There was a block glass walk in shower with white tiles, a built in black bathtub, and a white toilet and bidet. On the wall was a metal rack with a stack of white towels with black, red and grey striped hand towels and washcloths.

Off the other side of the bedroom was a huge 10' by 10' walk in closet. His bedroom was very masculine and she could see there was no thought of a woman being in his life when he designed it.

"Is this the only bedroom there is?"

"Yes, unless you want to sleep in the walk in closet I made from one of the smaller bedrooms."

Marilyn laughed! "I guess you weren't planning to have any company."

"No, I had no plans at all. Funny how things change," he said with a smile.

"Speaking of change," Marilyn said as she stared into his chest looking at his heart. "What about Stephanie?"

Allen grabbed Marilyn's hand and walked her back out and sat on the couch in the living room. He turned to look right into her eyes. "Stephanie is gone."

"But I thought you still loved her?"

"I do, but in a spiritual way now. It's different. It has been different since you came into my life."

"How is it different?"

"It's different because you're here and you fill my heart and soul with the love that I need now in my life. I can't lie; I did love her with all my heart. But that was years ago. And you're the present. I had no one in my life so I had nothing to replace her with. But you're the woman I love now."

Marilyn was happy that they talked about Stephanie. She understood what he meant. You can't go back and change the past. You have to live for today and tomorrow. Marilyn understood that more than anyone.

"And when I asked you to marry me I knew what I was doing. This is what I want. I want to spend the rest of my life with you."

"I want to spend the rest of my life with you too," Marilyn smiled. "But we have lots to work out yet."

He laughed at her. "You're really putting me through the test aren't you?"

She laughed at herself and how careful she was being.

"Well, I just want to make sure this is truly what you want."

"This is what I want Marilyn, and I want to make you happy. I want to open a gallery for you here in Manhattan, and you can go back to visit Miguel anytime you want."

She smiled. "You're always there for me Allen. I love you so much!"

Allen smiled as she kissed him softly on his lips.

"I want you to be happy. I know I'm asking a lot of you to move to New York, and I want the transition to be easy for you. So whatever you want, It's yours!"

That night Allen drew a hot bath for Marilyn. He filled it with bubble bath and put a bottle of white wine and some fruit, cheese and crackers on a fold up table so she could just relax.

He lit candles all around the bathtub. She had a nine hour nonstop trip from Rio to New York and he knew she was tired. She went into the bathroom and got undressed and got into the nice hot bath.

"Oh this is so wonderful Allen, thank you."

He came to the door as she poured water on her shoulders and back. He walked into the bathroom and took an exfoliating sponge and ran it down her back. Her body tingled from his touch.

"Would you like to join me?" Marilyn asked as she poured them each a glass of wine.

"I would love to," as he smiled at her while removing his watch from his wrist. Allen pulled his pullover sweater, tee shirt and socks off and then he let his jeans drop to the floor. He then removed his boxer briefs and stood there naked grabbing another washcloth and towel from the towel rack.

Marilyn looked at his body while he reached for the towel and she was impressed how he took care of his body. She already knew he was a runner and loved to spin and ride his mountain bike. But she could tell he did some weight lifting too.

"You take good care of yourself," she smiled at him as he got into the bathtub.

"And so do you," as he could see her naked body through the bubbles and water.

Allen got into the bathtub and pulled her body up on top of him as he kissed her neck and worked down to her breast. She moaned into his ear as he massaged her with some oil and soap on his hands.

He was ready to go inside of her. He pulled her up higher on his body. They both moaned from the pleasure of each other.

"I waited so long to do this," as he tried to catch his breath.

She moaned again and whispered "I love you" softly in his ear.

He pulled her harder and harder down on him, until a few minutes later she gave a large moan and sigh as her body tightened around him, and then he felt her go limp in his arms.

He then pushed himself deep inside of her for many more minutes lost in his pleasure for her. He then grabbed her tight and let out a large moan still holding onto her.

They both went quiet for a few minutes while they both stayed in each other's arms. Then Allen looked into Marilyn's eyes and said, "Baby, we're going to have a good life together."

The next day Allen took Marilyn downstairs to the main floor to see the area where he wanted her to set up her art gallery. Many people walked and drove by there every day on their way to work so it was the perfect location.

There were quite a few other businesses around like boutiques, salons, furniture stores, cafe's, restaurants, business establishments and law firms. Allen's practice was also just around the corner which was walking distance for him.

As soon as she walked in the front door she fell in love with the space. She thought it was a perfect size for an art gallery. The room was 50 by 50 feet wide which gave her 2,500 square feet of space to display her art collections. The ceiling was 14 feet high which gave it a glandular feeling then it actually was. She turned to Allen, "Are you sure you want me to have this space?"

"I sure am! It's all yours," as he smiled at her.

She walked around the room to see what she would do to turn it into a gallery. It had all the elements she needed other than it needed decorating and finishing touches. "I'll take it!" she shouted.

Allen laughed. "Then let's get started! But first we need to get some other dates taken care of first."

"And what date would that be?" she smiled at him knowing what he was talking about. She walked over to him and put her arms around his waist. "And do you have a date in mind?"

"Yes, as soon as possible," as he smiled at her.

"Okay!" Marilyn said with excitement!

"We'll get married in two months from today." The date will be August 16th."

Marilyn thought for a minute. "That sounds perfect. And where should we get married?"

"I think we should get married in Rio."

She was happy to hear he wanted to return to Rio. "That would be wonderful, but where?"

"Well, I was thinking it would be nice to get married on the beach."

"It's always been my dream to get married on the beach. There's a beautiful spot right below my pavilion, and we can have the reception following right after the wedding on the terrace."

Allen smiled, "I'll let you choose what kind of reception you want to have. I'm sure it will be beautiful!"

But there is one thing I would like to request," Allen added. "I would like to take a week's honeymoon vacation in Tuscany where my mother grew up. My parents still have the family farm and it is a beautiful place where we can spend some quality time together.

Marilyn just knew that Allen was so perfect for her. She already felt like they had been together forever. She looked into eyes, "That sounds like the perfect honeymoon to me!"

# Chapter 28

Marilyn headed back to Rio on the following Monday. She took a canvas painting back with her that she knew she could sell to an art gallery in Rio. She knew she could make a profit of at least twenty-thousand dollars on it.

She was going to love living in New York although she hated the fact that she was leaving Miguel again. But she knew he had his own life now. And now that he and Enesa were back together and having a baby, he would have his own life to tend to.

Miguel didn't have a phone and Marilyn didn't have any way of getting a hold of him. Miguel went into Chapada from time to time to get supplies. He promised her that the next time he went there he would call her from town.

Miguel didn't know she was engaged to Allen yet and about the wedding. She hoped he would call soon so she could arrange for him to come to the wedding and give her away. She was excited because by then the baby would be born. He promised her he would call as soon as he arrived.

As she walked in she started to feel uncomfortable. She never really thought about how she would feel returning to the pavilion after all that happened. She tried to block it from her mind but she couldn't get the memories out of her head. She poured a glass of Chamomile tea to try to relax.

She walked out onto the terrace and took a deep breath in. Then she closed her eyes for a few seconds smelling the fresh air from the garden and fresh mountain air. She had a beautiful high view and she could see all the sailboats waving on the water.

Then she started to feel at home again and thought about leaving this and it made her feel sad. But she loved Allen and knew she would get used to living in New York once she was settled in and her gallery was open. She thought about what she was going to do with the gallery. She started looking through some magazines for some ideas.

As she kept her mind occupied on Allen and the gallery it eased her mind of all the bad things that happened in the pavilion. And even though she loved it here it was never going to be the same again. Change for her was going to be a good thing, and she knew that Allen and she would return a few times a year to visit Miguel and enjoy the sandy beaches of Rio.

A few days later Marilyn was feeling at home again. The first night was the worst but Allen and she had the web camera on so she felt safe. The second night was much easier for her since everything seemed to be back to normal.

Then the phone rang and she just had a feeling it was going to be Miguel.

Marilyn excitedly picked the receiver up, "Am I an aunt yet?"

Miguel laughed, "Yes! You're an aunt! Cole was born eight pounds and five ounces the day before yesterday."

"I'm so happy!" Marilyn cried out! "How is Enesa doing?"

"She's doing great! She had him in two hours of going into labor and no complications. She was out of bed four hours after giving birth. She already had Cole outside in the garden. I think she loves him more than me."

Marilyn laughed. "I'm so happy for you both!"

"Thanks Aunt Marilyn, he said back laughing.

"Well, I have something to tell you too."

He laughed again, "Okay, what is it?"

"Allen and I are getting married!"

"Hurray!" Miguel shouted laughing. "I could see he really loves you Marilyn. He'll make you happy."

"I know Miguel, and I love him too. I just want to let you know that we're getting married in Niteroi on the beach just below my pavilion, and then a reception to follow on my pavilion terrace. And I need to ask you a favor."

"Anything, What is it?"

"I need for you to give me away."

The phone went silent for few seconds. "Then Miguel said, "I would love to give you away at your wedding. I'll be there no matter what! It's kind of sad to think that already I have to hand you over to another man, but I'm happy for you. And Allen will be a great brother in law and uncle to Cole."

Marilyn got choked up knowing that Miguel was feeling just a bit sad. He just got her back into his life and now she's leaving again.

"Miguel, I'm going to be living in New York."

The phone went silent again. "Well, I kind of figured that out when you told me you were getting married. I just want you to be happy and you have to follow your heart. I have a busy life now too. And no matter where we are, we will always be in each other's hearts."

Marilyn's eyes filled with tears. She reached down and touched the pendant with the picture of them in it. She never took it off since he gave it to her. "Yes Miguel, we will always be in each other's hearts. No matter how far!

"Allen and I are getting married on Saturday, August 16th. I would like to see you, Enesa, and Cole arrive on Friday, August 15th. Is that going to be okay with you? We will have a dinner reception for the wedding party that night."

"That's fine with me, and I can't wait for you to meet Cole!"

She smiled and said, "I can't wait either! I love you Miguel, and we'll see you soon!"

Marilyn called Allen and told him that Cole was born and everyone was doing well.

He was very happy to hear the news.

He also told her that everything was arranged with Michael, Alex, Quinn and Catherine.

Marilyn thought to herself, it was going to be such a beautiful wedding!"

Marilyn was busy getting the wedding plans together. She invited about fifty people who were long time friends of the family. She told Allen to invite whoever he wanted to invite. He told her that his parents were also flying in the day before the wedding. She couldn't wait to meet Rita and Avi.

Allen flew in two weeks later to stay with Marilyn for three days. He couldn't wait to see her and they had to meet with Marilyn's family priest to go over the wedding ceremony with him.

He would also brief them on their wedding vows and make sure this is what they truly wanted and understood the commitment involved with marriage.

They met him at the pavilion and he talked to the both of them about their relationship. Father Andrade then wanted to talk to Marilyn alone and Allen excused himself from the room and went out on the terrace to make a phone call to his secretary.

"Marilyn," said Father Andrade, "You have been through a lot over the last year. Are you sure you're ready for marriage?"

"Yes," said Marilyn. "I'm absolutely positive! I love Allen with all of my heart."

"But you just got over Emmanuel. I'm not so sure you're ready for this level of commitment."

"I know what you're saying Father, but I'm not so sure I really loved Emmanuel. He was there during some dark times in my life. But he gave me a false sense of security. He's a bad man, and thank God I learned what he was about before I married him. My life would have been a disaster!"

"Yes," said Father Andrade, "I do think it would have been a mistake. But why do you think now it is true love with Allen?"

"We have had so many experiences together in such a very short time. We haven't really seen the best of times yet. But no matter what we're still together and my love grows stronger and stronger for him. He was there for me every step of the way with Emmanuel. And he's the reason why Miguel and I are reunited. I know we're perfect for each other."

Father Andrade smiled at Marilyn. "I think you're right Marilyn. I don't ever remember you being so happy. You have had many tragedies in your life. I just want to make sure there will not be any more. I will marry you and Allen. It will be a perfect ceremony," as he patted her on the hand.

He got up and walked outside to Allen, "Allen, I will see you at the wedding practice the Friday before the wedding. You have a wonderful woman in your life. I give you my blessings!"

It was the day before the wedding and Allen, his parents, Michael, Alex, Quinn and Catherine all arrived together. Marilyn picked them up at the airport in a limousine and then took them right to the pavilion where she had a dinner party catered in her home garden. The Terracotta patio was edged with a continuous garden of mixed flowers and tall Royal palm trees throughout. There was a man made pond with water lilies and large goldfish that swam and made the lilies move through the water.

There was a built in stone fireplace and grill that the caterers were using to prepare the food. The table was set up in a "u" shape and sat in the middle of the garden. It had fresh flowers in white vases along the length of the tables.

There were little boxes at each place setting and inside the boxes were a mix of white chocolates shaped in starfish, sundials and sea shells. On the outside of the box it read, "*Thank you friends and family for sharing our happiness with us.*" *Love Marilyn and Allen.*

The table was topped with a white linen table cloth. The chairs were white fold up chairs with bright green palm tree cushions. White dishes with white and green napkins and silverware were stacked at the end of the table.

The food was going to be offered buffet style. Marilyn wanted the dinner to be very casual and let people eat and relax at their own pace. It would also give her and Allen a chance to sit with each and every one of their guests to have a small visit.

Everyone was so happy to be together and Allen's parents marveled at her garden and view of the water. She took everyone inside except Allen who was taking care of the caterers on the terrace.

They all loved her pavilion and her taste in decorating. Everything was white throughout including her couches and sofas and bedding.

The beautiful botanical green plants and flowers that lined the outside of the windows gave the inside a cozy and warm feeling. She had bright colorful area rugs over ceramic tiles, and pillows, vases and signature pieces that brought the house to life.

Her paintings were bright colored pastels of Brazil`s tropical birds and animals, landscapes, beaches, and waterfalls. They were all painted by a local artist and he designed them in a special series just for Marilyn. There were large wicker fans that hung in every room, including the front porch which also had wicker furniture and two large pots of ferns.

The house was white stucco with Terracotta colored clay roof. The garden terrace protruded out over the ravine and was held up by two large pillar posts to give a more glandular view of the waterfront and beach down below. Even at night the view was spectacular as all the high rise condos along the water were lit up and cast a light throughout the gardens and terrace.

Just as Marilyn was leading everyone back out onto the terrace, Allen appeared at the terrace doors. He smiled at her, "I have a nice surprise for you!"

When he moved out of the way and there stood Miguel with a big smile holding her little nephew Cole in his arms.

Marilyn was so elated to see them! She ran up to Miguel and Enesa and kissed them on their cheeks. Then Miguel held Cole out to Marilyn and she scooped him up in her arms. He was just the most beautiful baby Marilyn had ever seen!

He had a little round face with jet black hair and it was brushed all back and held in place with baby oil. He had big blue eyes, and his lips were round and bright red as if he had a hint of lipstick on. He had light olive color skin but his coloring was just like Miguel's. He was dressed in a blue knit sweater and white undershirt with matching cap and pants. He had on little white shoes and a light blue little ankle socks with little knitted sail boats all around the edge.

"He's just perfect!" Marilyn said as she walked up to Enesa. "He has blue eyes," Marilyn said with surprise!

"Yes, his eyes are the same color as my father's," said Enesa as she smiled looking down at her bundle of joy.

Marilyn turned to everyone who stood around basking in her glory over her little nephew. "Everyone,

I would like for you to all meet my beautiful little nephew Cole!"

The last one to show up before dinner was Father Andrade. He was 58 years old and was a stocky man who only stood about 5'6" tall. He was slightly balding and had thick heavy eyebrows. He walked onto the terrace and as soon as he spotted Miguel he walked up to him and shook Miguel's hand.

"You won't remember me Miguel, but I christened you when you were born. I have always prayed for you, and here you are! It is a splendid miracle to see you again."

"Thank you Father, said Miguel."

"Miguel, Marilyn told me that you have recently had a child. Congratulations!" as he smiled and patted him on the shoulder. "And Marilyn also told me you have a wonderful woman in your life. I would like to bless that relationship and marry you and Enesa this evening right here on the terrace if it would be okay with you?"

Miguel knew he wanted to marry Enesa and give her more children. He wanted to give her a daughter. He wanted Cole to have a relationship with his sister that he has with Marilyn.

"I would also like to christen Cole at the same time with your permission," asked Father Andrade.

"Yes, I would like him to be christened also. I would like my sister and Allen to be his Godparents."

Marilyn and Allen were thrilled! Enesa and Miguel were married just before dinner and everyone witnessed their wedding vows and the christening of Cole.

Enesa held Cole during the ceremony then handed him to Miguel while Father Andrade poured the christening water over his head. Cole let out a huge loud cry while the water ran into his eyes. Allen laughed and said, "He sure has a healthy set of lungs!"

# Chapter 29

It was the morning of Marilyn and Allen's wedding day and they could not see each other. Her phone rang and it was Allen. "I just wanted to say I wish you all the best today!"

Marilyn laughed at him. "Hi honey, are you sure you still want to do this?"

"I'll be there and not wild horses or anything else could keep me away!"

She laughed again. "I have to go now honey! I have to get ready to get married today!"

"See you later, and one more thing!" Allen shouted. "I love you!"

"I love you too and I'll see you soon!"

Marilyn got dressed with her wedding party and was wearing a satin platinum white bridal dress. It was strapless and had a faille trumpet pleated bottom with beaded detail on the bodice.

Her veil was fingertip length. It was platinum edged and beads ran through the netting to match her wedding dress. There were pearl buttons all the way down the back of her gown and stopped just below her waist.

Her hair was twisted up on top of her head and three white Orchids were pinned to the right side of the twist.

Alex, Enesa, and Catherine were wearing satin aqua blue cocktail length dresses. They were sleeveless also and cut straight across at the top and gathered into a twist at the waist.

They wore their hair up on top of their head like Marilyn's but only with one white orchid pinned to the side.

The flower girl wore a matching ballerina length satin white platinum dress with a big aqua blue bow around the waist and beaded with the same beading around the bodice as Marilyn's dress.

Allen's mother Rita came into Marilyn's room while she got dressed. "You look absolutely beautiful!" said Rita.

"Thank you," smiled Marilyn.

"And I hope you're going to call us mom and dad?"

"Yes I will . . . Mom!" As they both laughed.

Rita walked up to Marilyn and said, "I never thought I would see Allen this happy again. I'm sure you know about Stephanie."

"Yes I do. It was a tragic loss to Allen."

"Yes it was, and I'm so happy he has moved on to find love again," said Rita.

"I know Allen told you that I was engaged to someone. He's in jail in France for what he tried to do to us. I'm sure that being who he is, he won't spend the full five years for what he did. But I'm sure by the time he gets out he will have moved on. He knows it's over between us."

"I hope so," said Rita. "If not, please let us help you. We have a lot of contacts in France."

Rita pulled something out of her hand held pearl beaded purse.

"I want to give you something. It's something old to have for your wedding day. It's from Allen's great grandmother. When she and her husband and three children first immigrated to Canada, Allen's great grandmother worked in a clothing factory, or what we call a sweat shop."

She handed a white cloth handkerchief to Marilyn.

"She used to gather the left over cloth and thread, and she would make handkerchiefs. This one she made with butterflies. I want you to have it."

"This is beautiful!" said Marilyn.

Rita smiled, "She loved butterflies."

"What a beautiful story," said Marilyn. "I'll treasure this forever and pass it on to our daughter someday."

Rita smiled, "Thank you my dear. I'll go now and get myself ready for the wedding. I'll see you later." Rita put her arms around Marilyn and gave her a hug.

When Rita left the room, Marilyn choked back the tears as she ran her hand across the stitching of the handkerchief, and then tucked it into the ribbon of her bouquet of white roses and orchids.

When Miguel came into the room to get Marilyn, he looked at her and smiled. "I hoped I would see this day for you and here it is. You look so beautiful! And Allen is one lucky guy to have you."

Marilyn smiled up at him, "I'm so glad you're here too Miguel. Other than finding out you were still alive, this is the happiest day of my life!"

Miguel took Marilyn by the arm and walked her to the limo.

Allen, Michael and Quinn were standing on the beach when Marilyn got out of the limo. Allen looked to see her while Miguel opened the door and put his hand out to help Marilyn out. Alex walked behind her to lift her train and to carry it.

All the other women in the bridal party piled out of the limo looking at the beautiful setting where Father Andrade stood.

Allen couldn't believe how beautiful Marilyn looked. He thought he was the luckiest man in the world right now."

Michael and Quinn patted him on the shoulder and Michael asked, "Are you ready?"

Allen turned to look over his shoulder and said, "I'm ready."

Miguel led Marilyn up to the altar and Allen put his hand out to help her up the step. They stood in front of Father Andrade and he looked at them with a smile.

He began to say, "Friends and family we're gathered here today to witness the marriage of Allen and Marilyn. In the short time they have been together, they have had many challenges. But their love for each other is what makes them strong. God sometimes tests our love for some reason or another. Sometimes these tests will destroy the marriage, and other times it will make it stronger. Marilyn and Allen, I feel that your love for each other will grow with every one of God's challenges. And I believe in the short time I have seen you together you have a divine love for one another. I bless your marriage today and pray you never lose the love you have for each other. And with that being said, Allen, could you please repeat after me."

Just as Father Andrade was getting ready to speak to Allen, Allen looked at Marilyn and his face went cold! Then he closed his eyes while his body crashed to the ground hitting his head on one of the pillars going down!

Everyone gasped in horror as Allen lay on the ground while Marilyn knelt down right away to his side. At first everyone thought he passed out from nerves. But then as everyone looked on in horror, blood came running out from under Allen and down the altar.

Marilyn and Rita screamed out loud while Father Andrade ran to comfort Allen who was starting to move.

All the people at the wedding jumped up out of their seats devastated at what was happening!

"Allen, don't move!" cried out Michael, while he was at Allen's side to help him.

Quinn was already on his cell phone calling for an ambulance. Catherine was on another cell phone calling the police.

Avi looked up at the side of the coastal road above them and saw two men jumping into a black Mustang and when everyone heard the squealing of the wheels they all turned to see what was going on.

Marilyn's blood ran cold! She knew that Emmanuel had something to do with this. Michael had Alex take Marilyn and Rita away from Allen's side while Michael and Quinn got his tuxedo jacket and shirt off. Allen was shot in his shoulder. The bullet came from the front of his shoulder and was still lodged in his back before it could exit.

No one heard the gunshot so the shooter must have used a silencer. With no medical instruments, Michael and Quinn felt helpless. They could see the bullet but couldn't get it out.

Just then the police went speeding down the coast in four police cars. Their tires were spinning on the sand causing them to fishtail all the way up the beach. When they got there they all jumped out and there was an officer rushing to Allen's side.

"What happened?" The police officer shouted!

Avi ran to the police officer, "My son shot by two men in a black Mustang! They spun out and headed down that way!" as he pointed up the coastal road to show the police what direction.

The officer signaled to two other police officers who were parked at the top of the road. Then he dispatched up to them that the accomplices were in a black Ford Mustang and headed west on Coastal Boulevard. The two cops jumped into their cars and sped out in the same direction.

Just then the ambulance came down the beach and two paramedics jumped out and ran to Allen's side.

"We're doctors!" Michael yelled to the paramedics.

"What happened?" asked one of the paramedics.

Michael said, "He's been shot in his left shoulder. The bullet is lodged in the bone. That's all we can determine from our observations."

Allen laid there coming in and out of consciousness. He hit his head hard on the pillar of the altar and cut the back of his head going down.

Michael added, "He could also have a concussion."

"At least we hope that's all it is!" said Quinn.

The paramedics bandaged his shoulder so it wouldn't move, and they wrapped his head so he wouldn't bleed when they lifted him. They put him on a stretcher and then into the ambulance. He woke up just as they were ready to close the door.

"Did I at least get married?" he asked the paramedic.

Just then Marilyn jumped into the back of the ambulance and insisted, "I'm riding with him!"

The paramedic nodded and closed the door. On the way to the hospital Marilyn held on to Allen's hand.

"Can you hear me Allen?"

Allen gained consciousness as she talked to him. "Yes babe I can hear you. What happened?"

Marilyn put her head down and said, "You've been shot."

"Oh is that all?" he said to ease her fear.

She smiled at him, "Promise me you'll be okay!"

He looked at her still half conscious, "I'm going to be fine. What's one more episode in our life?"

Ten minutes later the ambulance arrived at the hospital and Allen was admitted and rushed to surgery. Within a few minutes everyone from the wedding party arrived at the hospital including Father Andrade.

"How is Allen doing?" he asked.

"He's in surgery right now." said Marilyn looking totally consumed.

Father Andrade put his arm around Marilyn and said, "Another test. You will get through this too," as he looked up and then sat her down. "Marilyn, I'm very worried. I thought with Emmanuel being in jail this would give you and Allen some time to get him out of your life. It looks like he isn't going to give up. I'm appalled he kept so many secrets hidden from you about who he actually is."

Marilyn thought about what father Andrade said. She turned to Father Andrade and asked, "Father, can you stay here while Allen is in surgery? I'll be back in a few hours."

Father Andrade looked at Marilyn with a surprised look on his face.

"I have to do this Father. I have to leave for just a few hours to get something."

She got up and ran down the corridor of the hospital with her wedding dress hiked up and gathered into her hands. Once outside, Marilyn jumped into the limo that drove the wedding party to the hospital.

She said to the chauffer, "Take me to my house as soon as possible!"

When she arrived at her house she ran in to her bedroom and removed her bridal dress, corset and white sandals. She threw on a black pair of pants, white blouse and black leather high heel pumps with a black leather waist length coat. She pulled the flowers from her hair and brushed her hair down. She ran back out to the limo and said, "Take me CRBC First National at 46 Centro and hurry!"

He pulled up to the bank and opened the door for Marilyn. She jumped out and ran inside the bank. She went up to the service desk and told the bank clerk she needed her safety deposit box.

The bank clerk took her inside to her safety deposit box and unlocked it and handed it to Marilyn. She then took her to another room with a desk and chair and left Marilyn inside alone.

She opened her safety deposit box and inside she pulled out another small metal black box.

Emmanuel on his last trip to see her asked her to put it in her safety deposit box. He told her that she was to keep it and if anything should ever happen to him, she was to take it to his father. She had to promise him she would never open the box herself.

Marilyn had completely forgotten about it with everything that went on between them. She looked all around the box and she found a key taped to the bottom. She took the key and unlocked it. Inside of it was a piece of micro fiche. She looked at the micro fiche and then put it back in the box and locked it. She then picked it up and put it in a briefcase. She gave her safety deposit box back to the bank clerk and left.

Once back inside the limo she said, "Take me to the National Library please."

At the library Marilyn asked to be led to the micro form reader and scanner. She inserted the micro fiche into the reader and enlarged it to view the contents.

The micro fiche contained some kind of an aerial view of a map. She stared at it looking to see if she could figure out where it was. As she looked, she could see a river and forest or jungle all around it. There was a red line that ran from a river into the jungle, and at the end of the red line was an "x" to mark a destination. Around the area there was a black circle.

Inside the circle there were little boxes with five digit numbers. Between the boxes were measurements between each box. As she looked at it she was thinking that the map looked like the Amazon Rainforest. As she looked again, she couldn't believe what she was seeing! She was looking at a map leading into Miguel's garden.

"What's going on?" she thought to herself. "Why does Emmanuel have a map of Miguel's garden? Why does he have everything mapped out and what do these numbers represent?"

She turned to a second page on the micro fiche. The second page contained an index and a description of each building in the garden. At the bottom of the page, it was dated six months before she even met Emmanuel.

Her thoughts swirled in her head. And then it hit her. Emmanuel already knew Miguel was still alive! He knew what was inside of the green houses. Emmanuel knew that Miguel had hundreds of cures that could save the world from sickness, cancer, and many other diseases.

Her heart leaped in her chest! It started to pound so hard she thought she was going to faint. She put her head back until she could catch her breath again.

She realized everything was a set up. Emmanuel was after Miguel's research and antidotes. He was going to sell the secrets of the garden for millions of dollars. The chance meeting at the art exhibit where they met was a set up. The engagement was a set up. His love for her was all a lie! Her mind swirled as she realized he used her to get to Miguel.

"How did Emmanuel know that Miguel was still alive? Why didn't he tell her Miguel was alive?"

Then she realized the plot. He wanted to reunite her and Miguel like some kind of hero. Then Miguel feeling indebted to Emmanuel, Miguel would give the antidotes to Emmanuel in return. But his plan backfired when she found out before Emmanuel could tell her.

She couldn't believe what was happening. He covered up his lies and deception every step of the way! And even after his plan was sabotaged, he continued to cover his tracks to hopefully win her back again so that he could continue his master plan.

Marilyn went to the last page of the micro fiche. She gasped as she realized she was looking at a high security floor plan blue print of the Council of State in France, which provides the executive branch of the French government with legal advice and acts as the Administrative Court of Last Resort.

The Council is primarily made up of high-ranking legal officers. In the right hand lower corner of the floor plan it was stamped with Veripirate, which is the national security advisory service to France as Homeland Security is to the U.S. It was stamped with a date on it. Marilyn thought to herself, "That was only six months ago!"

Also in the drawing there were boxes with passwords in each room. Some rooms contained more than one box with a password. She also realized that these were computer passwords. In one of the rooms it had a highlighted yellow box with a password and under the password it read, "Patents" on it.

"Why does he care about patents?" she asked herself.

Then she remembered having a conversation with Emmanuel and he stated that he was trying to work on a patent, and in his words he said, "The fucking process was taking too long and was costing too much money!"

She concluded that he was going to access the computers where the patents are stored and add the antidotes from Miguel's garden to expedite the process. She knew this would save him years to get a patent registered and save him millions of dollars.

She looked around making sure no one could see what she was doing, and then she pulled the micro fiche from the reader. Then she scanned the micro fiche and put it on to a computer disk. She then put it back in the metal box and placed it back into her briefcase. She looked once more to make sure she wasn't followed and returned back to the limo.

When she got back into the limo she said, "Take me back to the bank please." When she got there she returned the black box with the micro fiche back into her safety deposit box and then returned to the limo again. "Take me back to my pavilion as soon as possible!"

When she got there she put her wedding gown back on and redid her hair, then got back into the limo again.

When she returned to the hospital she found everyone in the surgical waiting room.

"Marilyn!" shouted Rita. "Where did you go? We were so worried about you!"

"I told her you would be back," said Father Andrade.

"I had to take care of something that couldn't wait. How is Allen?"

"He's still in surgery," said Michael. "Are you okay?"

"Yes, so long as Allen is okay, then I'm okay."

"I'm sure he'll be alright. He was coherent a few times which is a very good sign."

She smiled at Michael and patted him on his shoulder.

A half hour later the surgeon came out to talk to everyone. "Allen is fine. He's resting in recovery and he should be back in his room in a few hours. He was very lucky it missed his heart. The bullet lodged into his shoulder bone. It will heal completely in a few weeks or so. His cut on his head is also superficial. We bandaged it and he'll be fine."

The surgeon turned to Marilyn, "I'm sorry this ruined your wedding. But he'll be out of the hospital tomorrow and hopefully you can resume where you left off."

Marilyn thanked him and he walked away.

A few hours later a nurse approached Marilyn and said she could see Allen now. They moved him into a room. Marilyn followed the nurse down the corridor and into his room.

He lay on his bed fighting his sleep from the anesthesia. "I have been dying to see you," he said, "and pardon the pun," as he smiled at her.

She sat next to him. "Are you okay?" as she ran her hand over his forehead to push back his hair from his face.

"I'm good. I just wished he shot me after we said, "I do.""

"It will just be on hold until we get you back on your feet." Marilyn smiled down at him.

"Oh no!" he whispered. "We're going to say those words a lot sooner than that!"

Just then Father Andrade, Allen's parents and the wedding party walked into the room.

"Are you ready to finish your vows?" Father Andrade asked.

"I'm ready Father," said Allen.

Marilyn looked completely stunned! "Are you sure you want to get married in a hospital room?"

Allen looked up at her and smiled, "Why not, it will be a story we can tell our children someday."

The next day after Allen was released from the hospital, Marilyn brought Allen back to the pavilion where they thought it would be best to stay for Allen to recover.

When they walked up to the door, Allen tried to carry Marilyn over the threshold but couldn't with his shoulder being bandaged.

"Well, this isn't the way I wanted to start our honeymoon," said Allen.

Marilyn looked up at him with a sad look on her face. "I'm just glad you're alive. That's all that matters to me."

He leaned her against the frame of the door as he scanned his eyes up and down her body. "I have a broken shoulder, but the rest of me is working just fine!" as he stared hungrily into her eyes.

She laughed at him, and then she grabbed his hand and pulled him into the house and locked the door behind them!

# Chapter 30

The morning after Allen was enjoying resting on the terrace overlooking the water and watching all the sailboats go by.

Marilyn went to her computer. When she was living at the palace, she had all the people who and signed the registry into the palace put on computer disks. She did it just in case the original documents and registration books were ever stolen or destroyed.

She started a search on the computer for anyone with the last name of Sicard. Sure enough, On October 28th, 1983 she saw that Joséph Sicard, who was Emmanuel's father registered into the palace. Now there was a connection! She knew now that Joséph Sicard knew her father. But what kind of business could they have had? He was a lawyer and maybe his father hired him to do some legal work for him.

She wondered why he had dealings with an attorney from France. Maybe her father hired a French attorney since he was too well known in Brazil. Marilyn picked up the phone and called Emmanuel and Joséph's law firm and disguised herself as a clerk from the Brazilian Consulates office.

"Hello, my name is Juliana Mendes and I'm calling from the Brazilian Consulate's office. I'm calling to get some information on a man who had a legal matter with your law firm in France between 1983 and 1984. His name is Henry Luis Andre. He was from Rio de Janeiro."

The woman said, "Can you hold one minute and I'll check the computer to see if I can find a match to that name?"

"Yes I can," said Marilyn. Marilyn was put on hold while her heart was pounding!

When the woman returned to the phone she said, "Yes, he was a client of Joséph Sicard."

"Yes, that's the file I'm looking for. I was wondering if you could tell me the file number so I can retrieve it at the clerk's office."

"Hmm," said the woman. "This isn't a file. Mr. Sicard hired a detective for Henry Andre to track down a Miguel Henry Andre that was living somewhere in the Amazon."

"Can you tell me the date that he hired that detective?" asked Marilyn.

"Yes, the letter is dated November 18th, 1983."

"And what was the name of the detective?"

"His name was Jonathon Landry."

"Was he from Paris?"

"No, he was from Rio de Janeiro."

"And what was your name again?" asked the woman.

Marilyn quickly hung up the phone. She knew the woman was getting suspicious.

"Bingo!" Marilyn said to herself.


Marilyn searched the directory in Rio de Janeiro for a Jonathon Landry but nothing came up. Then she searched for detective agencies and found a Landry Security Company.

She called it and an older man answered the phone.

"Landry Security,"

"Hello, my name is Marilyn Andre. Are you Jonathon Landry?"

The phone went silent.

"What do you want?"

"I'm looking for a man who helped in an investigation to track down a child back in 1983. The boy's name was Miguel Henry Andre."

The man was very quiet again.

"What is it that you're looking for?"

"What I want to know is if that man was you?"

He didn't say anything for a few seconds.

"Hello," she said.

"Yeah, I'm here. Yeah, it was me and what do you want?" he asked in a harsh voice.

She took a sigh of relief. She knew if this man was willing to talk he could give her leads as to what happened between her father and Joséph Sicard.

"I was wondering if I could set up a meeting to talk to you."

"No," he said with a lazy nonchalant voice.

"I'll pay you for your time."

He hesitated. "Okay, but I get five hundred dollars an hour!"

"That's fine," she said.

"Can you meet me at the Antigua Restaurant off Coastal Boulevard in about an hour?"

"If you want to meet that soon then I want an extra hundred dollars. And I want it all in cash!"

"No problem, I'll see you then." as she hung up the phone.

Marilyn sat in the corner with sunglasses on when she saw him walk in. She knew from his voice it was him. He was dressed in a white dress shirt that looked like it had never been ironed. His pants hung down between his legs and his shoes were never polished and they were worn. His hair was a bit messed and she could tell he brushed it with his fingers. She could also tell he just shaved because he had a few knick marks under his chin. He had a bit of a pot belly but at one time Marilyn could tell he was very fit. He was about 5'10" tall with whitish grey hair. He had a limp from his right leg. He walked in and looked around then spotted Marilyn.

He sat down across from her and he said, "I forgot to tell you I charge extra for food and miscellaneous."

She smiled at him as he sat down.

"I'm Marilyn," as she put her hand out to shake his hand.

He never extended his hand and then said, "Yeah Okay, let's not get personal," as he looked around the room.

Marilyn smiled at him, "Mr. Landry, you don't look pure Brazilian."

My father was French and my mother was Brazilian. But my grandparents in Brazil raised me. It's a long story." He said still looking around the room.

The waitress came over to take their order.

Marilyn asked, "What would you like Mr. Landry?"

He puckered his lips, "I just want a beer right now."

Marilyn said to the waitress, "*Uma cerveja e um cha gelado por favor*," as she ordered an iced tea and beer for Jonathon.

While the waitress was gone Marilyn asked him if he remembered investigating the case for Henry Andre.

"Yes I remember. I never forget my investigations. But this one I really never forgot because it involved a kidnapping and a missing child. It was a very high profile investigation."

Marilyn was elated that he remembered about the kidnapping.

"Can you tell me what you remember about it?"

Just then the waitress brought their drinks and sat them down on the table.

"Can I get anything else for you right now?" asked the waitress in Portuguese. She looked at Mr. Landry as he shook his head no.

"I remember the man Henry Andre was desperate to find his son. He paid me a lot of money and it was all done through a law firm out of France. The attorney's name was Joséph Sicard."

"Why was an attorney from France hired by my father?"

He looked at her. "Your father was Henry Andre?"

"Yes," she said. "And the boy you were looking for was my brother."

He got nervous to talk.

"It's okay Mr. Landry. I know mostly everything. I just need to fill in a few blanks."

Even though she didn't know anything, she thought it would put him at ease to give her more information.

"I found the boy." He stopped and said, "I mean your brother, in the Amazon where I was told to look for him. He was being taken care of by a missionary family and a woman. Good looking woman at that!" as he smiled.

Marilyn gave him a dirty look to keep his mind on the investigation.

He scratched his head, "He was well taken care of."

"If you found him then why didn't they take my brother with them?"

"I never told them I found him."

"Why didn't you tell them?"

"I told them I couldn't find him." He took a big gulp of his beer, "But I did!"

"Why did you tell them you didn't find him if you were hired by them?"

"I thought that he looked happy and he didn't want to leave. He cried when he found out I was there to take him. They tried to hide him from me but I knew he was there. I was paid either way. I really didn't care if I returned him or not. I guess I thought the boy was better off where he was."

"But it was his father. My father!" Marilyn said back.

"Sometimes your own blood relatives aren't best for you. There was a lot of controversy about the kidnapping. Some say," and then he stopped talking.

Marilyn completed his sentence by saying, "And some say my parents did it, right?"

He nodded his head slowly yes.

"I did take the attorney with me to the place where your brother was being raised. He wanted to be there just in case I found the boy. He had all the legal documents to take him back with us. He had custody papers and legal actions if they didn't release him. But I said the hell with the courts! The boy was fine where he was. He had freedom and he lived in a beautiful house with good people. What more could you want for a kid? If I released him to the lawyer and your father, I don't know what would have happened to him. He was happy. That's all he needed."

Marilyn was happy that Mr. Landry made the decision he did. Who knows what kind of reaction Miguel would have received. He was right. Miguel told Marilyn himself that he was happy where he was and he didn't want to go home. The end result was that they reunited and Miguel was happily married with a beautiful little son.

"But I have to tell you that the missionary doctor had quite the racket going on in that place," added Jonathon as he took another gulp of his beer.

"What do you mean?" Marilyn asked.

"There were natives working for him and they were making gardens all over the place. Kind of like a little Garden of Eden.

He looked for the waitress to bring another beer.

"Even Mr. Sicard was quite impressed. He was very interested in knowing what they were doing in the garden. When no one was looking he was taking pictures and writing notes. He was asking the lady, I think her name was Ana, what they were doing in the greenhouses? But she was sworn to secrecy and didn't give him any information."

"Ah!" exclaimed Marilyn. "I wonder why he was being so curious?" she uttered out loud and catching herself.

"Well, I think they had some kind of medicine they were studying, and some big pond with all kinds of weird fish in it."

"Really?" said Marilyn. "Do you remember what they looked like?"

"Yes, I will never forget this one big black fish. He was in the middle of the pond all the time. It was a really weird looking one. Anyways, I have to get going. I have to get back to monitoring my houses. Do you have the money?" he asked with a smile.

She laughed at him and his quirky ways as she handed him six hundred dollars in cash.

"And you get the bar bill?"

Marilyn said, "I'll get the bill."

He gave her a little friendly wink and then got up and left.

# Chapter 31

She returned to the pavilion and Allen was on the phone with his office when she walked in.

"My beautiful bride just walked in so I have to go. Thanks for all you're doing and I'll call you tomorrow."

"Hello honey, was that Marge, your office manager?"

"Yes, she's taking good care of the office for me. Now what's going on with you? You're being awfully sneaky!"

She walked to him and put her arms around him.

"I know honey and I'm sorry. You won't believe what's going on. Let me make dinner while I tell you."

He rolled his eyes into the air and commented, "There's never a dull moment with you!" and then he smiled down at her.

When he heard what she had to tell him, he was really worried about what she had uncovered.

"Marilyn, if anyone finds out what you know, they're going to kill you!"

"I know, and this is the hard part. I don't want to get you involved."

"Marilyn, I'm already involved. I'm your husband!"

She smiled at him. "Allen, you're not going to like what I'm going to tell you. But it's for everyone's good and protection. I need to stay here while you go back to New York. I have to go see Miguel."

Allen just sat there and stared at Marilyn.

"That's not going to happen!" he rebelled.

"Allen, listen to me."

"No you listen to me! If you have to go see Miguel that's fine, I understand that. But you're not going without me. We're going together!"

"But you're in no condition to travel."

He turned and looked at her, "If Michael could travel in the condition he was in, so can I!"

Right after dinner the phone rang. Marilyn could see from the call display the call was coming from Landry Security Company.

"Hello," she said when she picked up the receiver.

"Hello Miss Andre?"

"Yes Mr. Landry, it's me, Marilyn."

"Oh hello, I was wondering if we could meet again? I have some more information for you that "I know" you will be very interested in hearing."

"What is it?" she asked.

"I have to tell you in person. I never do business over the phone."

"She thought for a minute and said, "Okay, Can you meet me at the same place tomorrow at one o'clock?"

"That's Fine," he said.

Then just before she was ready to hang up Jonathon said in a smiling voice, "Oh and Ms. Andre, I would suggest you bring some more cash with you. You know what I mean."

She laughed at him and asked, "How much is this going to cost me this time?"

"Just a measly five hundred dollars."

"She shook her head and said, "Okay, see you then."

When she entered the restaurant Jonathon was already seated in the same booth where they sat the last time.

Marilyn sat down. "Hello Jonathon, you said you have some more information for me?"

"Yes, I think you will find it most interesting!"

"Okay, I'm listening."

He looked down at her purse and then she remembered about the money. She took an envelope out with five hundred dollars in it and handed it to him.

He opened the envelope and took a quick glance and smiled at her. "I remember a conversation between your father and Joséph Sicard."

"What was it?" Marilyn asked curiously.

"I was doing some wiring in the reception area of Joséph Sicard's office, and I overheard Mr. Sicard and your father going over your father's will. Your father said that he wanted to make sure your brother was included in his will. Mr. Sicard read the will he drew up for your father and it stated that your brother was entitled to one third of the estate if he ever came back."

"But there was no mention of my brother in my father's will."

"Ah!" said Jonathon, "Just as I thought!"

"What are you trying to say Mr. Landry?"

"What I'm trying to say is that Mr. Sicard rewrote your father's will."

Marilyn looked at Jonathon with a perplexed look.

"Are you trying to say that Mr. Sicard has money from my father's estate?"

"Yes, that's what I'm saying."

"Did you overhear how much money?"

He laughed at Marilyn. "I never forget money, and it was for the amount of two and a half million dollars and one third of the palace. One third was to go to your mother, one third to you, and one third to your brother."

Marilyn leaned back in her chair, "Mr. Sicard has two and a half million dollars of my brother's money? But everything was willed to me and my mother."

He shook his head no. "Your brother was supposed to get a part of the estate. And I highly doubt your father would have changed his will since he died a few weeks later."

"How do you know he died a few weeks later?"

"I read it in the obituaries. Your father was a very prominent man."

"If Joséph Sicard changed my father's will, how can I prove it?"

"I have a tape of the conversation," said Jonathon looking around for the waitress.

Marilyn jumped up in her seat and leaned towards Jonathon, "How could you have a tape of the conversation?"

"I was there that day to wire the reception area and office of Mr. Sicard at his request. He had a meeting with someone in the French underworld and he wanted the conversation to be completely taped."

Marilyn listened very carefully to Jonathon while not saying a word.

"I had just got the bug set up and I recorded the conversation with your father and Sicard. It was only supposed to be a test. But when I heard the conversation I decided to record it. I never did trust that Joséph Sicard. He wasn't a trustworthy man. People thought he was, but he wasn't. I did a few investigations for him until he did me wrong on one of them. He cut me out of a deal and I lost thousands of dollars. But I knew I was going to get him back someday."

The waitress came over, "What can I get you today?" she asked in Portuguese. Jonathon said, "*Uma cerveja.*"

Marilyn also said, "*Nada para mim obrigado*" as she waited for Jonathon to continue.

"Joséph Sicard never thought your brother would resurface. He assumed your father would never find your brother again, and no one would ever be the wiser!

"Joséph was desperate in those days. He was growing the law firm and he would do whatever had to be done to get money. That's why he was having a meeting with someone in the syndicate. He was going to borrow some money."

"I see," said Marilyn with a very questioning look on her face. "So he knew after my mother died everything would be willed to me. And I was going to marry his son, and he keeps two and a half million dollars of my brother's money to line his own pockets."

"You're a very smart lady," smiled Jonathon.

The waitress returned and put the beer down in front of Jonathon and left.

"How do I get that tape from you?" Knowing this was going to cost her more money.

"Ten thousand dollars and the tape is yours." then Jonathon took a sip of his beer.

"Ten thousand dollars!" shouted Marilyn, then looking around to make sure no one heard her.

"That's peanuts! You get two and a half million dollars in return."

Marilyn thought about it and he was right. It was worth the deal if she could prove that Joséph Sicard changed her father's will, and has two and a half million dollars of her brother's money.

"Okay," said Marilyn. "I'll bring it with me tomorrow to your office. I'll be there at 9:00 o'clock in the morning." She smiled and got up and left.

The next day Marilyn met Jonathon at his office. He had all the shades drawn shut and a closed sign on the door. She knocked lightly and he answered.

She went inside and she couldn't believe the wires all over the office. There were alarm systems and tools everywhere. The whole office was in disarray with paperwork strewn about. She pulled out the envelope and waved it in front of Jonathon.

"You're not getting the money until I hear the tape!"

Jonathon looked at her and nodded his head no.

Marilyn turned and walked out the door and closed it behind her.

Then Jonathon ran behind her and swung the door open. "Okay!" he shouted at her.

She turned around and walked back in while he closed and locked it behind her.

He went over to an old cassette tape player and plugged in a tape. A voice came on and it was Jonathon in his younger days speaking into a microphone. He was saying, "Testing . . . testing."

Then she heard a voice that sounded like Joséph Sicard.

"Mrs. Laurent, can you bring Mr. Andre's will in please?"

"Yes Mr. Sicard," said Mrs. Laurent, his secretary.

Then Marilyn heard her father's voice.

"Thank you for doing this for me Joséph. I really appreciate your confidentiality regarding this matter."

"It's my job as your attorney to keep everything between us confidential Henry. Can I get you a drink?"

"I would love a scotch."

"I'll join you in that!"

Marilyn could hear Joséph pouring the drinks when his secretary walked in.

"Here it is Mr. Sicard and Mr. Andre. I just finished typing it up today. But I just want to clarify one thing since Mr. Sicard's handwriting isn't that legible."

Marilyn could hear a small chuckle from her father and Joséph.

"Mr. Sicard wrote that you wanted your son to get one third of the palace and the one third of the money from the estate?"

"Yes I did," said Henry.

"I didn't know you had a son?" she said.

There was silence for a minute.

"He's away at private school in Austria with some of my relatives."

"Oh! I would hope we can meet him someday," then she left the room.

Joséph said, "Henry, this is what I prepared for your will."

He read it to Henry as Marilyn carefully listened to every word on the tape. Sure enough it was stated in the will that Marilyn, Miguel and her mother were to receive one third each of the palace and one third each of the money from the estate.

Then she heard Joséph say, "I have an income statement for the estate value as of today's date, and I just need to verify that the money is correct. You have approximately four-million dollars in stocks and bonds. Two-million dollars in gold kept at First National in Rio de Janeiro, and you have 1.5 million dollars in a savings account in First National Bank as well."

"That's correct," said Henry. "Other than a few other little incidental accounts I have set up for day to day spending, that's the majority of it."

"So all together your net worth is approximately 7.5 million dollars plus the value of the palace as of this date?"

"Yes," said Henry.

"Okay then, I just need for you to sign the bottom right here and date it."

Marilyn could hear her father's pen scratch as he signed his name.

"Upon my death I want you to send this will to my attorney in Rio de Janeiro. Then he can take care of the estate from there."

"I have his contact information and I promise it will be forwarded to him. I understand completely what you must be going through. I know you don't want your attorney to find out until after your death that your son may still be alive. It must be hard for you."

"Joséph, I haven't slept one night since he's been gone. I hate myself for what I did!"

"Well, you did it for your wife and your daughter."

"Yes, and I hope someday before I die I can tell my son why, that's if he's still alive!"

After he signed the will her father said, "I'm glad this is out of the way. I have been meaning to make this change in my will for a long time. Now it's done."

"And I think you're doing the right thing by including Miguel just in case," said Joséph.

"Thank you again Joséph." as they shook hands.

She heard her father get up and walk out the door and closed it behind him.

After a few seconds Marilyn thought the tape was over and went to hit the button to stop it.

Jonathon reached down and grabbed her hand and said, "No wait, there's more!"

Marilyn waited and then she heard Joséph say, "Mrs. Laurent, can you come back in here please. We need to make a few changes again."

"Okay, I'll be right in," she said.

A few seconds later she walked into Joséph's office.

"We have to change Henry's income statement. Mr. Andre recently lost two and a half million dollars in the stock market. We have to change that number to 1.5 million dollars. Also, he wants to exclude his son again from the will. His son has a bad drug problem. Henry's wife Louisa is going to take care of him and his part of the estate so he doesn't spend it all at once."

"Smart idea," said Mrs. Laurent.

"Can I have those changes made as soon as possible?"

"Yes, I'll have it done today."

Then the door closed as Mrs. Laurent left the room and Jonathon stopped the tape.

Marilyn looked at Jonathon, "So he was banking on the fact my brother would never return wasn't he?"

"Yep, you got it!"

"So where's the money?" asked Marilyn.

Jonathon said, "Now that I don't know?"

Marilyn was enraged at what she heard.

"I'm going to put that man behind bars right next to his son!" Marilyn snapped angrily.

"You mean his son is in jail?"

"Yes, It's a long story."

"Ah," said Jonathon, "And the plot thickens!"

"Yes, and I want to thank you for this important information. I also have some other evidence that they have broken national security laws in France. I'll be taking this to the officials as soon as I can!"

"Oh?" said Jonathon.

"Well, let's just put it this way. When Veripirate, Frances home security enforcement agency, sees what I have in my safety deposit box at my First National Bank, Emmanuel and Joséph will be going to jail forever. If anything should ever happen to me and my husband Mr. Landry, please contact the authorities and tell them where it is."

Jonathon smiled and shook his head as Marilyn walked out the door.

# Chapter 32

The next day after meeting with Jonathon and listening to the tape, Marilyn and Allen flew into Manaus and shuttled to the Tishi Amazon Resort. Allen arranged with Yurah, Davi, Tutu and Nino to meet them there.

Luckily Marilyn and Allen had a night to celebrate their honeymoon at the resort. It was a perfect evening while they had a romantic dinner in their room by candlelight.

Then they basked in the hot tub with a bottle of champagne and chocolate covered strawberries. They made hot and passionate love long into the night making up for the time they lost. They talked about the honeymoon they had to miss and they decided to delay their plans until everything settled down. But the Tishi Amazon Resort was a wonderful way to celebrate their short honeymoon.

Right after lunch the following day they headed down the river. They arrived at the river's edge where they docked the boat next to the log in the water to go to Miguel's. They didn't waste time and headed into the rainforest as soon as they hit land.

They stopped at the waterfall to take a quick swim to refresh their bodies from the heavy rain and humidity. They ate lunch and then commenced back into the rainforest jungle and they could hear all the familiar sounds again. They could hear the Spider monkeys jumping from tree to tree above them. The cockatoos and other birds were calling each other.

All of a sudden they could hear the snort of a wild boar very near to them. Everyone stopped! They knew if there was one there were more. They all waited for the boars to show themselves as Yurah and Davi pulled their rifles from their harnesses.

They could hear it getting closer and closer, and then it walked slowly out of the ferns and into the opening. It looked at them and then and all of a sudden it fell over! Everyone stood wondering and confused. Then blood ran out of the boar as it took its last breath.

Yurah ran up to it and knelt down by its side.

"It's been hit by an arrow!" he cried out.

Everyone looked at each other. Someone was there! They all stood still and didn't know whether to move or not. Then all around them natives dressed with painted faces and bodies with feathered head dresses came out and surrounded them. Yurah and Davi stayed composed as the natives all circled them.

"Don't make any fast moves," said Yurah.

Then they spotted the chief with his face painted with a grand head piece on and gold all over his body. Everyone knew he was the chief.

Yurah talked to him in his native tongue. "Hello, we are just crossing through to get somewhere. We are not hunters. We are peaceful people!"

The chief looked at Yurah and then his eyes went to Marilyn. The chief walked up to Marilyn and looked her up and down.

Allen was ready to lunge at him, but Yurah warned him not to do anything or he would put Marilyn in more danger. He was a tall man with very black skin. He painted his face like a warrior and was in very good shape.

Marilyn thought that indigenous tribes like this were long gone for many years from the Amazon.

"Do you know these natives Yurah?" asked Allen.

"Yes, they are the Jiveru (Hee • va • ru) tribe. They used to be head hunters. I'm not sure if they still are. I thought they moved to the mountains years ago."

"What does he want with her?" Allen asked Yurah.

Yurah waved his hand at Allen to be quiet.

The chief finally did a full circle around Marilyn then stood looking into her face. She stared right back at him never taking her eyes from his. Then he laughed as he turned from her.

"You're a brave woman," he said to her.

Yurah translated what he said.

"Why do you come to the Amazon?" He turned to direct the question to Yurah.

"We are just passing through to see someone. We are heading to a destination in the rainforest."

"Where are you going?" asked the chief, as Yurah translated.

Then Allen spoke out. "Tell him the truth. Tell him we're going to see Marilyn's brother."

The chief turned to look at Allen. He walked up to him and put his face just inches from Allen's.

"Where are you from?"

Yurah translated, as Allen said, "I'm from America."

"Ah!" said the chief. "Is this your wife?" pointing to Marilyn.

"Yes, she's my wife."

"She's very beautiful," he said as Yurah translated.

"Thank you, yes she is!"

"Are you married?" Allen asked him.

Yurah translated and then the chief and all the native men around them started to laugh.

"Yes," he said. "I have twelve wives."

Yurah told Allen what the chief said and Allen raised his eyebrow, "Twelve? Wow, you're one busy man!"

Yurah translated to the chief and the chief and his men laughed again.

Then the chief walked up to Yurah again.

"Where did you say you were going?"

"We are going to find this woman's brother." as Yurah pointed at Marilyn.

"What is her brother's name?"

"His name is Natowa."

"Natowa!" yelled out the chief as he smiled at Marilyn.

"He's my friend!" Then the chief moved his gold chains aside to show a scar on his chest.

"Natowa saved my life once. He's a great healer. Tell him Rapau (Raup • ah) will come to see him soon!"

Yurah told Marilyn what he said and she nodded to him with a smile.

Then he walked over to the wild boar that lay dead on its side. He motioned for a few of his men to pick the boar up and then he turned and looked at Allen and Marilyn one more time. He put his head down to say good bye while he walked away.


They arrived in front of the garden. They walked down the path and a few native people ran up happy to see them. By now all the natives knew them and a few of the native men walked with them talking to Yurah and Davi. Marilyn went up to the house and just as she approached the door it opened and there stood Enesa.

"Marilyn!" said Enesa surprised to see her. "Are you okay?"

She grabbed Marilyn by the hand to lead her into the house while she saw Allen, Yurah, Davi, Tutu and Nino unpacking in the garden.

"Enesa, where's Miguel?"

"He's in the rainforest getting some plants he needs, why?"

"When Miguel gets back you have to come with us!"

"Why, what's wrong?" Enesa asked in surprise!

"You and Cole are in danger here. I don't know when, but there are people who are going to come and take over the garden. They're men of Emmanuel's. They want Miguel's research so they can sell it for millions of dollars!"

Enesa looked at Marilyn and said, "Come with me while I get Cole!"

They both rushed up the stairs and opened Cole's bedroom door that was Enesa's old room. Marilyn went to his crib and slowly picked him up not to wake him.

"You get him ready while I hold him."

Enesa rushed around his room gathering his things. When she had it all packed into his diaper bag they headed back down the stairs.

"Where are you going in such a hurry?" said a voice with a heavy French accent coming from the bottom of the stairs.

Marilyn, while still holding Cole in her arms, looked down and there stood Emmanuel and Joséph. She could hear people going through the house.

Enesa yelled out. "Please don't hurt my baby!" as she stood on the stairs behind Marilyn.

Marilyn turned to Enesa and handed her Cole. "What are you doing here Emmanuel?" she asked in a calm voice. "I thought you were in jail?"

Emmanuel and Joséph laughed.

"I'm a very powerful man my dear. My son will never go to jail over you," said Joséph as they both stared up smiling at her.

"You know what we're doing here," said Emmanuel.

Marilyn took a deep breath, "Where's Allen and the other men?"

They both stood at the bottom of the stairs just looking up at her.

"Allen and his guides are with my men," said Joséph.

Marilyn wanted to lunge at the both of them, but she stayed composed. "Where are they?" she asked again.

They both just remained smiling.

"You give me something and I'll return them," Joséph said back.

"What do you want?"

"I want Miguel to hand over the research and the antidotes."

"I can't make him do that!"

"Yes you can," Joséph said to her as he climbed the stairs and took Cole and the diaper bag out of Enesa's hands.

"Cute baby," he said to Enesa.

"Please don't hurt him!" as she pleaded with him and gently let him go.

"Then I suggest you tell your husband that we want all the research documents and the antidotes he has written down. We know he has them. So if you want to see your son again you will get them for us."

He smiled at Enesa and then walked back down the stairs with Cole in his arms to stand next to Marilyn.

"You make sure she gets them," as Joséph looked back down at Cole.

Enesa sat on the steps crying as Marilyn tried to comfort her.

"He won't hurt him," said Marilyn. "He's a cruel person but he doesn't have the heart to hurt a baby."

She hoped herself he wasn't capable of hurting a child. But the Joséph and Emmanuel she knew now seem to stop at nothing to get what they want!

Marilyn pulled Enesa up on her feet and walked her down the stairs and sat her on the couch. Enesa sat their crying curled up in a ball.

Marilyn turned around and two men stood at the front door guarding it. Joséph walked up to them and told them to stay there and keep an eye on Marilyn and Enesa as he walked out holding Cole.

Marilyn could hear Jaukeu on the porch talking at Joséph, "Hello, and welcome to the garden!"

"Shut up you stupid bird!" said Joséph going down the stairs with a scowl tone in his voice.

Marilyn knew there was no way out. She sat with Enesa for awhile on the couch and then she had an idea.

Marilyn got up and walked over to an end table where a vase with flowers in it sat on the table. She purposely knocked it over and it smashed to pieces when it hit the floor.

She turned to one of the men, "I need to clean this up."

The men just looked at her as she walked by them.

She walked into the broom closet off the hallway going into the kitchen. She closed the door slightly pretending to look for the broom and dustpan. She knew that room had the first window of the house that Miguel would see when he walked from the path into the garden. It was her only chance to warn Miguel that the garden was invaded.

She wrote with a dark pink lipstick she had in her pocket on the window, *"S.O.S.!"* Then she walked out passed one of the men looking up at him smiling with a broom and dustpan in her hand.

She knew Miguel would know what the "*S.O.S.*" meant from when they pretended to be spies in the palace. "*S.O.S.*" was their way of letting each other know when their parents were around. They learned it while watching an American spy movie.

The night fell and there was no sign of Miguel. Emmanuel was now back in the house and sitting in the kitchen while the two men still remained at the front door. Joséph was nowhere to be seen. Marilyn had no idea where Allen, Yurah, Davi and the two boys were. She told the men she needed to talk to Emmanuel. One of the men frisked her then he went into the kitchen.

He returned and said, "Go ahead!"

Emmanuel had opened a bottle of wine and was sitting at the table.

"Can I talk to you?" asked Marilyn.

He didn't look up and he didn't say a word. Marilyn pulled a chair up and sat across from him at the table.

"If I get you what you want what will you do with it?"

He laughed at her. "Come on Marilyn. You know what we'll do with it. You're not a stupid woman. Just like when you went to ask questions from Jonathon Landry."

"How did you know?"

"I knew because of your call display on your phone. His number was on it."

"You were in my house?"

"You were on to us and you knew what we wanted. We needed to get here before you ruined years of work and dedication to this project."

"So this is something you had planned for years even before you asked me to marry you, isn't it?"

Emmanuel looked at her with a straight face. "My father is the master mind behind it. I just followed suit. He knew what was going on in here when your father asked him to help him find your brother. He knew it was a gold mine. And now that you know what we're here for it's time to cash in."

Marilyn realized this was a set up from day one for Miguel. Even though Jonathon Landry told Joséph he didn't find Miguel, Joséph knew he was there. They have been watching Miguel's and Dr. Erikson's research and antidotes ever since.

Marilyn got up from the table and looked at Emmanuel. "Joséph has my brother's money from my father's estate."

Emmanuel laughed and said, "Prove it!"

He got up from the table and walked up to her. "I have a feeling you know more than you're telling us," said Emmanuel as he grabbed her under her chin.

She looked up at him, "If I help you, will you let everyone go?" almost pleading with him.

Marilyn realized what she just asked was a ridiculous question. Of course they wouldn't let anyone go. They cannot leave anyone alive so they couldn't link anything to them. She realized they were all going to die. Once Emmanuel and Joséph had what they wanted they would have everyone killed, including her baby nephew, Cole!

# Chapter 33

Marilyn sat in the living room with Enesa. She put her arm around her and said, "I promise everything is going to be okay. Cole is going to be fine."

She didn't really believe her own words but she had to give Enesa hope. She needed for her to stay strong.

Enesa said, "They must have Miguel."

"Why do you think that?"

"He hasn't come back yet."

Marilyn went over to another couch and grabbed Enesa a blanket. "You lay down and when you wake up I'm sure he'll be here."

Marilyn walked up to one of the men, "I have to go upstairs and get another pillow."

One of the men went up with her as she entered Miguel's room. She looked out the window towards the pond. She could see Eye Spy in the middle of the pond while the other fish swam around him.

There were two other men walking around the garden with guns. The natives were nowhere to be seen and the cliffs were not lit up tonight so the garden was dark except for the moonlight. Marilyn thought of something that Miguel had told her. He said that Eye Spy was very possessive over her, and he might kill or injure anyone that got too close to her. She knew somehow she had to get out to the garden to reach the pond. She grabbed a pillow off of Miguel's bed and walked back downstairs with the man following her. She put the pillow down next to Enesa.

Marilyn went back into the kitchen and by now Emmanuel had drank most of the bottle of wine. She reached into the wine rack and pulled out another bottle. "Can I join you?"

He just stared at her with his eyes glazed over, "Whatever."

She took the wine opener and popped the cork off and poured both of them a glass. "Cheers!" as she took a sip.

"What do you want?" he said looking at her with suspicion in his face.

"Emmanuel, I loved you once, I really loved you. But when I found out that you were just using me, I wound up hating you."

He looked at her, "Believe it or not, even though it started out that way, I did fall in love with you."

She looked at him to force a smile. "We had some good times together."

"I know you're here because you want to know where Allen is. That's what this is all about. He's safe." he paused for a moment then said, "For now!"

"I know you're not a cold blooded killer. I know you want the research papers and the antidotes, but I know inside you're not a killer."

He got up from the table and walked over to the sink where he poured his glass of wine down the drain.

"Get out of here," he said to her like he had no life left inside of him.

She got up and walked towards him. His face was hard and cold as he looked down inside the sink.

"I need to do something," she said in a calm voice.

"What is it?"

"I need to go to the pond."

"Why?" turning his head to look at her.

"When I stayed with Miguel he gave me a research project that needs to be done every night in order to keep the pond alive. He isn't here so it needs to be done. Enesa is in no shape to do it. If you want, you can come with me."

"I'll go with you so you don't do anything stupid!" he said with contempt in his voice.

They got to the pond with a clip board she grabbed from inside one of the greenhouses. She started to write some things down and then stared out at Eye Spy. She slowly moved around the pond pretending to document things while Emmanuel walked behind her drinking the wine from the bottle.

Eye Spy kept its eye on her everywhere she walked. She knew she had Eye Spy's attention so she stopped and turned to Emmanuel. She looked into his eyes and said to him, "Being with you again is stirring up my feelings for you. Do you still love me?"

He looked into her eyes and said, "Yes, I still love you." He reached out to pull her into his arms to kiss her.

All of a sudden Eye Spy started to move and the fish fled from around him to the bottom of the pond.

Emmanuel didn't know what it was doing so he grabbed Marilyn by her neck and threw her in front of him. "What the fuck is going on?" he shouted as he held on to Marilyn looking at the strange fish swirling itself around in the water.

Eye Spy started to transform. Its head transformed from a shark's head into a panther's. Then it grew fur and its legs disseminated out from its body while its long claws broke through from its paws. Its shark like teeth developed into fangs and it started to fiercely roar!

Emmanuel backed away still holding onto Marilyn then shouted, "Get it away from me!" while the panther swam to the edge of the pond. Then it leaped out of the water towards them. Emmanuel screamed and threw Marilyn loose from his grips from fear as the panther leaped and pulled Emmanuel down to the ground. Marilyn turned her head while she heard Emmanuel's blood curdling screams!

He screamed out to her, "*Aidez moi Marilyn!*" He was screaming for her to help him!

Marilyn ran towards the house to get away from his cries!

Just then the two men ran out of the house passing her to get to Emmanuel. Then she could hear fierce growls and roars from the panther as the panther ran after the two men. The men screamed for their lives!

She got to the door and ran inside and locked it throwing her back against the door.

Enesa jumped up crying, "What's happening?"

Marilyn grabbed her and sat her back down on the couch and told her to not say a word.

Everything outside went quiet after the men stopped screaming.

Marilyn knew the panther was roaming the garden looking for her. He would keep killing until he found her.

Then she heard another man screaming in French, "*Kill it!*" Then she heard him cry out one last time, "*Help me!*" Then everything went silent again.

All of a sudden there was a hard bang on the door!

"Marilyn, let me in!" It was Miguel.

She ran to the door and opened it as fast as she could! But when she opened the door the panther stood there waiting behind Miguel to pounce on him with blood on its fangs and fur. Then Miguel realized the panther was behind him.

"Shut the door," he said quietly as he stood there motionless looking at Marilyn.

But Marilyn couldn't do it!

"Marilyn, close the door!" Miguel said staring at her with such conviction in his face and voice.

She stood there crying knowing that Miguel would be the panther's next victim.

The panther moved slowly towards Miguel with its fangs straight out for him glaring into the back of Miguel's neck from its piercing green eye.

Marilyn shut the door half way so the panther couldn't see her. She saw a rifle from the two men perched up in the corner of the hallway and she grabbed it. She cocked the gun on pure adrenalin and swung the door open and shot the panther straight into its heart! The force of the gun knocked Marilyn to the ground, and then she instantly jumped back up!

Miguel screamed out at the same time, "No, don't kill him!"

The panther fell to the ground. It looked up at Marilyn for a moment and then its green eye slowly closed. It was dead.

Miguel slowly knelt down next to the panther and rubbed his hand over its fur.

Marilyn cried, "I'm so sorry Miguel! I had to do it!"

Then he got up and said, "I know, they would have killed him anyways," as tears filled his eyes.

Marilyn grabbed Miguel and pulled him into the house.

Enesa ran to his side and said, "They have Cole!"

He looked at Enesa, "I'll get Cole back! I knew something was wrong when Jaukeu didn't fly down the path to greet me. Then I saw the window in the broom closet and the message. I would have walked right into the ambush. I snuck in the back way so they couldn't see me. They have no idea I'm here."

Then he grabbed the rifle out of Marilyn's hands and walked back out onto the porch.

Just then Allen, who was holding Cole, walked out from the path of the cliff. He was being led by Joséph and another man who had a gun pointed at Allen's back.

You could see the rage in Miguel's eyes as the men neared the house. Marilyn pleaded with Miguel not to do anything to provoke Joséph.

Joséph yelled out to Marilyn, "You killed my son and my men you bitch!" as he had tears in his eyes looking around at the bloody massacre and seeing Emmanuel lying dead on the ground next to the pond. "Now I'm going to kill all of you!"

Marilyn's heart started pounding out of her chest. She ran to the door and threw it open. She went out onto the porch and started to walk towards him.

"No . . . kill me! They didn't do anything!" Marilyn yelled to Joséph.

Allen yelled out, "Marilyn, get back in the house!"

Miguel walked up next to Marilyn as they walked like a team together. Miguel had the rifle down at his side as he walked, knowing as soon as the man's gun went off to kill Allen he would shoot the man and Joséph dead!

The Pond

"I'll kill all of you by the time I'm done!" cried out
Joséph! "I want you to watch me kill your husband! *Le
tuer!*" Joséph yelled out in French, demanding the man
to kill Allen.

The man raised his gun from Allen's back to the
back of Allen's head. Miguel was raising his rifle to
shoot the man when a shot rang out from the bushes of
the path. The man went down dead not even knowing
what hit him!

Before anyone knew what was happening, men in
Brazilian officer uniforms ran up the path and grabbed
Joséph and threw him to the ground! Then another
special enforcement team with a logo of *Veripirate* on
their right chest and sleeves came running out and
handcuffed Joséph while he still lay on his stomach.

"What the hell is going on?" Joséph shouted!

The Veripirate officer spoke out, "Mr. Joséph Sicard,
you're under arrest for conspiracy against France's
National Security Enforcement Agency and also theft
of high security documents of The Council of State of
France!"

To Marilyn's disbelief, she saw Jonathon Landry
walking up the path. He walked up to Joséph leaning
down over him and said "Now we're even!"

Then the law enforcement agents pulled Joséph up
onto his feet.

Jauckeu flew up and landed on the ground in front
of Joséph and squawked, "Oh boy, you're in trouble!"

They took Joséph handcuffed and walked him down
the path and put him on an ATV and drove away.

Allen walked up to Enesa smiling and handed her Cole and said, "He's fine but he's a bit wet and hungry!"

Marilyn ran up to Allen and they threw their arms around each other.

Then Yurah, Davi, Tutu and Nino came walking out of the path.

The Brazilian enforcement agents went around the garden and bagged the bodies of Emmanuel and the men and took them away.

One of the enforcement agents walked up to Marilyn and asked her a few questions and then he said, "You have that man right there to thank for saving your lives," as he pointed to Jonathon. "He was the one that notified us what was going on and led us here."

Marilyn asked him, "But how did you know what Joséph and Emmanuel Sicard were up to?"

"Mr. Landry told us that you had something in your safety deposit box. We obtained a search warrant and found the micro fiche. We called Veripirate National Law Enforcement Agency in France and told them what we confiscated, and they sent their enforcement agents right away! It all made sense. They were coming here to get what they wanted and to kill all of you."

Marilyn smiled over at Jonathon and then walked up to him. "Thank you Jonathon, we would all be dead if it wasn't for you."

She went to reach over to give him a hug, but he pulled away and said, "Okay, let's not get personal!"

They both laughed as he walked away with one of the Brazilian law enforcement agents.

As he was getting ready to leave on an ATV, Miguel walked up to Jonathon and patted him on the back.

"My sister told me what you did for us. I want to thank you myself for all you have done. And I do remember you when I was a boy and you came to the garden with Mr. Sicard. Thank you for what you did for me."

Jonathon slapped Miguel on his back as he looked around the garden. "I'm sorry I couldn't have gotten here sooner. Now everything you worked for is destroyed."

"No, not completely," said Miguel. "Someday I'll finish what we started. I have everything documented."

Miguel walked back out to the pond and stood looking at all the dead fish. Everything in the pond was dead. Eye Spy shared its anatomy and DNA with everything in the pond. Because they were all one, as soon as he was killed everything died with him. Hundreds of fish were just lying at the top of the pond. The plants were lifeless and just floated or lay at the bottom.

It was already turning grey from the massive decomposition of the fish and plants. The antidotes were gone. Years of research were all destroyed. Miguel stood looking at the pond devastated by its death. It was a part of him. It took years to create and nurture it. It was all gone in just one second.

Enesa walked out of the house while Marilyn and Allen watched Cole. She walked up to him with tears in her eyes. She put her arms around him to comfort him. He turned to look at her.

'I feel I have failed your father."

"No Miguel! You didn't fail him at all! You did so much to finish what he started. You didn't destroy it, the outsiders of the Amazon did. Just like they have been destroying it for hundreds of years!

My father let his obsession obsess you too. There are still many ways you can continue your research. We still have thousands of plants to study and most of your research is documented. We just can't continue to get the antidotes. But there's still much more we can do."

Miguel looked at Enesa, "Yes, there's so much more we can do. My work is done here for now though, and it's time for us to move on and get Cole back to society where he can attend school someday."

Enesa shook her head in agreement with him. "But you must promise me one thing Miguel. You must promise that you will not return to the garden to do any research until Cole is grown. Once he's grown then maybe then we can return if we choose to do so. We need to make sure he has a normal life with a family someday."

Miguel agreed that the number one priority they have now is Cole and the other children they wanted to have. Miguel wanted them to be raised with both their parents. He knew the heartbreak of not having his biological parents and his sister in his life. He knew Enesa did too. He didn't want that for Cole.

Once inside the house, Miguel told Marilyn and Allen they would be leaving the garden to return to Rio de Janeiro. Marilyn was so happy to hear that he was ready to return home. The garden was beautiful but it was no place to raise a family because of the dangers of the Amazon.

"I have something to tell you," said Marilyn.

Miguel looked at Marilyn with uncertainty in his face. "What is it now?" as he smiled.

"Father left you two and a half million dollars and one third of the palace. Then when mother died, she left the palace and the rest of her estate to me since they thought, well you know . . ."

Miguel smiled at her.

"But now you're entitled to half of it. I just found out about it myself and I'll explain it to you later. But right now I would love to see you move back into the palace with Enesa and Cole. The lease is up in a few months. You can live at my pavilion until then."

Enesa smiled at Miguel. "It would be wonderful to raise Cole in the place you were born."

He looked at her and said, "Yes, and we can start on a sister for Cole. And I hope she'll be as wonderful of a sister to him as my sister is to me." He walked over to Marilyn and hugged and kissed her on her cheek. "We'll take you up on that offer!"

Marilyn was elated! "Then get your things ready and let's get out of here!"

"I have a few things I have to do before I go," said Miguel. "You all go without me and I'll follow you in a few days. The Brazilian Law Enforcement Agency has asked me to stay and help them document some things. And I need some time to get some things together."

"Enesa and Cole can come back with us," said Marilyn.

Allen shook his head in confirmation.

Miguel walked up to Enesa and Cole. He kissed them both and said, "I'll see you in a few days.

# Chapter 34

When Marilyn was back in her pavilion, she received a phone call from Franck Sicard, Joséph Sicard's brother and partner at the law firm.

Marilyn called her lawyer earlier that day to tell him she was going to start the legal process to get Miguel's inheritance from Joséph back.

"*Bonjour Marilyn*, How are you?" Franck said with a heavy French accent but spoke to her in as much English as possible.

"Hello Franck, I'm well. I'm sorry for everything that has happened."

"Don't be Marilyn. We're sorry for everything my brother and my nephew put you and Miguel through. Please accept our apologies. My brother will have a long time in jail to think about the trouble he's caused. They're going to let him out to attend Emmanuel's funeral, but he'll be going back and spending quite some time thinking about what he did."

"It's no reflection on you Franck. I know you had nothing to do with it."

"*Merci* Marilyn and I'm happy that you have a fine husband in your life now. Your life with Emmanuel would have been hell!

I'm calling to let you know that we have a check here for Miguel in the amount of 2.75 million dollars. The amount breaks down to two and a half million dollars which was his inheritance plus interest. Is that going to be sufficient for him? There's no need for legal proceedings Marilyn. We just want to cooperate fully and get Miguel what he's entitled to."

"I think he'll be very happy with that Franck, and thank you."

"If you need anything please don't hesitate to contact me at my office."

"I will Franck. Take care and I'll have Miguel get a hold of you soon."

"*Prendre pour l'instint Marilyn.*" Franck said and he hung up the phone.

After the law enforcement agents were gone from the garden, Miguel buried the panther next to the pond. Then Miguel walked back out to one of the greenhouses and went inside.

He went over to a large cupboard and opened it. Inside of the cupboard was a test tube filled with a clear blue fluid with two embryos the size of thimbles inside of it. There was a heat lamp mounted above the embryos.

Also growing in the bottom of the test tube was a seedling plant that was just beginning to sprout. It was also connected by a wire that split off and joined to the two embryos.

The embryos were so transparent at this early stage that Miguel could see their hearts beating through their skin.

Miguel looked on to the two embryos and said, "I'll come back someday to finish my work. But right now I cannot finish what I started with you."

Miguel pulled out a pair of rubber gloves from a drawer and slipped them onto his hands. Then Miguel reached up and picked the test tube up, and with tears in his eyes he disconnected the wires from the two embryos and seedling plant. He watched on as the two embryos stopped moving. Then he could see the two hearts stop beating at the same time.

He took the test tube and walked to the pond and reached down and gently dumped the embryos and plant into the water. He looked on to all the dead fish and plants as they were lifeless floating on top.

He stood for a bit longer and then turned to walk away. When he turned around, all of the native people were standing behind him. The natives had become his family too. Many of them spoke English learning it from Dr. Erikson and Miguel.

"You're leaving the garden Natowa?" One of the native men, Haazig (Hah•zig) said sadly.

"Yes, I have to leave Haazig. I have to get Cole into civilization so he'll be ready for school someday."

"But the rainforest and garden will miss you!" Haazig turned and ran his hand to show Miguel all the native people standing around him sadly looking on.

"I'll miss all of you too," said Miguel.

Tears again filled his eyes. "This garden became my life," as he looked around. "It took years and years of research to hopefully someday free the world from disease and sickness. We were so close. We were almost there, and now it's all gone! It's going to be hard to leave, but I have to leave so that Enesa and our children can have a normal life. The life I didn't have. Watch over the garden for me Haazig, and please take care of Jaukeu." Miguel watched Jaukeu in the distance sitting on his perch dancing up and down. "I promise I'll come back someday," as he patted Haazig on his shoulder.

Miguel went over and grabbed a green canvas sack and threw it over his shoulder as he walked out of the garden.

He came to the end of the path and stood inside the Magnolia trees. He turned back to look down the path one more time and he could see the pond in the distance.

He reached into his shirt pocket and pulled out a capped vile with the purplish grey fluid inside of it, and then he put it back. He turned and walked out of the Magnolia trees into the rainforest and he was gone.

*"Marilyn, the pain is over. It's no secret anymore. Now we are free."*

*She looked up at Miguel, "Yes, you and I and mother and father are free!"*

*To my Readers:*

*Thank you for reading "The Pond" and I hope you enjoyed it as much as I enjoyed creating it. The characters are purely fictional, and even though some of the places that are portrayed in the book are real; some of the native tribes and villages names were changed.*

*The story is fictional, but some of the content is based on facts that actually happened at one time during the Rubber Tree Holocaust in Brazil.*

*I wrote "The Pond" to allow my readers to explore the beauty of the Amazon and take you on a mesmerizing trip of adventures and places with a beautiful story to be told between Marilyn and Miguel.*

*Thank you again, and I hope "The Pond" is a book that you'll read over and over for it has many adventures to explore.*

*Michelle Dubois*

# About The Author

Born in Western N.Y., Michelle travelled with her parents and five other siblings between United States, Mexico and Canada. Her parents finally settled in Colden N.Y. where her latter childhood years were mostly spent. When her parents retired, they returned back to Canada and settled in Southern Ontario.

Michelle married a Canadian and after ten years of marriage she divorced and raised her one son Christopher, now getting ready for university in the fall. Michelle pursued a career in real estate in Southern Ontario where she still sells new homes and lives in the same subdivision where she works.

"The Pond" is Michelle Dubois' first published novel. Almost two years in the making, her critics have given "The Pond" fantastic reviews and going as far to say "I didn't want the book to end!" She is also in the process of writing the movie script knowing that not only will "The Pond" be a bestselling novel, but also a big screen box office hit as well. Michelle feels that being a writer is a new endeavor for her and is anxious to write her next novel.

*A special thank you to:*

*My mother*
*My son Christopher*
*Cathy and Mark*